Alexander Cunningham

Reports of a Tour in Bundelkhand and Rewa in 1883-84

And of a tour in Rewa, Bundelkhand, Malwa, and Gwalior, in 1884-85 - Vol. 21

Alexander Cunningham

Reports of a Tour in Bundelkhand and Rewa in 1883-84
And of a tour in Rewa, Bundelkhand, Malwa, and Gwalior, in 1884-85 - Vol. 21

ISBN/EAN: 9783337194086

Printed in Europe, USA, Canada, Australia, Japan

Cover: Foto ©Andreas Hilbeck / pixelio.de

More available books at **www.hansebooks.com**

Archæological Survey of India.

REPORTS

OF

A TOUR IN BUNDELKHAND AND REWA IN 1883-84;

AND OF

A TOUR IN REWA, BUNDELKHAND, MALWA, AND GWALIOR, IN 1884-85.

BY

MAJOR-GENERAL A. CUNNINGHAM, C.S.I., C.I.E.,

ROYAL ENGINEERS [BENGAL RETIRED],

DIRECTOR-GENERAL OF THE ARCHÆOLOGICAL SURVEY OF INDIA.

VOLUME XXI.—PARTS I AND II.

"What is aimed at is an accurate description, illustrated by plans, measurements, drawings and photographs, and by copies of inscriptions of such remains as most deserve notice, with the history of them so far as it may he traceable, and a record of the traditions that are preserved regarding them."—LORD CANNING.

"What the learned world demand of us in India is to be quite certain of our data, to place the monumental record before them exactly as it now exists, and to interpret it faithfully and literally."—JAMES PRINSEP.

CALCUTTA:

PRINTED BY THE SUPERINTENDENT OF GOVERNMENT PRINTING, INDIA.

1885.

PREFACE.

IN this volume I have brought together the reports of my last two tours in Bundelkhand and Rewa, during the cold seasons of 1883-84 and 1884-85. During these tours I visited many places which had not been reported upon by the officers of the Archæological Survey. The most notable of these places were the great forts of Kâlanjara and Ajaygarh, the strongholds of the Chandels of Mahoba, and their religious capital of Khajurâha, which possesses the most famous collection of magnificent temples in Upper India. I have taken the opportunity of giving a complete account of all the Chandel inscriptions at present known. These continue the genealogy for several generations after the fall of Mahoba.

On the south bank of the Jumna, a short distance above Allahabad, I visited a large ruined temple, which had been seen and sketched about 50 years ago by Major Kittoe, who calls it the shrine of Karkotak Nâg.

At a short distance, on the way towards Allahabad, I visited a stone building at Chilla, which is said to have been the dwelling-house of the two Banâphar heroes Alha and Udal. It is surrounded by a fortified enclosure, and is important as being one of the very few old dwelling-houses that now exist.

In Rewa I made the discovery that the whole valley of the Tons River had been held by the Kalachuri Rajas of Chedi for at least two centuries prior to the advent of the Bâghel Râjputs. In the previous year my Assistant Mr. Garrick had found a short inscription on rock near the northern boundary of Rewa giving the name of Gânggeya Deva, the Kalachuri Raja of Chedi, in the beginning of the 11th century. The name of his son Karna Deva is still remembered by the people in connexion with the fort of Gûrgi Masaun, the old capital of the district. Its foundation is attributed to Karan Dahariya, or Karna Dahaliya, Dahal being a well-known name of Chedi. Raja Karna reigned in the middle of the 11th century. Another inscription of the Kalachuri kings was found by my servants on a slab in one of the northern passes of the Rewa territory. It bears the name of Râja Nara Sinha Deva *Dahaliya*, and is dated in the Samvat year 1216, or A.D. 1159. Two later names are preserved on copper-plates belonging to the large village of Kakareri, also in northern Rewa. These are Jaya Sinha Deva in A.D. 1175, and Vijaya Deva in A.D. 1196. I have found no traces of the Kalachuri kings of a later date than the last, even in Chedi itself. I conclude, therefore, that the Bâghel Râjputs, who now hold the country, must have obtained possession in the very beginning of the 13th century. This is rendered absolutely certain by the mention of two very curious names as the rulers of the country in the middle of the century. These names are given by the Muhammadan historians as Dalaki wa Malaki, which I have identified with the two contemporary princes of the Bâghel chronicles called Dalkeswara and Malkeswara.

In Rewa also the waterfalls of the Tons River at Kevati-Kund, Chachai, and Jhirna were visited. At the first place an old Pali inscription had been found a few years ago by Mr. Markham. On my visit a stûpa carved in outline was also found, proving that the cave was of Buddhist origin.

The numerous sources of the Ken or Kiyan River were next visited, with the expectation that some ancient sites might be found. Many old places were discovered, but most of the temples were in ruins. One very curious temple was found near Ganj in the Ajaygarh territory; the whole of the outer faces of the walls being carved to imitate rock-work. At

Lakhuria, only a short distance, a very important inscription was discovered. It bears the name of Raja Prithivi Sena of Vâkâtaka, in conjunction with that of his tributary Vyâghra Deva. The former was the father of Rudra Sena of Vâkâtaka, and the latter was the father of Jayanâtha, whose copper-plate inscriptions have been found near Uchahara and at Kâri Talai. As these are dated in the years 174 and 177 of the Gupta era, the Lakhuria inscription of his father Vyâghra may be referred to the year 150 of the Gupta Kâl, shortly after the death of Skanda Gupta. In fact it may have been the death of the great Gupta prince that led to the occupation of this part of the country by the king of Vâkâtaka.

A still older inscription was afterwards found in a cave near the top of the Ginja hill, about 40 miles to the south-west of Allahabad. The hill is an isolated peak of the Vindhyan range, 1,326 feet in height above the sea, and about 800 or 900 feet above the plain. The top is a narrow ridge of perpendi-cular sandstone rock about 200 feet in height. On the south face the cliff overhangs considerably, forming a large open hall, or rock shelter, about 100 feet long, and from 40 to 50 feet broad, and varying in height from 20 to 25 feet outside. It is closed at the two ends by rough walls, but the whole of the front is now open. On the rock at the back there is an ins-cription of two lines in red paint, with several rude drawings of men and animals. The characters of the inscription are of the earliest Gupta forms ; but the opening is worded in the well-known style of the shorter Indo-Scythian inscriptions, as follows :—

> Mahârâjasya Sri Bhima Senasya
> Sam (vatsare) 52, Gimha pakshe 4,
> divasa 12, etaya purvvayam, &c.

"In the reign of Maharaja Bhima Sena in the year Samvat 52, in the 4th fortnight of the hot season, the 12th day. On that date, &c."

I take Bhima Sena to have been the Hindu Raja of Ko-sâmbi during the reign of the paramount Indo-Scythian king

Huvishka.   The date, if referred to the Seleukidan era, corresponds with A. D. 140.

At Madanpur, about 50 miles to the north of Saugor, a new
inscription of Prithvi Râja Chauhan was discovered.   It records his conquest of the country of *Jejâkabhukti*.   The same
spelling of the name I have since found in a Mahoba inscription.   This then was its original form, which soon became
shortened to *Jejâhuti*, as written by Abu Rihân, just as *Tirabhukti* became *Tirahuti* and *Tirhut*.   The usual Brahmanical
derivation of the name of Jajhautiya, from Yajur-hota, is thus
proved to be erroneous.

The last discovery which was made in the beginning of the
present year was that of a Buddhist stûpa at Râjâpur, about 100
miles to the south of Gwalior.   The stûpa is almost intact ; but
it is quite plain, and possesses no railing and no inscriptions.

A. CUNNINGHAM.

CONTENTS.

PART I.

PART II.

PLATES.

———

PART I.

REPORT OF A TOUR IN BUNDELKHAND AND REWA

IN

1883-84.

ARCHÆOLOGICAL SURVEY OF INDIA.

REPORT OF A TOUR IN BUNDELKHAND AND REWA IN 1883-84.

PART I.

1.—KOSAM, OR KAUSÂMBI.

IN his account of the famous city of Kausâmbi, the Chinese pilgrim Hwen Thsang describes two holy places which I failed to identify at my previous visits. These were the rock-cave of the venomous serpent, and the ancient brick-chamber in which the famous Bodhisatwa Vasubandhu composed his treatise named the *Vidyâ-mâtra-siddhi-shâstra*, for the refutation of the doctrine of the Hinayâna.

The first place is thus described by the pilgrim :[1] "At 8 or 9 *li*, or 1½ mile, to the south-west of the town there is a rock-cave of a venomous dragon. After overcoming this dragon Buddha left his shadow in the cave. But, though this fact is recorded in history, there is nothing to be seen at the present day."

At my previous visits I had looked for this cave on the bank of the Jumna to the west of the city just outside the village of Pâli. The south-west bearing is quite impassable, as the general course of the Jumna above the city is from north-west to south-east. Before going to Kosam (which I have previously identified with the ancient Kausâmbi), I visited the hill of Prabhâsa, or Pabhosa, as it is generally called, as I had a suspicion that the *rock-cave* might be found in the *rocky* hill. It is true that the hill of Pabhosa is 3 miles to the north-west of the great fort of Garhwâ, but it

[1] Julien's Hwen Thsang, Vol. II, p. 286.

is not more than 2 miles from the present villages of Kosam and Pâli, which formed the old city outside the walls of the fort.[1]

On reaching the hill of Pabhosa I found that there was not only a cave high up in the face of the hill, but that there was also a Nâga, or serpent, of which everybody had heard, but which no one had seen. The serpent is believed to have his head in the Jumna while his tail remains in the cave, which is more than a quarter of a mile from the river. The Nâga is said to be seen once a year at the time of the Diwâli festival.

The cave is artificial, and is simply an old quarry with a pillar left in front for the support of the roof. In front there is a Jain temple, and there are three standing Jain figures cut in the rock above. The Jain temple was built by one Hira Lâl about 40 years ago. The whole face of the hill in front is now a mere mass of débris, the refuse of the quarry above. The room is said to be large enough to hold four bedsteads: it has two windows, as well as a door. On an eminence near the foot of the hill to the east there is a tank called Deo-Kund, with a small temple on its bank.

The Chinese pilgrim mentions that there was a stûpa of Asoka, about 200 feet high, beside the cave, but no traces of such a building could be found. It is very probable, however, that the present Jain temple occupies the site of some ancient building. The pilgrim also notes that close by there was a site where Buddha used to take exercise, and a second stûpa containing some of his hair and some nail-parings. Sick people used to visit the place, and pray for their recovery.

On the faces of the rock at several points there are short inscriptions, which may be only records of the quarry-men. They are all, however, written in characters of the Gupta period. One of them gives the name of *Vasu Deva;* a second reads *Savahâvinse;* while a third gives the name of *Yasa,* and a fourth reads *Adahâsisam.* The quarries are, there-

---

[1] See Plate II for the position of the Pabhosa hill.

fore, as old as the time of the Guptas, from 200 to 400 A.D., and the cave and its legendary Nâga were, no doubt, in existence at the period of Hwen Thsang's visit to Kausâmbi in A.D. 636.

In searching for the brick-chamber of Vasubandhu to the south-west of Kausâmbi, I was led, by the pilgrim's description of its height being equal to that of a pavilion of two storeys, to examine a cave near the villages of Garauli and Gopsahsa, both to the south-east of the great fort. The cave has been excavated in a huge earthen mound, named Tikri, which rises from 45 to 50 feet above the general level of the country. Owing to its commanding position, overlooking the Jumna, the mound was used as a survey station, and it is probable that a few feet at the top were added by the surveyors. The excavation consists of two rooms facing the east. The outer room was 11 feet long by 8 feet 3 inches deep, with a doorway, 4 feet wide, leading into the inner chamber, which is 11 feet 6 inches broad by 13 feet 3 inches deep. This inner chamber has a long raised seat or couch on the south side. Both chambers are now only 4½ to 6 feet in height. They had been inhabited lately by a fakir.[1]

On the eastern face, just halfway up the slope, or about 15 feet above the ground, there is a brick wall, which appears to have been the back wall of another chamber. There are quantities of broken bricks at the foot of the mound, and in the fields close by, where fragments of stone are also found. The brick wall I take to be the remains of a lower storey, which agrees with Hwen Thsang's account of the residence of Vasubandhu as an ancient chamber of bricks—" d'un pavillon à deux étages."[2] I could find no trace of the great monastery of kiu-shi-lo, or Gosirsha, with its stúpa 200 feet in height. The name of Gosirsha, or Gosira, appears to be preserved in that of the neighbouring village of Gopsahsa; but there are no remains of walls now visible, although there are numerous fragments of stone and quantities of broken bricks scattered about.

---

[1] See Plate II for the position of the Tikri mound.
[2] Julien's Hwen Thsang, Vol. II, p. 286.

2.—RITHORA.

One mile and a half to the north-west of Mhow Ghat, and within sight of Kosam, there are two ruined temples, of small size, but of fine workmanship. The larger one is only $10\frac{1}{2}$ feet square outside, with a portico on the north in front of the entrance, supported on two nicely carved pillars. The temple has fallen backwards, and the enshrined figure is lying inside crushed beneath the roof. On the face of the door-step there are represented two crocodiles, each carrying two women with children in their laps. There is a figure of Káli outside, from which it may be inferred that the temple was dedicated to the worship of Siva. The pillars are of early mediæval style.

The second temple is similar to the first, and was also dedicated to Siva, as it still possesses a group of Hara-Gauri. The entrance doorway also is similar to that of the other temple ; but the jambs, which are still standing, have figures of the Ganges on her crocodile and the Jumna on her tortoise.

3.—BAR-DEWAL.

For my knowledge of this fine old temple I am indebted to an almost forgotten work of Major Kittoe.[1] He calls the building a " Temple of Karkotak Nág," but this name is now quite unknown. His account of it is so very brief that I may give it in full :—

"The elegant ruin represented in the accompanying plate [2] is situated on the bank of the Jumna, on the Bundelkhand side, a few miles below the town of Mhow. It is dedicated to Siva under the denomination of Karkotak Nág. The work is executed in a most exquisite and elaborate style, in hard, close-grained sandstone. The greater part, indeed the main body, of the building has long since fallen to the ground ; the only portion remaining, and which I have faintly attempted to represent, is that still existing of the Nandi Sabha (or portico), in which Siva's bull Nandi is always placed. It is not

[1] Illustrations of Indian Architecture, by Markham Kittoe : Calcutta, Thacker and Co., 1838, long folio.
[2] I have given a representation of Kittoe's view in Plate IV, reduced to two-thirds of the original.

known who erected this truly beautiful specimen of Hindu sculpture and architecture. There is a small village close by, the superstitious inhabitants of which informed me that a huge black serpent, or nâg, inhabits the temple, and is occasionally visible."

This is all that he says regarding the temple, the rest of his notice being taken up with an account of the serpent Karkotak Nâg, and the story of Nala and Damayanti.

The temple is situated on the south bank of the Jumna, on a high bluff point close to the village of Kutharo. It is just 11 miles to the east of Mhow Ghât, and 25 miles to the west-south-west of Allahabad. Its position is rather inaccessible, as there is nothing but a pathway ascending and descending for 11 miles through the ravines of the Jumna on the west, and a similar pathway on the east for 4 miles, from the large village of Partâbpur, where the great stone quarries are situated.

The Bar-Dewal must have been a magnificent temple. Its position on a high projecting point overlooking the Jumna is a very fine one, and both in size and in decoration the fane was worthy of its site. It is, besides, raised on a plinth or platform of 11 feet.[1]

It is a lingam shrine of Siva—and the name given to it by Kittoe of Karkotak Nâg is quite unknown. The entrance is to the east, as usual with lingam shrines. It consists of the usual sanctum containing the lingam with the entrance on the 'east. The Mahâ-mandapa, or great hall, is 25 feet square, the roof being supported on four magnificent columns, each upwards of 14 feet in height. These are placed 8 feet 8 inches apart on a raised platform 1 foot $3\frac{1}{2}$ inches in height. On each of the four sides immediately opposite each pillar there is a square pilaster nearly 10 feet high, at 5 feet distance ; and between each pair of pilasters there are two octagonal pillars of the same pattern as the larger columns, and of the same height as the pillars. The architraves covering these pillars are massive beams about 2 feet square in section, and very elaborately ornamented on

---

[1] See Plate III for a plan of the temple.

each face. Between each pair of pillars there was formerly a cusped arch, of which one was still *in situ* when Kittoe sketched the temple.

The central roof of the Mandapa has fallen down ; but a portion of the side roof still remains, exactly as it was seen by Kittoe. The usual arrangement that I have seen is to cover this portion by overlapping stones, projecting one over the other from the outer and lower rows of pillars until the space between the two rows of pillars is roofed over. But in the present example the arrangement is quite different, the whole of the surrounding veranda, as it may be called, being roofed in by long sloping slabs which are very deeply cut with three horizontal recesses, which imitate the courses of the overlapping roofs. In these recesses there are rows of small seated Nâga kings, with snakes' hoods over their heads. On the west side three of these sloping slabs still remain *in situ*, and at the north corner there is a single slab of wedge shape, that is, narrow at the top and broad at the bottom, showing that the same arrangement of roof was continued at the angles.

In the accompanying plan I have attempted to restore the temple from the existing remains, either *in situ*, or lying on the ground below.

The dimensions of the platform were obtained from the existing angles.

The four great columns of the central hall, C, are still standing in their places.

Of the smaller pillars those marked P¹, P², are still *in situ*, as well as the base of P³. The positions of the others marked P. have been fixed on the authority of two small projecting brackets at right angles, on each of which were once supported the ornamental cusped arches, similar to those between the larger pillars. The presence of these small brackets shows decisively that there must have been four pillars on each of the three open sides of the hall. Only four of these pillars are now lying on the ground—two on the north side, and two on the south side ; but there are also some short architraves which once spanned these spaces, and some

narrow roofing slabs which could not have formed any part
of the roof of the great central hall.

With these remains still existing it seems certain that
there must have been a small porch, or hall, on each side to
the north and south, and a third on the east side forming
the entrance. I could not find any trace of the flight of
steps, as the whole of the eastern front is now a confused
mass of large stones.

Externally the view from the east would have presented
three pyramidal domes in front; the middle one being higher
than the others, with the tall spire of the sanctum behind.

The people differ as to the meaning of the word *Bar*.
Some say it refers to a Bhar Raja who built it, but others refer
it to a Bar, or Banyan, tree which grew near it. I think, however, that it was more probably only the *Barâ Dewal*, or
" great temple." There is a large village on the bank of the
Jumna 1 mile to the west called Barha, and this may have
given its name to the temple.

When Kittoe saw the temple just 50 years ago, the light-
cusped arches between the pillars of the Mandapa were still
in their places, as shown in his sketch. They fell down some
years back, and three of them are said to have been taken
to Allahabad by a Saheb.

There is no inscription now remaining, the only writing
being a pilgrim's record of the last century.

There are plenty of large bricks lying about, but they
could not have belonged to the temple itself, as it is built
entirely of stone. Perhaps there was a surrounding wall of
brick, with some subordinate buildings.

4.—RIKHIAN CAVES.

In the face of the hill nearly due south from Bar Dewal,
and about a mile and a half distant, there are two large caves
known by the name of Rikhian, or the dwellings of the
Rishis. They are apparently old quarries, partly built up in
front with dry stone walls to form rooms. Two pillars help
to support this roof. The larger cave is $34\frac{1}{2}$ feet long by

17½ feet broad, and 6½ high. Inside, against the back wall, there is a large collection of statues, which were most probably taken from the Bar Dewal Temple after it had become ruinous. The principal statue is a figure of Vishnu with 12 arms. It is 4 feet high by 2½ feet broad. There are also figures of Kâli and Ganesa, and of 42 goddesses, which arc most probably a portion of the Chaunsat Joginis, as several of them are represented with animals' heads. Amongst them is one with a leonine head and another with a porcine head, &c.

The second cave is 22 feet long by 16 feet broad, and 7 feet high, with one pillar in the middle to support the roof. It has a projecting porch in front of the entrance built with squared stones. It has also two holes, or small windows, to give light. Inside there is a seated figure of a three-headed goddess with 16 arms. It is 2 feet 8 inches high, by 1 foot 9 inches broad, and most probably represents Dûrgâ.

Outside there is a small temple with a sanctum only, 4 feet 10 inches square, and a flat roof, 9½ feet high. Two other temples in ruins are close by.

There is also a large tank, 600 feet in length, which is supplied by a small stream coming over a waterfall.

The place is considered holy, and is visited by numbers of pilgrims.

5.—CHILLA.

Chilla is a pretty, well-wooded village on the south side of the Jumna, 12 miles due east from Bar Dewal, and the same distance to the south-west of Allahabad. It is celebrated for its possession of a large stone dwelling-house, which is said to have been the residence of the two famous Banâphar heroes, Alha and Udal.

The building stands in the middle of a small fortified enclosure called Kot, which has a thick earthen rampart, faced with stone both inside and outside, and four towers at the corners. It has also a ditch all round, with a stone counterscarp.

The house itself is a square of 46 feet, each side divided by pillars and walls into 25 small bays, in five rows each way.

To the north is the entrance, with a long slab seat on each side, covered by a low roof, supported by short pillars. The middle compartment is open to the sky, and thus forms a small courtyard.[1] The five compartments on the south side form five separate rooms, each with its own door. The two compartments on the north-west are walled in to form a separate room with its door to the south. Similarly the two others on the north-east form a single room with a door to the west. Each of these rooms is lighted by a stout stone trellis, and two similar trellises give light to the inner parts of the body of the building. Each compartment is between 7 and 8 feet square, and the total height is 8 feet 10½ inches.

The roof is flat. Four pillars of the same pattern, but less massive, are now used to support some broken slabs of the roof. These are said to have been brought from above, where they supported a canopy where the inmates used to sit.

With its massive ramparts, which completely covered the building from view, the place was capable of being defended for some time.

All the doorways are slightly ornamented, but more especially the door sills. The corner rooms and side-walls have stout stone trellises of a simple pattern. The pillars also are slightly decorated. There are no inscriptions, but the letter *n* of an early form was found in two places. From its form I should judge that the building must be as old as the 8th or 9th century.

This building is of some interest, as so few specimens now exist of early Indian domestic architecture. I have given in other volumes plans and descriptions of a stone dwelling-house at Ranod, and the fine palaces of Mân Singh at Gwalior; the former belonging to about the 8th century, and the latter to the early part of the 16th century A.D. A very interesting specimen of an intermediate period has been found by Mr. Beglar in Râjputâna in a palace of the famous Prithvi Raja, which, therefore, belongs to the latter half of the 12th century A.D.

---

[1] See Plate V for a plan of this building.

Outside the enclosure of Kot there are numerous remains
of a large stone temple, in richly carved stones and broken
statues, which would seem to show that Chilla was once a
place of some importance.

6.—CHITRA-KUTA.

The holy hill of *Chitra-kuta*, or the " many-hued peak, "
is famous as the residence of Râma, Sitâ, and Lakshman
during their exile from Ayodhya, and also as the abode of
the sage Vâlmiki, the reputed author of the Râmâyana. It
is situated on the left, or west, bank of the Paisuni River,
about 5 miles to the south-west of Karwi, and 50 miles to
the south-east of Banda. Its praises have been sung by
Vâlmiki himself as the—

> " Auspicious hill ! where all day long
> " The lapwing's cry, the Koïl's song,
> " Make all who listen gay ;—
> " Where all is fresh and fair to see ;
> " Where elephants and deer roam free. " [1]

A paved foot-path, with a continuous belt of small temples,
encircles the foot of the hill, which is crowded with pilgrims
at all times of the year. The temples, however, are all
modern, and there are no inscriptions. Fragments of sculpture and pieces of carved stone are found lying about the
foot of the hill, but there is nothing to show that the place
is an old one. Kâmtâ is the name of the village close by the
hill, and the hill itself is often called *Kâmtâ*. The true name
is *Kâmadâ-giri*, or the " hill of the giver of plenty," or the
" desire-giving hill." The hill itself is still covered with
jungle, but there are no Rishis, as the Brahmans of the present day all live in comfortable houses below.

Of late years the small town of Sitapur, situated also on
the left bank of the Paisuni River, 1 mile to the north of
Kâmtâ, has rivalled the fame of the holy Chitra-kuta. Here
the river Paisuni forms a long straight reach, both broad and
deep, on the banks of which there are numerous temples

[1] Griffith's Râmâyana.

and bathing ghâts, or flights of steps leading down to the
water. Some of the temples are said to be old, but they
are all so smudged with whitewash that it is quite impossible to judge of their antiquity. The name of Sitâpur is,
however, quite modern, as it was given by Charan Dâs near
the beginning of the present century. The old name was
Jaysinghpur.

I saw many thousands of pilgrims on their way to Kâmtâ
and Allahabad from Bhilsa and Sâgar. There was also a
widowed Râni from Ratlâm. They came by different routes
through Hirapur and Panna, as well as by Ajaygarh and
Kâlanjar. There were also many pilgrims from Chattisgarh
and Raypur in the Central Provinces, who had come by
Amarkantak and Sohâgpur to Rewa, and then by Jetwar and
Mârkandi on the railway, and thence over the hills to Râsin
and Kâmtâ.

Whatever age may be assigned to the Râmâyana, it is
certain that the story of Râma and his exile to the famous
hill of Chitra-kuta must be still older. We know, indeed, that
the story is certainly as old as the second century B.C.,
as it is represented amongst the sculptures of the Bharhut
stûpa as an illustration of the Dasaratha jâtaka of the Bud-
dhists. In the Râmâyana we read that Râma on his depar-
ture from Ayodhya went first to Sringiverapura on the Ganges
(now Singor), and, after crossing the river, paid a visit to the
sage Bharadwâja, whose hermitage was at the junction of the
Ganges and Jumna. Bharadwâja told him to go to the hill
of Chitra-kuta on the Mandâkini River. As these two names
still survive in the holy hill of Chitra-kut and the small river
Mandâkin which joins the Paisuni a little below Sitâpur, there
can be little doubt as to the correctness of their identification. But there is a third name in the immediate vicinity
which seems to offer a conclusive proof of the Chitra-kuta of
Bundelkhand being the actual place intended by the poet.[1]
This is the hill of Prasravan, which, as it is coupled with the
Mandâkini, can only be another name for Chitra-kuta itself.
Prasravana means literally "a cascade or waterfall," and might,

[1] See Griffith's Râmâyana, Vol. III, p. 298.

therefore, be applied either to a hill or to a stream. In the present instance I believe that it may be identified with the Paisuni, or Parsaroni, as it is also called. Now, this stream is famous for its cascades, and on that account must have received the name of the Prasravana Nadi, or "waterfall river." In the same way the hill of Chitra-kuta would be called the hill of Prasravana.

Similarly I believe that the Godâvari stream searched for in vain by Lakshman was not the distant Godâvari River which rises at Nâsik, but the holy Gupt-Godâvari, or " hidden Godâvari," which rushes forth from a cave in the hill a few miles to the south of Chitra-kut. But whatever may be thought of this identification of the Gupt Godâvari with the Godâvari River, it is certain that the Gupt Godâvari corresponds exactly with Bharadwâja's description of the Chitrakuta Hill, whence Râma and Sita would—

" See the foaming torrent rave
" Impetuous from the mountain cave.[1]

The Chitra-kut Hill of Bundelkhand still further corresponds with the Chitra-kuta of Vâlmiki in the various hues of its rocks from which it has derived its name, or, as Mr. Griffith has rendered it,—

" There a silvery sheen is spread,
" And there, like blood, the rocks are red ;
" There shows a streak of emerald green,
" And pink and yellow glow between ."[2]

I have thought it necessary to give all these small coincidences, as Mr. Beglar has brought forward some very plausible arguments to prove that the Chitra-kuta of Bundelkhand is not the Chitra-kuta of Vâlmiki. His chief objection is the want of a torrent issuing from a mountain cave. But this I have now supplied in the Gupt Godâvari, which is a place of pilgrimage. Mr. Beglar proposes the hill of Râmgarh 150 miles to the south-east of Rewa and 160 miles to the west-south-west of Hazaribagh. It is true that a torrent issues from the Ramgarh Hill, which so far agrees with the

[1] Griffith's Ramâyanâ, Vol. II, p. 206.   [2] Ibid. Vol. II, p. 375.

Chitra-kuta of Rama. But it is equally true that the Râmgarh Hill is 200 miles from Allahabad, and therefore does not
agree with Bharadwâja's description of Chitra-kuta as being
only a " short distance" from the junction of the Ganges and
Jumna.[1] Mr. Griffith says "4 leagues," which I take to be
yojanas, equal to about 30 miles, instead of 60. But this is
something very different from the 200 miles direct, or 250
miles by road of Râmgarh from Allahabad. Then there is a
very serious difficulty about a chariot getting to Râmgarh,
which stands in one of the most hilly and inaccessible districts
in India. I do not think that a poet would take a chariot there
even in a dream.

There are several claimants for other places connected
with the wanderings of Râma, as well as with those of the
five Pândus. Thus, there are three places named Bairât, and
several named Kundilpur, as well as two districts called Mat-
sya-desa.

7.—GUPT GODÂVARI.

The Gupt Godâvari, or " concealed Godâvari," is a small
stream which issues from a cave in the hills about 9 miles
to the south-south-west of Chitra-kuta. The stream is
one of the objects of pilgrimage. It is from 8 to 10 feet
broad and 3 feet deep, and falls into the Godai Nala. The
end of the cave, it is said, has never been reached. There is
a long Nâgari inscription inside, but it is quite modern.

8.—GONDA, OR GODA.

Gonda is a large flourishing village 1 mile to the south
of the present high road leading from Karwi to Banda. It is
13 miles from Karwi, and stands on the old road going to
Kâlanjar on the south-west and to Banda on the north-west.

To the east of the village, where an embankment has been
thrown across the valley between two ranges of hills to form
a tank, there is a pair of old temples standing together on the
same platform. They are simply known as Chandeli Man-
dar, or the "Chandeli Temples," as all old buildings are

---

[1] Wheeler's Ramâyâna, p. 190.

designated throughout Bundelkhand. By some they are attributed to Alha and Udal, and king Parmâl. But the attribution
is very doubtful, the only certainty about them being their
Chandel origin. Both temples have the river goddesses
Gangâ and Yamunâ at the bottom of their door jambs, but
they are not standing on their symbolic animals, the crocodile
and tortoise. The animals, however, are present, but are
made very small, and are mere accessories at the feet of the
figures.

The larger temple is built on the usual plan of an entrance
hall, a central hall, and a sanctum with the door to the east.
It is 55 feet long by 48 feet 9 inches broad, and is still about
40 feet in height above the plain, but not more than 30 feet
above its own terrace. It was originally dedicated to Vishnu,
as there is a figure of that god over the middle of the entrance doorway. On each of the two sides there was a pillared portico, to which on the south side was attached a
small temple 13 feet square outside, with the entrance on the
north leading into the mandapa of the larger temple. This
small fane was dedicated to Lakshmi, as shown by her figure
over the centre of the entrance door. But at some later
date both temples were appropriated by the Saivas, who
placed lingams inside, which are still *in situ.*

The spire of the smaller temple is now gone, but nearly
the whole height of the spire of the larger one is still standing, saving only the *kalas,* or pinnacle. The lower part is
perpendicular, but the upper part is sloping with a very
slight curve. On the perpendicular sides there are two rows
of figures, each 2 feet in height. Amongst these are—

<blockquote>
7 figures of Siva.
1 figure of Kâli, skeleton goddess.
1   „   of Ganesa.
6 figures of Vishnu.
1 figure of Brahma.
1 standing male figure not recognised.
1 figure broken.
4 figures lost.
</blockquote>

TOTAL 22 the full number.

In the upper part of the spire the angles only were ornamented, all the middle spaces being left quite plain.

The roof of the mandapa of the great temple is altogether gone, and the stones now cover the floor, and prevent
accurate measurements being taken.

I searched in vain for inscriptions. There are a few pilgrims' records ; but as none of them are dated, they are of
little value. Such as they are, I have given them in the plate
below the plan of the temple.[1]

> *A. On left jamb of Vishnu Temple.*
> *tasâla *dasala.
>
> *B. Inside Vishnu Temple.*

1. Krita Sri Râwat Totai Vinikoti patithâ.
2. Ma ** sara Deva miti.

> *C. Inside Lakshmi Temple.*
> Vasu Devaii Bhasara.
>
> *D. On left jamb of entrance.*
> Arjuna Deva.

9.—RÂSIN, or RÂJAVÂSINI.

The old town of Rasin, or Râsin, is situated on the high
road leading from Banda to Kâlanjar, and just midway between Karwi and Kâlanjar. It is 29 miles distant from Banda.
It lies at the foot of a granite hill, and its numerous mounds,
ruined temples, and broken sculptures, all show that it must
once have been a place of considerable consequence. In the
time of Akbar it was one of the mahals of Sirkâr Kâlanjar
of the Suba of Allahabad. There are also many fine old
tanks, of which I obtained the following names, but the list is
said to be very incomplete :—

1. Adhika.
2. Amarâdei, on the hill.
3. Bahubâri, on the hill.
4. Bathkhor.
5. Chachai.
6. Chandâ-Maheswari, on the hill.
7. Chandi Talao.

[1] See Plate VI, both Temple and Inscriptions.

8. Chungwa Bhungwa.
9. Dhamsarâ.
10. Dudkhhari.
11. Godika.
12. Kariyâ.
13. Khalukhal.
14. Kuthli.
15. Palti Pokhara.
16. Pothra.
17. Puraniya.
18. Rasandai, on the hill.
19. Sarwâ Karwâ.

Four of these tanks are shown in the accompanying map of Râsin.[1] The Adhika Tal is a very fine sheet of water; but nothing is known regarding any of the makers of the tanks. The name of Râsin is said to be only a contraction of Râjbansi, but from one of the inscriptions it would appear that the old name was *Râjavâsini*, or the Royal Residence, which would naturally be shortened to Rajâsin and Râsin.

The positions of the antiquities of Râsin are all marked in the accompanying map by the letters A, B, C, D, E, F.

A.—On the side of the road, at the foot of the hill and to the north of the town, there are several Sati pillars, with a large standing female figure holding a child in her left arm, and several fragments, including a four-bracket capital, with human figures on the faces, and smaller figures in the angles.

B.—Is a small mound on the east side of the road faced with squared stones. On the top are several statues, of which the most prominent is a figure of Ganesa. The platform was certainly the site of a temple, and it is accordingly now called *Sivâla*, or the "Temple of Siva," and sometimes also *Ganesa* from the principal figure. But amongst the broken sculptures I found many fragments of a colossal figure, which after some trouble I succeeded in fitting together as a colossal figure of the skeleton goddess Kâli, 8 feet high and 4 feet broad. The figure has 24 arms, and is surrounded by a number of small skeleton females of the same kind, both sitting and standing. The goddess herself is represented

[1] See Plate VII.

standing on the back of a prostrate male figure. She has a deeply sunken stomach with a very long-tailed scorpion between the ribs.

On the mound there are several other sculptures, such as the goddess Devi (Durgâ) with ten arms, a Mahesasuri Devi, and two Nandis, a large figure of Hanumân, 6 feet high, and the upper half of a statue of the Narasinha, or man-lion, of life-size. But the principal figure is the colossus of Kâli, which must certainly have been the statue enshrined inside, and which would therefore have given its name to the temple.

C—The principal object in this group of ruins is the entrance doorway of a temple, which is still standing apparently *in situ*, with some fragments built into a piece of rough wall on each side. The site is accordingly known simply as *Darwâja*, or "the Door." Amongst the stones collected here there is a complete pilaster, 5 feet 2 inches in height, and a piece of a twelve-sided pillar. There is also a ten-armed figure of Durgâ, and several Sati stones, of which one bears a nearly obliterated inscription.

D—Is a Sivâla built of old materials.

E—Is a temple of Ratannâth, built on the top of the hill overhanging the town. It is not very old, and bears no inscription.

F—Is the famous temple of Chandâ Maheswari, which is situated in a dense jungle on the top of the hill, about 1 mile to the east of the town in a direct line, but nearly 2 miles by the winding pathway. The building is much smaller than the Gonda temple, and has no figures on the outside, but only simple mouldings. The sanctum is only 12 feet outside, and 8 by 7¾ feet inside, with a niche in the back wall, and a lingam in the middle. The mandapa, or hall, in front is slightly oblong, being 18 feet 8 inches by 17 feet 7 inches. The hall is open at the sides, with two broad seats, 3½ feet wide, backed by sloping parapets. There is a small portico in front, 9 feet wide by 6 feet deep. The enshrined statue of the goddess has four arms, and is 2 feet in height. Close by there is a tank hewn out of the rock 80 feet by 50 feet.

There are two inscriptions on the temple : 1st, an old record of the Chandeli period in two long lines, without date The beginning is lost, and there is no King's name ; 2nd, a record of seven short lines, dated in Samvat 1466 (A.D. 1409), which I read as follows :—

1. Siddhih !—Samvat
2. 1466 varshe Chaitra
3. Sudi 7 sane—Râjâ
4. dâsah Sri Râjavâsinya
5. Paramârddi Mahipateh-
6. tasya bhrityosti jai Pâlah,
7. Samogha Sura Pâlajah.

" In the Samvat year 1466, on Saturday, the 7th day of the waxing moon of Chaitra (Saturday, 23rd March 1409 A.D.), the king's slave in Râja-vâsini (the royal residence of Paramârdi, lord of the earth, whose servant was Jai Pâla Samogha, the son of Sura Pâla).[1]"

I take the name of Paramârdi to refer to the Chandel king of two centuries earlier than the date of the inscription. Râja-vâsini I suppose to have been his royal residence, and perhaps to have been founded by him. It is, however, quite possible that there was a second Paramârdi at the date of this inscription in A.D. 1409, although no certain records of the Chandel Princes have yet been found of a later date than Samvat 1372, or A.D. 1315, of Vira Varmma II.

10.—MARPHA.

The great fort of Marpha is but little known, although it is as large and as lofty as either Kâlanjar or Ajaygarh. It is situated on a high projecting hill, just 4 miles to the south of Râsin, and 12 miles to the north-east of Kâlanjar.[2] I passed under the fort and within a mile of its walls on my way to visit Bilhariya temple, which is just 2 miles to the south of the fort. I did not visit the place myself, as it had been previously explored by both of my Assistants, Mr. Beglar and Mr. Carlleyle. The inscriptions spoken of by Pogson[3]

[1] See Plate XIV for a *fac simile* of this inscription.
[2] See the map in Plate I for the position of Marpha.
[3] Pogson's Bundelas, page 135.

are not old, and are of very little value. There is one long
inscription of three lines, dated in Samvat 1404, or A.D.
1347. It records a dedication. Two others in small letters
are Jain records of the Mula Sangha, dated in Samvat 1407
and 1408. They contain no kings' names, and are confined
to the names of the donors of the statues dedicated, and of
the high priest at the time of dedication. I can find no
mention of Marpha in any of the Muhammadan historians,
and I am inclined to think that it was not occupied as a fort
until Kâlanjar had fallen.

The missionary Tieffenthaler, who visited Marpha in the
middle of the last century, states that it was also called
Mandefa. But I suspect that both the names are only
corruptions of the original, which, from the inscription of
Samvat 1404 mentioned above, would appear to have been
Madharppa.

This inscription is dated in *Samvat 1404, Kârttika Sudi
14 Gurau*, in the *Sidhitungarâjye*, or during the reign of
Sidhitunga. There is nothing like this name either amongst
the Bâghel chiefs of Rewa or the Chandel princes of
Kâlanjar.

The fort is now nearly deserted, and is overrun with jungle,
in which both tigers and leopards find cover.

11.—BILHARIYA.

Ten miles to the south of Râsin, in the midst of the
valley, overlooked by the great fort of Marpha, there is a
small stone temple on the top of a rocky hill called *Bilhariya
Math*, or the Bilhariya temple. It is about 18 miles from the
Majgowa station of the Jabalpur Railway, but the road lies
over an uninhabited hill tract, and is now very rarely used.

The hill is 70 feet high. On the lower terrace towards
the south there are the remains of two other temples, which
have been dismantled to furnish materials for a small fort, at
a short distance to the north, near the village of Bhagalan-
purwa. Its walls are built entirely of squared stones, amongst
which I recognized door jambs, pillars, amalaka fruit pinnacles, mouldings of many kinds, and several roofing slabs.

The temple on the hill is a small one, but it is highly ornamented, and is otherwise remarkable for its picturesque situation.   It consists of a sanctum, 11¾ feet outside and 4¼ feet inside, with a portico in front, 9 feet square.   The spire is still standing with the lower amalaka fruit *in situ*, but the upper part of the pinnacle is gone.   On the outside there are two rows of figures, of which the lower ones are 19 inches in height.   I recognized the following :—

North . { Lakshmi, four-armed, seated, being anointed by two ele. phants.
Siva and Pârvati, standing.
Nearly naked female, exposing her person.
Siva standing with Nandi.

West . { Siva with trident.
Vishnu.
Siva naked, with sword and skull.

South . { Ardhanâri, half male, half female figure.
Naked female.
Saraswati, four-armed.

The temple was dedicated to Vishnu, who is represented over the centre of the entrance with Brahmâ on his right and Siva on his left, and the Navagraha, or nine planets, arranged between them.

12.—KÂLANJAR FORT.

The fort of Kâlanjar is one of the most famous places in India.   In A.D. 1023 it withstood the army of Mahmud of Ghazni, but was shortly surrendered, and the Raja was received into favour on presenting some highly complimentary verses to the great conqueror.[1]   In 1545 it held out against the redoubtable Sher Shah, and was not captured until the besiegers had been roused to fury when their king had been mortally wounded by the bursting of a shell in the trenches. In 1812 it repulsed the assault of a British force under Colonel Martindell, but the fort was surrendered on the following morning, as the Raja doubted whether he would be able to

[1] Brigg's Ferishta, Vol. I, p. 67.

withstand a second assault.	The terms were very favourable, as he received an estate of equal value in the plain.[1]

Kâlanjar is situated 90 miles to the west-south-west of Allahabad, and 60 miles to the north-west of Rewa.	The fort stands on an isolated flat-topped hill of the Vindhya range, which here rises to a height of 800 feet above the plain. The lower part of the ascent is tolerably easy, but the middle portion is very steep, while the upper part is nearly perpendicular and quite inaccessible.	The main body of the fort, which lies from east to west, is oblong in form, being nearly a mile in length by half a mile in breadth.	At the north angle there is a large projecting spur nearly a quarter of a milè square, which overhangs the town; and on the middle of the southern face there is another projection of about the same size, but triangular in shape.	The distance between the extreme points of these two projections is nearly 1 mile. The whole area is therefore considerably less than 1 square mile, while the parapet walls are nearly 4 miles in length.[2]

Kâlanjar is often compared with Gwalior, under the belief that the two forts are about the same size.	But Gwalior is $1\frac{3}{4}$ mile in length by half a mile in breadth, with a parapet of rather more than 5 miles in extent.	Kâlanjar, however, has the advantage of Gwalior in height, being upwards of 800 feet above the plain, while Gwalior is under 400 feet. But the water-supply of Gwalior is permanent and good, while that of Kâlanjar is uncertain, and has failed on several important occasions.

Kâlanjar has been occupied from the most remote times. According to Wilson, it is mentioned in the Vedas as one of the *tapasyasthânas*, or "spots adopted to practices of austere devotion."[3]	In the Mahâbhârata it is stated that whoever bathes in the lake of the gods in Kâlanjar acquires the same merit as if he had made a gift of 1,000 cows.[4]	In the Padma Purâna it is named as one of the nine holy places in Northern India.

[1] Pogson's Bundelas, p. 142.
[2] See Plate VIII for a map of the fort.
[3] Sanskrit Dictionary, *in voce*.
[4] Atkinson, Gazetteer of Bundelkhand, Art. *Kalanjar*.

" Renuka, Sukara, Kasi, Kâli, Kâla, Bateswarâh, Kâlanjara, Mahâkâlâ, Ukhala nava Kirttnâh,"—that is, " Renuka
(near Agra), Sukara (Soron on the Ganges), Kâsi (Benares),
Kâli, Kâlâ (or Karra on the Ganges), Bateswara (two of the
name), Kâlanjara, Mahâkâla (or Ujain), are the nine famous
Ukhalas."

But all these notices refer solely to the sanctity of the
hill as the resort of *tapaswis*, or holy ascetics. The overhanging rocks afforded shelter to the Rishis, and the rain
water percolating through the rocks from above gave them
drink. The hills of Asirgarh and Gwâlior were similarly
occupied by holy ascetics before they were made into fortresses. At the former the famous saint Aswathâma gave his
name to Aswathâmagiri, and at the latter place the holy hermit Gwâlipâ gave his name to Gwali-âwar. But the name of
Kâlanjarâdri, or the hill of Kâlanjara, is said to have been
derived from Siva himself, who, as *Kâla*, or " Time," causes
all things to decay (*jar*), and who is therefore the destroyer
of all things, and the god of death. *Tapaswis*, or ascetics,
of Kâlanjara were therefore devoted to the worship of Siva.

The oldest historical mention of Kâlanjara as a fortress is
in A.D. 1023, when the place was besieged by Mahmud of
Ghazni during the reign of the Chandel Raja Ganda[1] Deva.
Its erection as a fortress is universally attributed to Chandra
Varmma, the traditional founder of the Chandela family.
But the inscriptions are silent as to Chandra Varmma, and
give Nannuka as the founder of the family. There is, besides,
good evidence to show that Kâlanjara was a famous fortress
even before the rise of the Chandelas. The Kalachuris of
Southern India claim descent from a son of Siva, named
Krishna, by a Brâhmani mother, who slew the king of Kâlan-
jarapura, and *afterwards* took possession of the " nine-lakh
country of *Dâhala Mandala* " (or Chedi).[2] Now the Chedis,

---

[1] The Raja is called Nanda by the Muhammadan historians, but his true
name was Ganda, as recorded in all the inscriptions. In Persian letters, G might
easily be changed to N by the substitution of a point for the " markaz " of
" Gâf."

[2] Rice's Mysore Inscriptions, p. 64.

or Kalachuris, had possession of Dâhala Mandala (Tipurra or
Tewar on the Narbada) as early as the 6th century, when
they came into contact with Mangalisa Chalukya. Their
occupation of Kâlanjara must, therefore, have occurred some
time earlier. I have already suggested that this event may
have given rise to the Chedi or Kalachuri era, which, as I
have shown, dates from A.D. 249. But the fort of Kâlanjara must already have existed for some time before it
attracted the notice of the Kalachuri chief Krishna. It
seems highly probable, therefore, that the fortress may have
been founded at least as early as the beginning of the Christian era.

The actual history of Kâlanjara begins in A.D. 1019, when
Mahmud of Ghazni advanced to the frontier of the Kâlanjara
Raja's dominions. The Raja collected a large army of
36,000 horse, 105,000 foot, and 640 elephants to oppose
him. The result is thus related by the historian Nizâm-ud-din
Ahmad[1] :—

"When the Sultân approached his camp, he first sent an ambas-
sador, calling upon him to acknowledge fealty and embrace the
Muhammadan faith. Nanda refused these conditions, and prepared
to fight. Upon this the Sultân reconnoitred Nanda's army from an
eminence, and observing its vast numbers, he regretted his having
come thither. Prostrating himself before God, he prayed for success
and victory. When night came on, great fear and alarm entered the
mind of Nanda, and he fled with some of his personal attendants,
leaving all his baggage and equipments. The next day the Sultân,
being apprized of this, rode out on horseback without any escort,
and carefully examined the ground. When he was satisfied that there
was no ambush and strategical device, he stretched out his hands for
plunder and devastation. Immense booty fell into the hands of
the Musalmâns, and 580 of Nanda's elephants, which were in the
neighbouring woods, were taken. The Sultân, loaded with victory and success, returned to Ghazni."

No reason is given by the historian for Mahmud's retire-
ment. Ferishta, however, suggests that Mahmud must have
been apprehensive about what might occur in the Punjâb and
other countries in his rear, and was satisfied with what he

---

[1] Elliot's Muhammadan Historians, by Dowson, Vol. II, p. 464.

had done that year.   It seems more probable, however, that
Mahmud retired because he was doubtful of the result, and,
like a prudent general, he went back to Ghazni to return with
a large force.

Accordingly in A.H. 413 (A.D. 1022, or according to
Ferishta one year later), Mahmud again undertook an expedition against the territory of Nanda (Ganda Deva).[1]

" Having reached the fort of Gwâlior, he besieged it.   Four days
after, the chief of the place sent messengers promising 35 elephants,
and solicited   protection.   The Sultân agreed to the terms, and
from thence proceeded to Kâlanjar.   This is a fort unparalleled
in the whole country of Hindustân for its strength.   He invested this
fort also, and after a while, Nanda, its chief, presented 300 elephants,
and sued for peace.   As these animals were sent out of the fort without riders, the Sultân ordered the Turks to seize and mount them.
The enemy perceiving this was much surprised, and Nanda sent
a copy of Hindi verses in praise of the Sultân, who gave it to the
learned men of Hind and other poets who were at his court, who
all bestowed their admiration upon them.   He was much pleased
with the compliment, and in return conferred on him the government
of 15 forts, besides some other presents.   Nanda acknowledged this
favour by sending immense riches and jewels to the Sultân, who
then victoriously and triumphantly returned to Ghazni."

Kâlanjar is not mentioned again until after the occupation of Delhi by the Muhammadans, when Kutb-ud-din Aibak
advanced to besiege it.   According to the historian Hasan
Nizâmi[2]

" The accursed Parmâr, the Rai of Kâlanjar, fled into the fort
after a desperate resistance in the field, and afterwards surrendered
himself, and 'placed the collar of subjection' round his neck, and
on his promise of allegiance, was admitted to the same favours as his
ancestor had experienced from Mahmud Subuktigîn, and engaged to
make a payment of tribute and elephants, but he died a natural death
before he could execute any of his engagements.   His Dewân, or
Mahtea, by name Aj Deo, was not disposed to surrender so easily
as his master, and gave his enemies much trouble, until he was compelled to capitulate, in consequence of severe drought having dried up
all the reservoirs of water in the forts.

[1] Tabakât-i-Akbari, in H. M. Elliot's Muhammadan Historians, Vol. II,
p. 467.
    [2] Tâj-ul-Maasir, in H. M. Elliott's Muhammadan Historians, Vol. II, p. 231.

"On Monday, the 20th of Rajab, the garrison, in an extreme state of weakness and distraction, came out of the fort, and by compulsion left their native place empty, and the fort of Kâlanjar, which was celebrated throughout the world for being as strong as the wall of Alexander, was taken. The temples were converted into mosques and abodes of goodness, and the ejaculations of the bead-counters and the voices of the summoners to prayer ascended to the highest heaven, and the very name of idolatry was annihilated. Fifty-thousand men came under the collar of slavery, and the plain became black as pitch with Hindus. Elephants and cattle, and countless arms, also became the spoil of the victors."

The full name of this Raja was *Paramârddi Deva*, but he is usually known even to this day as *Parmâl* Raja, and to him the downfall of the Chandel dynasty is universally ascribed. According to Ferishta the Raja was assassinated by his minister, who again hoisted the Hindu flag on the fort.[1] But the place was soon reduced by the failure of the spring which supplied the garrison with water.

The government of Kâlanjar was entrusted to Hazabbar-ud-din Hasan Arnal, and the fort thus became a part of the Muhammadan kingdom of Delhi. But it soon fell into the hands of the Hindus, probably during the weak reign of Aram Shah in A.H. 607, as it is related by Minhâj that Iltitmish sent a force against Kâlanjar in A.H. 631, when the Raja fled.[2] The army returned with much plunder, but the fort remained in the possession of the Hindus.

Again, in A.H. 645 (A.D. 1247) Minhâj gives an account of a Raja with the mysterious name of Dalaki-Malaki, who occupied a hill fort to the south of the Jumna, who managed to escape from his fort while his women and children fell into the hands of the Muhammadans.

Four years later in A.H. 649 (A.D. 1251) the Muhammadan troops from Bayâna, Sultânkot, Kanauj, and Gwalior were sent to ravage the territories of Kâlanjar.

Again, in A.H. 653 (A.D. 1255) Malik Kutlugh Khan, who had married the king's mother, rebelled, and being obliged to fly, took refuge in Kâlanjar.

---

[1] Brigg's Ferishta, Vol. I, p. 197.
[2] Raverty's Tabakât-i-Akbari, p. 733.

During all this time the fort was in the hands of the
Hindus, and so it most probably remained for nearly three
centuries more until it was taken by Sher Shah in A.D. 1545.
During the strong reign of Ala-ud-din Khilji it might, no doubt,
have been taken easily, but that king was too intent upon the
plunder of the rich states of Southern India to care for the
capture of a fort which had already been plundered by his
predecessors.   The shortness of Tughlak's reign alone prevented the annexation of Gwalior, Kâlanjar, and other similar
places.   From the time of Muhammad Tughlak, when the
Muhammadan dominions began to break up into a number of
small states, Kâlanjar remained in the quiet possession of
the Hindus under the descendants of their old Chandela
Rajas.

In A.H. 937 (A.D. 1530), a few months after his accession,
Humâyun invested Kâlanjar, but gave up the siege on the
Raja expressing his fealty.[1]

In A.H. 952 (A.D. 1545) Sher Shah laid seige to Kâlanjar.   According to Ahmad Yâdgâr his reason for attacking
the place was because the Raja refused to give up Bir Singh
Deo Bundela, who had sought refuge with him.[2]   On Friday,
the 9th of the 1st Rabia, while standing in the trenches, the
king was badly wounded by a shell or rocket, which rebounded
from the wall of the fort.   On being carried to his tent he
gave orders for an immediate assault.   The historian Albas
Khan[3] says—

" Men came and swarmed out instantly on every side like ants and
locusts, and by the time of afternoon prayers captured the fort, putting
every one to the sword, and sending all the infidels to hell. About the
hour of evening prayers the intelligence of the victory reached Sher
Shah, and marks of joy and pleasure appeared on his countenance.
Raja Kirat Singh, with 70 men, remained in a house. Kutb Khan
the whole night long watched the house in person lest the Raja
should escape. Sher Shah said to his sons that none of his nobles
need watch the house, so that the Raja escaped out of the house, and
the labour and trouble of this long watching was lost. The next day
at sunrise, however, they took the Raja alive.

---

[1] Elliott's Muhammadan Historians, Vol. V, p. 189.
[2] Dowson's Note in Elliott's Muhammadan Historians, Vol. IV, p. 407.
[3] Târikl-i-Sher Shah in Elliott, Vol. IV, p. 409.

" On the 10th Rabi-ul-awal, 952 A.H. (May 1545), Sher Shah went from the hostel of this world to rest in the mansion of happiness, and ascended peacefully from the abode of this world to the lofty heavens. The date was discovered in the words *azálash murd*, ' He died from fire.' "

When Islâm Shah reached the camp at Kâlanjar his first act was to order the Raja's execution.

In the early part of Akbar's reign the fort of Kâlanjar came into the hands of the Bâghel chief of Rewa, Raja Râmchandar, who in A.H. 977 (or A.D. 1569) made it over to Akbar. After that it remained for upwards of 120 years in the undisturbed possession of the Mughal kings of Delhi. Towards the end of the reign of Aurangzeb the fort was captured by the bold Bundela chief Chhatr Sâl. Apparently no attempt was made to recover it, and on the accession of Bahâdur Shah in A.D. 1707, the Emperor confirmed Chhatr Sâl in all his conquests.

On the death of the Bundela chief his dominions were divided between his sons, and the fort of Kâlanjar became part of the state of Panna, under the rule of Raja Hardeo Shâh. At the beginning of the present century the fort still belonged nominally to Panna, but was actually in the possession of a family of Brâhman brothers named Daryau Singh, Gangâdhar, and others. Daryau Singh and Gangâdhar were confirmed in their possession by the British Government. But as Daryau presuming on the strength of the fortress, gave shelter to bands of plunderers, and openly defied the British authority it was determined to take Kâlanjar from him, and thus to reduce his power of doing mischief. Kâlanjar was accordingly invested by Colonel Martindell in 1812, and, though his assault was repulsed, yet the chiefs were so doubtful of making a successful resistance that they surrendered the fortress the next day on the condition of receiving an estate of equal value in the plain below.[1] Since then Kâlanjar has remained in the hands of the British Government. At first it was held by a regular garrison, but since

---

[1] Pogson's Bundelas, and Gazetteer of Bundelkhand.

the mutiny the walls have been dismantled, and the fort is
now held by a party of police.

The antiquities of Kâlanjar were first noticed by Pogson,
but they have since been very fully and ably described by
Lieutenant Maisey (now General) in an interesting paper
accompanied by numerous illustrations.   I can add but little
to his account of the antiquities of the place, but I have been
fortunate in obtaining several inscriptions, and more especially
some early ones, which escaped his notice.

There are two entrances to the fort of Kâlanjar, of which
the principal is on the north side towards the town, and the
other at the south-east angle leading towards Panna.   This
latter, which is still called the Panna Gate, is now closed.
The other entrance is guarded by seven different gates, which,
beginning from below, are named as follows :—

1—Alam, or Alamgiri, Gate.

2—Ganes Gate.

3—Chandi, or Chau-burji, Gate.

4—Budh-bhadr Gate.

5—Hanumân Gate.

6—Lâl Darwâza.

7—Barâ Darwâza.

The number of seven gates suggested to Colonel Pogson
that Kâlanjar must have been the "seat of solar worship"
which he supposed to be confirmed by the name of *Ravi-
chitra*, "the former word signifying the sun, and the latter a
holy place."   But *Rava-chitra* simply means "sun-spotted;"
and it is further unfortunate for the solar theory that during
the Hindu rule there were only six gates, the lowest gate
named the Alam Darwâza, having been added during the
reign of the Emperor Aurangzeb Alamgir.

There is an ascent of about 200 feet up to the lowest
gate, which is a battlemented building in the modern Muhammadan style.   Over the archway outside there is a rhyming
Persian inscription of three lines, recording the constructing
of the gate by Muhammad Murâd, during the reign of the
Emperor Aurangzeb, when it was made as strong as the " wall

of Alexander." The following is the text of this inscription,
as given by Lieutenant Maisey :—

الله هوالغني '

شد مرمت چون قلع كالنجر   شاه اورنگ زیب دین پرور

ساخت درها محكم و خوشتر   چون محمد مراد از حكمش

سد عظیم چو سد اسكندر   از خرد سال جستمش ميكفت

The date is given in the numerical value of the letters in
the words سد عظیم, which represent—

$$60 + 4 + 70 + 900 + 10 + 40 = 1084 \text{A.H.},$$

or A.D. 1673, in the 15th year of the reign of Aurangzeb
Alamgir, after whom the gate received its name of Alam
Darwâza.

Above this there is a steep ascent, chiefly by steps, to the
second gate called the *Ganes Darwâza.*

At a short distance higher up in the bend of the road
stands the third gate, named the Chandi Darwâza. As noted
by Lieutenant Maisey, there is, in fact, a double gate, with four
towers,.on which account it is also known as the Chau-burji
Darwâza, or " gate of the Four Towers." At this gateway
there are several pilgrims' records of various dates, as given
by Lieutenant Maisey, with the following dates : Samvat 1199,
1572, 1580, and 1600. The latest of these, Samvat 1600, or
A.D. 1543, records the final capture of the fort by Sher Shah
a mistake of two years. On the rock close by there is a much
older inscription of fifteen lines, of the later Gupta period,
which appears to have escaped the notice of Lieutenant
Maisey. It is very nearly complete, but not in very good
order. I can find neither date nor king's name in it.

The fourth gate, named Budha-bhadra Darwâza, is the gate
of the " auspicious planet Mars (Budha)." It is also named
the *Swarga-rohana*, or " Heaven-ascending Gate," owing to
the stiff climb required to reach it. It possesses only one inscription of a pilgrim, dated in Samvat 1580, or A.D. 1523.

The fifth gate, or Hanumân Darwâza, is so named after a
figure of the monkey-god carved on a slab resting against the

rock. There is also a reservoir called Hanumân-kund. There are, besides, numerous rock sculptures, which are very much weather-worn. Many, however, are still quite recognizable, such as Mahâdeva and Pârvati, Ganesa, the Bull Nandi, and the Lingam. Two inscriptions of pilgrims were noticed by Lieutenant Maisey, dated in Samvat 1530 and Samvat 1580. On the ascent beyond there are many weather-worn figures carved on the rock representing Kâli, Chandika, and the Lingam. There is also a small cave, or niche, containing a broken figure of Honumân. There are several short inscriptions of pilgrims, with the dates of Samvat 1560 and 1600.

The sixth gate, called the Lâl Darwâza, from its red colour, stands near the top of the ascent. To the west of this gate, in the Raoni, or *faussebraie*, immediately above the Bhairava-kund, there is a colossal figure of Bhairava cut in the rock. Here also are two figures of pilgrims represented carrying water in the usual manner in two vessels fixed to the end of a Banghi pole. Near one of them there is the following inscription in well-shaped Gupta characters :—

Samâdhigata pancha-mahásabda-Sâmanta Sri Vasanta.

"The illustrious Sâmanta Vasanta (the possessor of the title of) pancha-mahasabdha."

The expression of *Samâdhigata pancha-mahasabda* is commonly applied to *Sâmantas,* or petty chiefs, as I am informed by Pandit Bhagwân Lâl Indraji. I take the figure of the water-carrier to represent the Sâmanta himself.

Carved on the rock outside the Lâl Darwâza there is a long inscription of sixteen lines, which is unfortunately too much obliterated to be readable. In the fourth line I see the name of *Kâlanjarâdri,* or the "Hill of Kâlanjara."

A short ascent leads to the seventh, or uppermost gate, called *Bara Darwâza,* or the "Main Gate." As it stands now, it is undoubtedly modern, and its late date is confirmed by the only inscription attached to it of Samvat 1691, or A.D. 1634.

Inside the fort on the north face are four places of note named Sîtakund, Sîtasej, Pâtâl Gangâ, and Pându-kund.

Sîtasej is a small cave, or recess, containing a stone bed and pillow for the use of a hermit.

The Pâtâl Gangâ is a large deep well, or reservoir, cut in the rock. The water is deep, and is constantly dripping and trickling from the roof and sides. The oldest inscription found here is of Samvat 1339, or· A.D. 1282. The next is of Samvat 1500, or A.D. 1443; and a third of Samvat 1540, or A.D. 1483. Next comes a record of the Emperor Humâyun in Persian, dated in the year A.H. 936, or A.D. 1529-30. The latest is of Samvat 1640, or A.D. 1583, during the reign of Akbar.

The Pându-kund is a "shallow circular basin, about 12 feet in diameter," into which the water is constantly trickling from the crevices in the.horizontal strata of rock. This *kund* is undoubtedly old, as it possesses a short inscription in Gupta characters reading "*Manoratha*   *   *

Near the middle of the east face there is a natural hollow, in the bottom of which has been excavated in the rock a small reservoir with steps all round. This is called the *Budhi*, or *Burhyia Tâl.* Its waters are believed to possess very great healing powers, as the leprous Râja Kirat Brim, or Kirtti Varmma, after having bathed in the tank, found himself healed. This Raja is commonly called Krim Koth, or "Krim, the leper."

At the south-east angle is situated the Panna, or Bansâkar Gate, which is now closed. The latter is the old name, the former having been given since the British occupation. It is covered by a small outwork. There are three gates. There are some pilgrims' records of Samvat 1550 and 1600, and near the Bhairon-ka-Jhirka, or Bhairava's well, there is an old record of Samvat 1195, or A.D. 1138, and a single sculpture of a pilgrim carrying two water vessels on a banghi-pole. Above the kund there is a colossal figure of Bhairava carved in the rock. The oldest pilgrim's record is Samvat 1194, or A.D. 1137. Amongst other figures there is a second water-carrier.

Near the middle of the south face is the *Mrig-dhâra*, or "Antelope's Spring," a small pool in an inner chamber of the rampart into which water is constantly trickling. It is no doubt supplied, as suggested by Lieutenant Maisey, from the great reservoir of Kot-Tirth on the high ground close by.

Kot-Tirth is a large reservoir, nearly 100 yards in length, with several flights of steps and many remains of sculpture. Kot-Tirth, or the " Fort-Holy Place," is the chief object of pilgrimage in Kâlanjar. In the south-east corner there is said to be a deep hole, and this was probably the original holy pool of the place, which was eventually enlarged to its present size. The Brâhmans declare that it is fed by springs ; but as it occupies the highest ground in the fort, and there are no higher hills in the neigbourhood, its only feeders must be the springs of heaven during the rainy season. The name is also written Koti-Tirth, or the " ten million places of Pilgrimage," and Koth-tirth, or " the "Leprosy place of pilgrimage," where lepers are cured by bathing.

The great lingam of Nilakantha is situated in an outwork in the middle of the west face of the fort. The upper gate, leading into the outwork, is attributed to Raja Parmâl, or Paramârdi Deva, who reigned from A.D. 1167 to 1203. There are several inscriptions, but all of the 16th century of the Samvat, being dated respectively in Samvat 1540, 1547, 1557, and 1574. A second gate, which leads into the court-yard of the temple, has no inscription. But on the rock on the right hand of the descent there are numerous small caves and niches, with many statues and several inscriptions which will be noticed presently.

The actual shrine of the Nilakantha lingam is a small cave with the remains of a fine *mandapa*, or hall in front. The façade of the cave has been very rich, but it is now much broken and hidden by numerous coats of whitewash. On the jambs of the door there are figures of Siva and Pârvati with the Ganges and Jumna Rivers. These are of the Gupta period. The pillars of the hall are later, and belong to the time of the Chandels. The roof of the Mandapa is now gone, but most of the pillars and pilasters still remain, forming a square with four on each side, and four in the middle. In roofing, the corners were cut off to form an octagon, as shown in Lieutenant Maisey's plan.[1] The lingam is made of a dark-blue stone, $4\frac{1}{2}$ feet high, and has silver eyes. It is at present the chief object of worship at Kâlanjar, and, to judge by the pilgrims' records, it has been equally popular for many centuries.

Just outside the Mandapa of Nilakantha there is a deep *kund*, or rock-cut reservoir, called Swarga Rohina ; and to the right of the kund in a rock recess, or niche, there is a colossal figure of Kâl Bhairav, 24 feet in height, standing in 2 feet of water. The sculpture is 17 feet broad. It is mentioned by Abul Fazl as being 18 cubits in height.[2] The figure has 18 arms, and is ornamented with the usual garland of skulls, with snake earrings and snake armlets, and a serpent twined round the neck. In the hands are various objects, of which the most prominent are a sword, a bowl of blood, &c. Beside this statue there is a figure of the skeleton goddess Kâli, 4 feet in height, which is now standing in water upwards of a foot in depth. The water trickles from above and falls on these figures. Beyond this sculpture there is a closed postern in the wall of the outwork, above which, on the outside, there is an inaccessible cave.

13.—KÂLANJAR INSCRIPTIONS.

In arranging the Kâlanjar inscriptions I have begun with those inside the fort, which have dates. There are several older records both inside and outside, but as it is difficult to arrange them chronologically, I have placed them at the end of the account. Two of these belong to the Gupta period.

The earliest dated inscriptions at Kâlanjar are found in the temple and on the rock of the Nilkanth outwork. They are limited to a period of 72 years during the reigns of Madana Varmma and his son Paramârddi Deva, immediately prior to the Muhammadan conquest in A.D. 1203. The

[1] Bengal Asiatic Society's Journal, 1847, p. 193.
[2] Ain-i-Akbari, Vol. II, p. 29.

latest is in fact dated in the preceding year, Samvat 1258, or
A.D. 1201-02.   These inscriptions are the following :—

A.—Plate X.—Pillar in Nilkanth Temple.

Deva (?) Sri Nilakantha
ma (?) nityam pranamiti.
Aum! Sam 1186 Mahârâja Sri
Madana Varmma Deva ‖ mahâ
pratihâra Sangrâma Sinha‖
Mahâ Nâchani Padmâvati‖
lânshuh Auji.
Adoration to Nilakantha
-was made   *   *   *   *   *   *

Aum! In the Samvat year 1186 (A.D. 1129) during the reign of
the fortunate king Madana Varmma Deva, the chief door-keeper,
Sangrâma Sinha, (and) the chief dancing-girl, Padmâvati—written by
Auji.''

The inscribers were, no doubt, two of the permanent attendants attached to the Nilakantha shrine, one being the
chief door-keeper and the other the chief of the dancing-girls.

The last words *lânshuh Auji* I have given as explained
by a Brahman.

B.—Plate X.—Piece of Broken Pillar.[1]

Aum! Samvat 1187 Jyeshtha Sudi 9
Sri mad Madana Varmma Deva‖
Kâlanjarâdri Sri Tri
-salka * rdi ârâ * na Sri (*end*)

(Incomplete).

"Aum! In the Samvat year 1187 (A.D. 1130), on the 9th day of
the waxing moon of Jyeshta, during the reign of the fortunate
Madana Varmma Deva, on the hill of Kâlanjara, Sri Trisalka ''*   *

This inscription is incomplete, as it ends abruptly with the
word Sri in the 4th line.

C.—Plate X.—Rock near Nilakantha.

This inscription is engraved on the rock to the left, or
north, side of the temple of Nilakantha.   It was copied by
Lieutenant Maisey, but the text and translation afterwards pub-

---

[1] Now lying at the police station in the town; and said to have been brought from
the temple of Nilakantha.

lished by the editors of the Bengal Asiatic Society's Journal (1848, p. 321) contain so many errors that I have no hesitation in giving a fresh reading of the text —

1. Aum Swasti! parama bhaṭṭâraka Mahârâjadhiraja parameswara parama-ma
2. heswara Sri Kâlanjarâdhipati Sri Man Madana Varmma Deva charanambu
3. jârâdhan tatparo dhimân dharmmaparâyana Maharajapu
4. -tra Sri Solhaṇa suta mahâ Sahaṇika maha selaita Kuma
5. rakula Kamalaṅdu Mahârâjaputra Sri Vachha Râjaḥ‖ Deva Sri
6. Kavidyanka Achhoda Râüt Sri Udanaḥ‖ Deva Sri Ni
7. lakanthasya Sutradhâra Sri Râma suta Rupakâra Sri Laha
8. ḍa tad Babri Rupakâra Sri Lakshmi-dhara sântyo mûrtti rèshi
9. teti‖ Samvat 1188 Kârttika Sudi 8 Sanai‖.

"Aum-Swasti. During the reign of the supreme lord, the king of kings, the mighty sovereign, the chief of Kâlanjara, the fortunate Madana Varmma Deva, then Maha Selaita, the Mahâ Sahanika, son of the king's son Solhana, together with Sri Vatsa Raja Deva, the son of Prince Kamalandu * * * and the Râüt Sri Udanah, set up this image of Nilakantha.

"Sculptors Sri Lâhada, son of the architect Sri Râma and Sri Lakshmidhara.

"The Samvat year 1188 (=A.D. 1131) on the 8th day of the waxing moon of Karttika, on Saturday.

D.—Plate X on Rock near Nilakantha beside a figure of Narasinha.

1. Aum! Dikshita Sri Prithvidhara sutaḥ Ṭhakkura Sri Sa
2. lhaṇa Pabhuvatasya tanayena *Th*akkur Sri Nri Sin
3. hena Deva Sri Nri Sinhasya Mûrttiriyam Kârâpi
4. teti‖ Samvat 1192 Jyeṣṭha sudi 9 Ravan.

This is No. 5 of Lieutenant Maisey's inscriptions, but the editors of the Bengal Asiatic Society's Journal have misread the well-known title of *Thakkur* as *Sarkkâra.*[1] Immediately below it there is a second inscription to the same purpose,

---

[1] Bengal Asiatic Society's Journal, 1848, page 322.

but with the name of Râlhaṇa, instead of Salhaṇa. It reads
as follows :—

Lower half of D.

1. Aum !   Dikshita Sri Prithivi-dhara Su
2. -taḥ Râlhaṇa ; tat Sutena Sri
3. Nri Sinhena Nri Sinha Mû
4. -rttih Karapiteyam.

" Aum!   This image of Nrisinha was caused to be made by Ṭhakkur Sri Nrisinha Deva, son of Ṭhakkur Sri Salhaṇa Pabhuvata, son
of Dikshita Sri Prithivi-dhara, Samvat 1192, Sunday, 9th day of the
waxing moon of Jyeshtha (A.D. 1135).

" Aum !   This image of the Nrisinha was caused to be made by
Sri Nrisinha, son of Râlhaṇa, son of Dikshita Sri Prithivi dhara."

E.—In a kotri or cell to the north of Nilakantha.

This inscription of 7 lines is in good order, but unfortunately it conveys no information of any interest.   It opens
with a dedication to Śiva, and closes with the date of *Samvat
1194, Chaitra badi 5 Budhau*.   It is simply a record of two
Brahmans (*dwija*) of the Bharadwâja gotra.   The date is
equivalent to A.D. 1137, Wednesday, 23rd February.

F.—Broken Inscription on Rock to north of Nilakantha.

This inscription is unfortunately broken on both sides
and rather more than one-half of the lower part on the right
is gone.   There are 20½ lines of the small letters, and 7½
lines of much larger letters.   At first I thought that there
were two distinct records ; and this is quite possible, but as
the latter part is joined to the former in the middle of a line,
it looks more like a continuation.   As the words *Mahesa
mûrtti* occur in the 6th line, I conclude that the record most
probably refers to the great lingam of Mahesa, or Nilakantha.   In the 12th line I see the name of Kâlanjarâdri, or
"hill of Kâlanjara," and in the last line there is the date of
Samvat 1195, or A.D. 1138, in the middle of the reign of
Madana Varmma.

G.—On Pavement of Nilakantha Temple.

1. Samvat 1222 Kshatravansodbhava Sri Lakshmana Suta Vâsu
   Deva nityam pranamati.
2. Pameṇa suta Sri Vara || Hara Deva suta Vâsabhu nityam
   praṇamati.

These two lines simply record the visits of pilgrims to the shrine of Nilakantha in S. 1222, or A.D. 1165. The first line gives the name of Vâsu Deva, the son of Sri Lakshmana, of the exalted Kshatra race. The second line gives the names of Pamena's son Sri Vara, and Hara Deva's son Vâsabhu.

H.—On a large black stone, inside the Temple.

This is No. 1 of Lieutenant Maisey's inscriptions.[1] It consists of 32 lines. The date has been wrongly read by the translator as Samvat 1298, or A.D. 1241, instead of 1258, or A.D. 1201, which it actually is, and which it certainly ought to be, as Paramârddi Deva, the chief object of the record, died soon after the capture of the fort on 27th April 1203 A.D. The translator has not given any version of the first 24 lines, as they contain only a eulogistic and glowing address to Siva and Pârvati.

The remainder of the inscription is given as follows :—

25. "He, the greatest of kings, having drunk, like draughts of honey and curds, the shining fame of the kings, his enemies, introduced a rule for collecting the land revenue without resistance from any foe (or he became the husband of the earth, which without resistance completed the ceremony of marriage).

26. "Some having been easily made prisoners and kept in his own house, were afterwards released. In a moment he caused some of them to wander from house to house ; some he made to enjoy happiness ; some, the fathers and children, with unceasing compassion for them, were seeking safety for their life within the walls (of some castle). Of the long arm of this king his enemies were afraid as of their *fatal* enemy.

"27. The king of Dashârna, like the wind of the Malaya mountain, kisses sportively the lips of the maidens, red like the pomegranate, seizes them by their beautiful tresses, removes the garments that shine brightly on the high bosoms of the maidens, and easily dries the perspirations occasioned by sport from the brows of the fair.

"28. By whom was not the king Paramârdi Deva esteemed? He was the god with the uneven arrows upon the earth, like a spiritual guide in the mysteries of love. Hundreds of maidens who approached his bed, and hundreds of foes who fell at his feet, were rejected by him.

[1] Bengal Asiatic Society's Journal, 1848, page 313.

" Thou firmament move on, and ye quarters of the world, proceed ; and thou earth enlarge !   Ye who have witnessed the widespread fame of former kings, now behold the rising glory of the fame of king Paramârdi, which, like a pomegranate bursting by the swelling of its seeds, extends over the world.   Seeing the gifts of this king, who gives even more than is requested, and hearts of the Divine Jewel (*Vishnu's Chintâmoni*) and the heavenly cow (Kamadhenu, who grants all wishes) would have burst with shame if the former were not a stone, and the latter an animal.

"The king Paramârdi, having conquered his enemies, himself composed with his innate faith this eulogy of Purâri (Siva).

"Oh, ye venerable ones ! although my liberality is great, still my high qualities will not be remembered by vicious persons ; meditate therefore on such works as may satisfy your minds.

"The able Padma, the favourite of the valiant king Paramârdi, the grandson of an eminent artist, the son of Anrina, and superior to all artists, has, in company with Deoka, his younger brother, composed and inscribed this praise of the husband of Girija :—

"'As long as the earth, clad in the garment of the atmosphere, which is adorned with the garland of stars, joining, like two resplendent breasts, the eastern and western mountains ; as long as the earth rests upon the bed of the hood of the serpent-king, so long let this work of the king Paramârdi endure.' "

" Dated Monday ; the 10th of Kârtika Sudi, Samvat 1298.   May prosperity and success attend ! [1] "

It is curious to remember that just 18 months after this bombastic record was composed, king Paramârdi gave up his fort to Kutb-ud-din Aibak.   The inscription is dated Monday on the 28th October A.D. 1201, and the surrender took place on Saturday the 27th April A.D. 1203.

J.—Sandstone Slab in Nilakantha.

This inscription is also given by Lieutenant Maisey.   It is carved on a soft yellow slab, and is in a very imperfect state, all the right half being missing, so that the translator was not able to make out very much of it.   It mentions several of the Chandel kings by name, ending with Vira Varmma, who was the son of Trilokya Varmma, and the grandson of Paramârdi Deva.   Its date must therefore be close to A.D. 1250—

---

[1] Bengal Asiatic Society's Journal, 1848, pp. 316 and 317.

during the period when the Hindus had recovered possession of the fort. The following translation is copied from the Journal of the Bengal Asiatic Society [1] :—

"(The meaning of the first six lines is ambiguous.)

"7. Was born Bijayapâla. From him sprang Bhumipâla, who, with his sharp sword, destroyed many kings.

"8. His son made low the kings, as Agastya made low the mountain (the Vindhya Mountain). Having conquered the southern country, he speedily defeated the immense army of Karna.

"9. * * * * which was watered by the flood of tears of the gazelle-eyed females of the king of Mâlwa * * *

"10. His son Jaya Varmma Deva, who was devoted to the worship of Nàrayana (unintelligible).

"11. Being wearied of government the king made it over to * * Varmma, and proceeded to wash away his sins to the divine river * *

"12. They departed their lives, and obtained all their desires in the next world.

"13. After him Madana Varmma assumed the reins of government * * * (unintelligible).

"14. He in an instant defeated the king of Gurjara, as Krishna in former times defeated Kansa. He undertook an expedition to conquer the world * * * *

"15. The younger brother of king Madana was Pratâpa Varmma who was most powerful.

"16. He was concerned for those * * * * * * who were sick, and who were distressed ; * * * * who were lame and weak.

"17. * * * He had double mouths and double eyes (?). He, the Lord, ever endowed with the eminent qualities of a hero. (The rest unintelligible and obliterated.)

18. He made the eyes of the women of * * warm (with passion) and confounded the hearts of his enemies * * Kamala (Lakshmi) who was against * * in the field of battle, * *

"19. * * he looks as a hero * * (unintelligible) * *

"20. * * (unintelligible).

"21. * * (unintelligible).

"22. * * He who delighted the hearts of all the learned

_____
[1] Bengal Asiatic Society's Journal, 1884, pp.319 and 320.

Vira Varmma, disdaining pleasure, subduing all his desires.

"23.   *   *   (unintelligible).

"24.   *   *   (unintelligible).

"25.   *   *   he caused various temples, gardens, ponds and tanks to be made at places   *   *

"26.   *   *   who was a patron of archers   *   *   *   who, like thousands of Sumeru, bestowed gold in Tula   *   *   *

"27. Who established the images of Siva, Kamala, and Kâli in splendid houses   *   *   *

"28.   *   *   (unintelligible).

"29   *   *   *   they, being tired, followed his steps in the order of their ranks.   This eulogy was   *   *   *   by a person named Valluki Vira."

K.—Plate IX.—In a cell near Nilakantha.

This inscription is older than any of the preceding, but unfortunately the beginning of the first line is lost, and I can find neither date nor king's name.   It records the setting up of a symbol of Maheswara.   The characters may belong to the 8th century.

L.—Plate IX.—Near the Ganes Gate.

This is a fine inscription of 15 lines.   I see the name of *Bhava Nâga* in the 10th line, and in the 1st line there is mention of the *Pânduvânam-kula.*   The characters belong to the later Gupta period.   It is the oldest long inscription yet found at Kâlanjara.

M.—Outside the Lâl Darwâza.

This is a long inscription of 16 lines, but it is so much injured that very little is readable.   I can see *Kâlanjarâdri,* or the " hill of Kâlanjara " in the 4th line, and something like Samvat 1226 at the beginning of the last line.

In the fort there are many other short records of pilgrims who paid their devotions at the shrine of Nilakantha and other places.   I got 27 of these records, of which—

1 was dated in Samvat 1366

1   ,,   ,,   1423

18 between 1500 and   1600

7 between 1600 and   1700

Two of them were found near the north gate, one in the Bhairon cave, two on the pillars of the Nilakantha temple, and twenty on the steps of the Kot Sâgar, or Kot Tirath tank.

Outside the walls of the fort on the north face, and about halfway up the hill, there is a small isolated rock some 15 feet long by 10 feet in height. On this rock there is sculptured a famous lingam named Balkandeswara, and, beside it, the figure of a pilgrim carrying Ganges water at the two ends of a banghi-pole. Over the head of this figure there is an old inscription of one line of Gupta characters, 1 inch high, which reads as follows :—   (See Plate IX—P.)

Samâdhi gata pancha-mahâsabda Sâmanta Sri Vasantah.

There is a similar figure with the same inscription down in the plain below, which will be noticed presently.   See Q.

On the back of the rock there is a figure of Mahesasuri Devi.

On the north face of the hill, and about 60 or 70 feet above the plain, there is a fine stone-walled tank called *Gangâ Sâgar*, 160 feet in length by 120 feet in breadth. It has a continuous flight of steps on three sides, and only a narrow flight in the middle of the fourth side. A long flight of steps leads to the top of the embankment. The whole of the steps and walls are formed of cut stones, including numerous carved pillars, bracket-capitals, and broken statues. On this site there has once been a very fine temple, as shown not only by these remains, but by a colossal figure of Vishnu, 13 feet in length, reclining on the serpent Ananta. There is also a head of a colossal boar, or figure of Varâha, built into the walls. There are no inscriptions ; but it seems highly probable that the inscribed figure of a water-carrier, now fixed in a shed a short distance below, must have been taken from this site.

The figure of the water-carrier called *Sarwan Bâbâ*, is 6½ feet high by 3 feet broad. I suppose that the original name may have been *Saravâha*, or the "water-carrier," but the people are unanimous in calling it Sarwan, which was the name of the son of Raja Dasaratha's sister. The story is similar to that of the Raja of Benares, as told in the Buddhist legend of the Sâma-Jâtaka. The name Sarwan is well known in Northern India, and there are several popular songs founded on his story. His father and mother were blind, and were entirely dependent on him for their food. He is said to have carried them about in a banghi; hence the identification of the water-carrier as Sarwan was very natural. The Brahmanical account is found in the Mahâbhârata, where it must certainly be an interpolation. The abstract of it, as given by Wheeler, is as follows[1] :—

" There is a curious episode in the original, in which Dasaratha declared that all his misfortunes had arisen from his having been cursed by a pious recluse whose son he had accidentally slain. The story is told at considerable length; but the main points are comprised in the following extract from the Adhyâtma Râmâyana :—

" ' Being in his younger days fond of hunting, the Mahâraja went one night to the side of a pond, where the sage Sarwan was procuring water. Sarwan attended on his father and mother with the purest affection. Both parents were blind, and Sarwan was in the habit of placing each of them in a separate basket, and slinging them across his shoulders; and in this fashion he conveyed them to all the places of worship then existing in the world. On the present occasion his parents had complained of thirst, and Sarwan had slung the baskets over the branch of a tree and gone down to the pond with a vessel to procure water. The Maharaja, hearing the footsteps, thought it must be a deer, and shooting an arrow in the darkness towards the sound, it pierced the breast of Sarwan, who thereupon fell to the ground. The Mahâraja, perceiving he had shot a man, hurried to the spot, and was at once thrown into the deepest affliction. Sarwan, however, said :—[1] Be not distressed, O Mahâraja! I am a Vaisya, and not a Brahman, so that the heinous sin of the murder of a Brahman will not fall upon thy head. My parents, however, have performed sundry religious observances, and should their anger be raised against thee, they would reduce thee to ashes. Give them first a little water to allay their thirst, and then address them with humility and respect.' The Mahâraja then drew out the arrow, and Sarwan expired. The Mahâraja then did as he was directed, and explained the circumstances to the bereaved parents, and expressed his deep contrition. At the request of the parents he then collected

<hr />

[1] See Wheeler's Râmâyana. Note, page 159.

wood for the funeral pile, and they then sat upon it, and directing the Maharaja to fire it, were consumed with their son. Before this was accomplished, however, the old man uttered the malediction that he, like them, would die out of sorrow for the loss of a son."

The popular account, which is current amongst the people at the present day, is much fuller than Wheeler's abstract. Shortly after his parents became blind, Sarwan married a girl named Sânwal, who is said to have been of an evil disposition. She had a cooking-pot made with two divisions, in one of which she cooked the rice with milk, making *khir*, and in the other she cooked the rice with curd (or *chhâch*), making *mâheri*. The former she kept for her husband and herself, and the latter she gave to her husband's parents. After some time the old man complained that ever since his son's marriage their food had become very bad. Sarwan then managed to change plates with his father, and dipping his finger in the coarse food he became aware of his wife's duplicity. Ashamed of his wife's conduct he got a *kânwar*, or bânghi-pole with two baskets, and placing his parents in them, he put the bânghi on his shoulder and started off on a pilgrimage. After passing through several places they reached Ayodhya. As the old people were thirsty, Sarwan hung up the bânghi on a mango tree, and took a vessel to fetch some water. On reaching a tank, surrounded by deer, he stooped down to fill the vessel, when he was suddenly wounded in the side with an arrow, shot by Raja Dasaratha, who mistook him for an antelope. As he fell, Sarwan called out " Râm ! Râm!," which attracted Dasaratha's attention. Then Sarwan begged the Raja to take some water to his parents, who were in the bânghi hanging on the mango tree near at hand. Dasaratha took a lota of water to the blind couple, who, hearing a strange voice, demanded who he was. The Raja then told the whole story, and the bereaved parents at once cursed him, saying—

> Jas kinâ tum Sarwan sokâ,
> Tas hui he tum Râm birogâ.

"Like as you have caused grief through Sarwan,"
"So shall you suffer grief through Râm."

Then the two blind people died, asking the Raja to have their bodies burned along with that of their son.

After a time when Râma was about to leave Ayodhya on his 12 years' exile, the curse of the blind parents came to Dasaratha's mind, and he told the whole story to his wife Kausalya—

Tâpas Andh Sâp sudhi âî,
Kausalâ hi sab kathâ sunâî.

The legend is undoubtedly an old one, as it forms the subject of one of the Buddhist Jâtakas. It is not found amongst the existing sculptures of Bharhut; but it is represented on the back of the western gateway of the Sânchi stûpa, and on the eighth step of the staircase of the Jamâlgarhi stûpa.[1] In neither of these representations is there any trace of the banghi. On the contrary, the two blind parents are represented seated in the former sculpture in front of their *pansals*, or leaf-roofed huts, and in the latter in a sort of arbour, where they are receiving the pot of water from the hands of the king. In these Buddhist sculptures, however, the king is not Dasaratha, Raja of Ayodhya, but Peliyaka, Raja of Benares. This story, as related by Spence Hardy, is as follows[2]:—

"When Gotama Bodhisat was born in a former age, as Sâma, son of the hermit Dukhula, he rendered every assistance to his parents, who had become blind when he was sixteen years of age. It happened that, as he one day went for water to the river, the king of Benaras, Peliyaka, entered the forest to hunt, and as Sâma, after ascending from the river, was, as usual, surrounded by deer, the king let fly an arrow, which struck Sâma just as he was placing the vessel to his shoulder. Feeling that he was wounded, he turned his face towards the spot where his parents dwelt, and said, 'I have no enemy in this forest; I bear no enmity to any one;' though, at the same time, he vomited blood from his mouth. Thus he reflected, 'I have omitted the exercise of *maitri-bhawana*, and some one has sent against me an arrow; for what reason it can be I cannot tell, as my flesh is of no use, neither my skin; I must therefore make enquiry.' After saying this to himself, he called out, 'Who is it that

[1] See Fergusson's Tree and Serpent Worship. Plate 36, fig. 1, and the 8th step of the staircase, which is now in the British Museum.
[2] Eastern Monachison, p. 275.

has shot me?' and when he learnt that it was the king, he related his history to the monarch, and said that his greatest grief arose from the thought that his blind parents would now have no one to support them, and would perish. But when the king perceived the intensity of his grief, he promised that he would resign his kingdom, and himself become the slave of his parents, rendering unto them all needful assistance in the stead of their son. Soon afterwards Sâma fell down senseless from the loss of blood ; but a dewi, who in the seventh birth previous to the present, was his mother, having perceived that if she went to the spot important consequences would ensue from her interposition, left the dewa-loka, and remaining in the air near the king without being visible, entreated him to go to the *pansal* and minister to the wants of the blind parents of Sâma. The king was obedient, and went to the place, where he informed the hermit and his wife that their son was slain. On hearing of his death, they uttered loud lamentations, and requested to be taken to the place where he had fallen. They were, therefore, brought to it, when the mother, in placing her hand upon his breast, perceived that it was warm ; at which she rejoiced greatly, as she knew by this token that he was not dead. She therefore resolved upon repeating a *sacha-kiriya* for his restoration, and said, ' If this Sâma has in any previous period obtained *kusula*, by the power of this virtue (*sacha*) may the consequences of this calamity be removed ! if from the time of his birth until now he has been continent and true, supported his parents, and excelled in the acquisition of merit ; if I have loved him more than my own life ; if we, his parents, possess any merit what-ever ; by the power of these virtues (*sacha*) may the poison pass away from the body of Sâma, as the darkness vanishes at the rising of the sun ! ' On the utterance of these words, Sâma revived, and sat up ; after which the *devi* also said, ' If I have loved Sâma more than any other being, by the power of this *sacha* may the poison or this arrow be destroyed ! ' Then by the united *sacha-kiriyas* of the devi and his parents, Sâma was restored to perfect health. The parents also received their sight, and the *devi* repeated the ten virtues of a king to Peliyaka, by attending to which he was enabled to reign in righteousness, and was afterwards born in the deva-loka, as Sâma and his parents were in the Brahma-loka."

Here, again, in this Buddhist version there is no trace of the Banghi story. At the present day the Banghi is an essential part of the legend ; and forms a pictorial frontispiece to the lithographed copies of the " Sângît Raja Sarwannâth."

14.—AJAYGARH FORT.

The fortress of Ajaygarh is situated just 20 miles by road to the south-west of Kâlanjar. It stands on a lofty, flat-topped spur of the Vindhya Hills, within sight of the River Kiyân, or Ken, which is only 8 miles distant. It is of about the same height as Kâlanjar, or between 700 and 800 feet above the plain. The lower part of the hill, which is of granite, is not very steep, but the upper part, which consists of a reddish sandstone, is very abrupt and quite inaccessible. The size of the fort has been very much under-estimated, as being only about 1 mile in circuit, whereas it is only a very little smaller than Kâlanjar, as may be seen at once by a comparison of their plans.[1] The fort is very nearly 1 mile in length from north to south, and only a little less from west to east. It is nearly triangular in shape, and the circuit of its walls is just 3 miles, that of Kâlanjar being under 4 miles.

The foundation of Ajaygarh is referred to an unknown raja, Ajay Pâl. But the name of Ajaygarh is not found in any of the inscriptions, the name being invariably given as Jayapura-dûrgga, or the " Fortress of Jayapura.[2] "

The fort has two gates ; one to the north being simply called Darwâza ; and the other to the south-east, called the Tarhaoni Gate, as it leads directly upon the village of Tarhowan, at the foot of the hill. In the inscriptions I find mention of the Kâlanjara-dwâra, or Kalanjar Gate, and this must be the " Darwâza " on the north, as it leads directly towards Kâlanjar.

Near the northern gate there are two tanks excavated in the rock, which are known by the name of Gangâ-Jamnâ. Almost exactly in the middle of the fort there is a large tank cut in the rock called Ajay-Pâl-ka-Talao. It is evidently old; but the black stone figure on its bank, which is called Ajay Pâl, is clearly a statue of the four-armed Vishnu.

Near the southern end of the fort there is another tank called Parmâl Tâl, or the Reservoir of Raja Paramârd.

---

[1] See Plates VIII and XI, which are drawn on the same scale.
[2] Bengal Asiatic Society's Journal, 1837, p. 887.

Close by there is a ruined temple of the Chandel times, which is also attributed to Raja Parmâl; and at a short distance there are two other temples standing together, which are simply known as Chandeli Mahal. All these temples are in ruins.

The largest of the three temples is 60 feet long by 40 feet broad, with its entrance to the west. The northern portion has fallen down. The walls of the standing portion are very richly ornamented.

The second temple, of the same size, also faces the west. This also was very highly decorated. But all the numerous figures which once adorned its walls are now gone, except that of a single four-armed female.

The third temple near Parmâl's tank is slightly smaller than the others, its dimensions being 54 by 36 feet. The angles of the sanctum seem to have been laid out on the circumference of a circle.

On the rock at the Tarhaoni Gate there is a row of eight goddesses (the Ashta-sakti), of whom seven are sitting and one standing. They are each 3 feet high and 3 feet 10 inches broad, in separate frames. They are roughly executed. Their names are written below them, amongst which I could read *Sri-Chandi, Sri-Chamundâ, Sri Kâlikâ*, and also the name of *Jayapura-dûrgga*. Both Durgâ and Kâli are amongst the figures.

Close by there is a long inscription cut in the rock, 7 feet by 2 feet 4 inches. It contains several names of the Chandel Rajas, beginning with Kirti Varmma and ending with Bhoja Varmma. The characters are of the square form called *Chitra-varna*, or "Ornamented letters." There are also several rows of small Jain figures sitting with their hands in their laps. Near these there is a cow and calf, and a four-armed goddess sitting with a child in her lap, and with five pigs above one another on her right side, and eight pigs in pairs above one another on her left hand. This is evidently the figure of *Shashti*, the goddess of fecundity.

There is no mention of Ajaygarh by name in any of the Muhammadan histories. I once thought that it might be the stronghold of the mysterious *Dalki-wa-Malki*, which was captured by Ulugh Khan, the Wazir of Naseruddin Mahmud, in A.H. 644, or A.D. 1246. The fort was certainly in existence some time before, as it is mentioned in the earliest of the Ajaygarh inscriptions as Jayapura-dûrgga, in Samvat 1208, or A.D. 1141, during the reign of Madana Varmma. Now we learn from another Ajaygarh inscription, dated in Samvat 1345, or A.D. 1288, that Nana, the grandson of Malika, was the minister of the Chandratreya kings, that is, of the Chandel Rajas. We learn also that he was a contemporary of Raja Bhoja Varmma, the grandson of Raja Trailokya Varmma, who was therefore a contemporary of Malika. I thought, therefore, that the strange combination of names in Tiloka wa-Malika might represent the joint names of Tilaki (Trailokya) and his minister Malika. It is true that only one raja is spoken of; but the conjunction *wa* " and " would seem to show that there must be two distinct names. That Trailokya Varmma actually possessed Ajaygarh we learn from another inscription dated in Samvat 1269, or A.D. 1212, which was found outside the tank of Pâtâl Sar inside the fort.

The position of the stronghold of Dalaki wa-Malaki is described by Minhâj as being " in the vicinity of the Jumna between Kâlanjar and Karra." But in the position here indicated there are no defiles, and no mountains and no jungles, as described by Minhâj, and I have accordingly given up this identification in favour of another, wnich will be discussed in my account of Bâghelkhand.

15.—AJAYGARH INSCRIPTIONS.

The inscriptions found in Ajaygarh belong chiefly to the later period of Chandel history after the occupation of Mahoba and Kâlanjar by the Muhammadans. The latest historical records at Kâlanjar belong to the reign of Paramârddi Deva; but at Ajaygarh we have the series continued from Madana Varmma by one inscription of Trailokya Varmma, the son of Paramârddi, followed by three of his grandson Vira Varmma I, two of his great-grandson Bhoja Varmma, and one of his grandson's grandson Vira Varmma II. The following is a brief account of these inscriptions:—

A.—Plate XII.—On Jamb of Upper Gate.

1. Aum! Samvat 1208, Mârg-ga badi 15
2. Sanau ‖ Jayapura dürggiye sa-
3. mast lokânâm Râüt Sri Ve-
4. da Kshatriya-Jâtiya Kortia
5. grâmiya Râüt—Sri Jauna Pâ-
6. la putra annena kî dâ bhudye Si-
7. rothayena pralipâdanam atam
8. Bhadranantam Sri Sri Karanika
9. Thakkur Sri Ghal * era, Thakkur Sri
10. Jâlhanam | Thakkur Sri Mahidhara Tha-
11. kkur Sri Pâsala | varetha lahaḍanḍa bhrâ |
12. tiyana 13, Sankali âjan 52
13. Patairena ḍiya vettakara 1 Sri Soma
14. marâjasya gramohoddhi * ta ni grâ-
15. miya bhâga pâthâ Widyârddâh Sana
16. sa Kshechâsya dranâh ‖ Râjyena Sri,
17. man Madana Varmmanah ‖ Thâ-Sri-
18. Sutradhâra Suprata-

"In the Samvat year 1208, on Saturday, the 15th day of the waxing moon of Mârgga [Saturday, 10th November 1151 AD.], in the fort of Jayapura, for the use of all people, the Râüt Sri Veda, a Kshatriya by caste, of the village of Kortiâ, the son of Râüt Jauna Pâla, built a (*Sirotha ?*)

.   .   .   .   .   .Sri Sri Karanika, Thâkkura
Sri Ghala—bera | Thakkur Sri Jâlhana Thakkura
Sri Mahidhara | Thakkura Pâsala   .   .   .   .   .
"during the reign of Sriman Madana Varmma, Sculptor, Suprata.

B.—Plate XII.—On Jamb of Upper Gate Samvat 1237.

1. Samvat 1237 Ashâdha
2. Suddhi 2 Some-Jayapura-dûrgi-
3. ya Samast lokânam Râüt
4. Sri Virena Tejlaputra Kshatri-
5. yam Koṭia grâmiyam anenu
6. Durbhikshenaiyâ pâdanam mârgga da
7. sutri dhâna dresavo suta prabhriti pra-
8. tipadanakshatam [1] todanamta rava
9. Sri Sri Karana varetho 13—   (? varegi)
10. Samkala â 12, patairasya
11. nauli cha

" In the Samvat year 1237 (A.D. 1180), on Monday, the second day of the waxing moon of Ashâdha, in the fort of Jayapura, for the use of all people, by the Râüt Sri Vera, the son of Tejla, a Kshatriya of the village of Kotiâ, during a time of famine, a *bauli* (well) was built on the road. May his successor preserve it."

(*The remainder has not been made out.*)

As the week day of Ashâdha Sudi 2 was not Monday, but Wednesday, I conclude that *Some*, or Monday, was a mistake of the writer for *Saumye* or Wednesday.

C.—*Plate XII.—On jamb of Upper Gate.*

1. Samvat 1243 Jyeshtha Sudi ‖ Budhe
2. Jayapura-dûrggiye Samast lokâ-
3. nâm Râüt Sri Sihada, Râüt Sân-
4. tana putra, Kshatriya Jâtiye, ko-
5. tiâ grâmiya anena chautre ni-
6. vârana Sri pratipâdanam kritam ta-
7. danântaramba Sri Sri Karana vare-
8. *tha* 103 Samkali â 53-swasti.

"In the Samvat year 1243, on Wednesday, the 11th day of the waxing moon of Jyeshtha, for all people the Râüt Sri Sinhada, son of the Râüt Sântana, of the Kshatriya race, of the village of Kotia, established a Chautra."

(*The remainder has not been made out.*)

The week day should be *Sunday*, 1st June A.D. 1186, and it is probable that it should be read *Rave*, or Sunday instead of *Budhe*.

D.—*Plate XII.—Outside Tank of Patal-Sar.*

1. Aum! Samvat 1269, Phâlguna badi (?) Sanaw; Raja Sri Trai-lokya Va-
2. rmma Devav ijaya râjye..

(*The remainder of this inscription has not been read.*)

It is said by a Simla Pandit not to be Sanskrit, but some vernacular dialect. It is the only record yet found of Trailokya's own reign. The day of the month is obliterated, but as the week-day is certain, the date must be either the 2nd or the 9th of Phâlguna badi, equivalent to either Saturday the 9th, or Saturday the 16th February, A.D. 1213   His father Paramârddi was assassinated in A.D. 1203. This is

the only inscription of Trailokya that has yet been found.
But his name occurs in several of the Ajaygarh inscriptions
as the son and successor of Paramârddi and the father of
Vira Varmma I.

E.—Plate XIII.—Rock Inscription.—15 lines.

Eight lines to left of crack in rock ; seven lines to right of crack.

This long inscription is engraved on the rock, with a
crack dividing it into two portions.   The left-hand portion of
seven lines is bounded by the crack, and the record is continued
by eight more lines on the right hand.   The following abstract
gives the substance of the inscription, as read by a Simla
Pandit :—

"From Chandra sprang the Chandravansa race, in which was
born Raja Kirtti Varmma, whose songs the learned still sing for his
glory. His son was Sulakshana Varmma, who conquered Malwa.
To him was born Jaya Varmma, whose son was Prithvi Varmma,
whose son was Madana Varmma. Next came Trailokya Varmma, the
destroyer of his enemies, whose sons were Yaso Varmma and Vira
Varmma. The latter became Raja, and married the daughter of
Raja Govinda, the lord of the earth (*kshitipati*), named Kalyâni
Devi, who was equal to Pârvati. For the increase of her own merit
she presented to the Brahmans the *Amrita-Kupa*, or "Pool of Amrita"
(now called the Gangâ Jumnâ Tank), and also a temple. The
record was composed by Ratna Pâla, the son of Hari Pâla. In the
year of Vikrama (Vikrama Vatsara) . . (date in words, apparently
Samvat 1312) . . . in the reign of Sri Mad Vira Varmma, on
Thursday, the 13th of the waxing moon of Vaisâkha (Thursday, 22nd
April 1255 A.D.)"

I have failed in tracing the Govinda Raja mentioned in
this inscription. He may, perhaps, have been the Raja of
Nalapura, or Narwar, the predecessor of the famous Châhada
Deva, the gallant opponent of the Muhammadans.

F.—Plate XIV.—On wall of Temple.

    1. Aum I Aswavaidya Tha : Bhojakasya putra A-
    2. bhaya Deva Iswara nityam pranamati Vi-
    3. RA VARMMA râje, Samvat 1325, Vasta gotrah (? Vatsa).

"Abhaya Deva, son of Thakkur Bhojaka, of the Vatsa gotra,
offered his adoration to Iswara during the reign of Vira Varmma in
the Samvat year 1325 (A.D. 1268.)"

G.—Plate XIV.—On Rock near figure of Ganes.

This inscription gives the genealogy of the Chandela Rajas from Kirtti Varmma down to Vira Varmma I. It is doubly dated, first in words in lines 19 and 20, as follows :—

" Sâgarânala-vedendu yukte Samvatsare varshe Mâghamâsi site pakshe trayadasyam Vidho-dine."

Here *Sâgara,* the Ocean, stands for 7, or the seven seas ; *anala,* or fire, stands for 3 ; *Veda* stands also for 3 ; and *Indu,* the moon, for 1. The whole date is therefore 1337, by joining together the oceans with *fire,* the *Vedas,* and the *moon,* in the white half of the month of Mâgha, on the 13th Monday (*Vidho-dine*). The date is then repeated more concisely in figures, as " Samvat 1337, Mâgha Sudi 13 Some, or Monday, the 13th of the waxing moon of Mâgha, in the Samvat year 1337 (Monday, 3rd February, A.D. 1281).

This inscription, as explained by a Simla Pandit, records the setting up of a statue of Vinâyaka (Ganesa) by Ganapati, the minister of Vira Varmma.

H.—Slab in Indian Museum, Calcutta.

The slab bearing this long inscription is now in the Indian Museum in Calcutta. The text, with a specimen of the letters, and a translation, was published in the Journal of the Asiatic Society in 1837.[1] It records the genealogy of Nâna, one of the ministers of the Raja Bhoja Varmma in Samvat 1345, or A.D. 1288. (See verse 24, where he is called " Minister of the Chandrâtreya race." He set up an image of Hari (or Vishnu) in the port of Jayapura (*Jayapura-dûrgge*) in honour of his forefathers.

The inscription was composed by Amarapati and written in *Chitravarnâm,* or "ornamental letters," which, we thus learn, was the name given to the peculiar square characters in common use throughout the Chandel dominions and the neighbouring countries from about 1115 to 1400 A.D. The inscription is itself of little value.

[1] Bengal Asiatic Society's Journal, Vol. VI of 1837, p. 885.

I.—Two long lines, 7½ feet, large letters.

1. Aum namah Sri Kedaraya Kayastha Vâstavya
   . . Kata *jayapura-durggaya* Thakkur Sri Vidana tatputra
   . . Sri.ja Thakkura Sri . . . . . devenasansta, Sri
   Kedâra,Pârvati, Vrishabha, Krishna Sri * Kâtâ.
2. Kâyastha vâstavya.

J.—Plate XV.—At the Tirhawan Gate.

This inscription of 15 lines in very large letters is carved on the rock near the Ashta Sakti. It has not yet been translated, but I have noted the following names :—

Line 4.—Sri Kirtti Varmma.
   ,, 5.—Paramârddi.
   ,, 13.—Sri Bhoja Varmma.
   ,, 14.—Sri Mad Bhoja Mahi Mahendra.

I cannot find any date in it, but, as we have an inscription of himself, dated in Samvat 1345, or A.D. 1288, and another of his son, dated in Samvat 1372, or A.D. 1315, the inscription may be assigned to about A.D. 1300.

K.—Near a female figure—11 lines.

1. Samvat 1346 samaye.
2. . . . . . . Jayapura-dûrgge.
3. . . Mahârâja Sri Bho-Varmma De-

This inscription is too much injured to be readable. Several of the letters are quite clear, but they are all isolated, except towards the end, where I can read *pâla* and *tasya.* The *ja* of Bhoja is omitted in the original.

L.—Over a female figure.

1. Samvat 1349 || Jyeshtha badi 14 Sukre dine
2. Sadhu || Mana Suta ama Deva putra Arjuna tasya bhâriyâ-
3. Gângo || nityam damaya . . ha Iswara pranamati || Sri. ||

"In the year 349 (A.D. 1292,) on Friday, the 14th of the waxing moon of Jyeshtha, Gângo, the wife of Arjuna, son of Ama Deva, the son of Manu, performed adoration to Iswara.

M.—On upper round step of Temple.

1. Phulahe Raushahne putra Jyarti
2. tranamati . cha || Sam. 1371.

I cannot satisfactorily read the name of the pilgrim who made this record of his visit to Ajaygarh in Samvat 1371, or A.D. 1314. It looks like Jyaitu, the son of the flower man Raushan.

N.—To west of gateway outside.

This long inscription of 12 lines is too much injured to be easily read. It belongs to the reign of Vira Varmma II, as it is dated in Samvat 1372, or A.D. 1315. It has been so repeatedly whitewashed over that the letters are now filled up.

O.—Plate XIV.—On pillar of gate.

1. Aum ! Ganapataye namah‖ . . . Jayapurvva, &c. &c.

I can make out nothing of this inscription, and a Pandit to whom it has been shown declares that it is not Sanskrit. The name of Vira Nripa occurs in the 12th line, and the date is in the last two lines—" Samvat 1372 Paush badi 10 Sanau," or Saturday, the 22nd November 1315.

P.—On rock outside gate—4 lines.

In 4th line name of Kirtti Varmma.

16.—BACHON, or BACHAUND.

Bachaund, or Bachon, as it is commonly pronounced, is a large village situated under a hill on the left bank of the Kiyân, or Ken River, 15 miles to the west of Ajaygarh, to which state it now belongs. It contains about 500 houses, · and upwards of 2,500 inhabitants. There is a fine large tank called the Bilhariya Tâl, faced with boulder stones, and to the north of the village there are many broken sculptures and other remains, which show that Bachon was formerly a place of considerable importance. Amongst these there was—

    1 figure of the Vâman Avatâr.
    1 group of Hara Gauri.
    1 figure of Vishnu.
    2 lingams.

Several old carved pillars of small size.

1 broken slab with the following inscription in 12 lines—

1. (Swas) ti Samvat 143 (3)
2. Sâke 1298 . .
3. . . nibhi Nâga
4. sahum jatto so râmo.
5 Bhilama Deva râjo.||
6. Vachhiuni-Sthâno
7. . Sri Gopâla Devahya.
8. . namo.

(The rest not made out.)

The name of the place is most probably given in the 6th line as *Vachhiuni-Sthâna,* or Bachhiun. The Raja Bhilama Deva, mentioned in the 5th line, must be one of the later Chandels. Unfortunately we do not possess the genealogy of the later Princes, so that it is impossible to identify him. The date of Sake 1298, or A.D. 1376, lies in the middle of the reign of Firoz Shah Tughlak, when the Delhi empire was weak, at which time both Kâlanjar and Ajaygarh were in the possession of the Chandel Rajas.

17.—KHAJURÂHA.

I have already given a long account of Khajurâha, with a detailed description of its principal buildings, which form by far the finest group of Hindu temples now existing in Northern India.[1]

Khajurâha, or Kharjurpura, is first mentioned by name by Abu Rihân in A.D. 1031, who calls it the capital of Jajâhuti.[2] There are no traces of fortifications, but it is probable that Khajurâha may once have been a walled town, as the people refer the name to a pair of gold *khajur* trees (date-palms), which, they say, were fixed on one of the city gates. A more natural derivation would have been from the khajur trees, amongst which the town was originally situated. At present, however, there are not many of these trees in the neighbourhood.

[1] See Archæological Survey, Vol. II, p. 412, and Vol. X, p. 16.
[2] Reinand's Fragments, p. 85, Text, and p. 106, Translation. See also Elliott's Muhammadan Historians, by Dowson, Vol. I, p. 57.

The name of the place is found in the inscription of Ganda
Deva, dated in Samvat 1056, or A.D. 999. It comes immediately after the date " Sri *Kharjuravâtika Râja Dhanga
Deva râjye*," which has been entirely misread by Sutherland
as " *Sri Prithvi-pati Râja Sri Banga Deva râjye*."[1] *Kharjuravâtika* would thus appear to have been the original form
of the name, which was shortened by dropping the *v*, thus
making *Khajurâtika* and *Khajurâha*.

The place is afterwards mentioned by Ibu Batuta, who calls
it *Khajurâ*, " at which there is a lake about a mile in length,
and round this are temples in which there are idols. At this
place resides a tribe of Jogis with long and clotted hair. Their
colour inclines to yellow, which arises from their fasting.
Many of the Moslems of these parts attend on them, and
learn (magic) from them." As Ibn Batuta visited the place
about A.D. 1335, I infer from the tolerance of the Hindu
ascetics that Khajurâha was still in the possession of the
Chandel Princes, while the Moslems were in occupation of
Kâlanjar and Mahoba. It is almost certain that the Hindus
still held Ajaygarh, as there are at least two inscriptions in
that fort, dated in Samvat 1372, or A.D. 1315, during the
reign of Vira Varmma II.

At the present day Khajurâha is only a small village. In
1852 it was said to contain only 162 houses, which would
give a population of less than 1,000 persons. But in 1874 I
was told that there were 350 inhabited houses, which would
give a population of about 2,000 persons. The Brahmans,
who form one-sixth, are of two classes, Kanaujiyâ and Jajhotiâ.
There are a few Chandel thakurs, or zamindars.

I searched diligently for other ruins, in the hope that
some older remains would be found. The oldest was a triangular fragment of a large inscription in Kutila characters,
bearing the names of Harsha Deva and Sri Kshiti Pâla Deva
Nripati. If it belongs to the time of Harsha Deva, the father
of Yaso Varmma, and the grandfather of Dhanga Raja, its
date must be about A.D. 900.

[1] Bengal Asiatic Society's Journal, Vol. VIII, p. 175.

The oldest building now standing at Khajurâha is, no doubt, the oblong hypæthral temple of Chaunsat Jogini, or the "sixty-four female goblins," who drink the blood of the slain. As I have described this curious building in a former report, I need only mention here that it is an oblong quadrangle, 102¼ feet by 59½ feet, situated on a low rocky hill, 25 feet above the level of the plain. It contains 64 small cells distributed round the sides, and one large cell in the middle of the back wall. It is built entirely of granite, and is therefore, no doubt, older than all the other temples of Khajurâha, which are built of sandstone. In my Report I ventured to assign its age as prior to A.D. 900, and this assignment I am now prepared to verify by two short inscriptions which I found on the pedestals of two small statues of the enshrined Joginis. The cells are small, being only 2 feet 4½ inches broad by 3 feet 9 inches deep. The figures are therefore small. I found only three of them now remaining, the largest of which was 3 feet in height, and the others 2 feet 3 inches in height. The largest with eight arms represents the goddess Bhainsa-suri Devi, killing the buffalo demon. On the pedestal is inscribed the name of *Hinghalâj*. On one of the others I found the name of Maheswari. As the characters of these records appear to be older than those of the dated Khajurâha inscriptions, with the single exception of those on the statue of Hanumân, which bears a date in three figures only, I conclude therefore that the Chaunsat Jogini Temple must be older than any of the other temples at Khajurâha, of which one at least dates as far back as Samvat 1011, or A.D. 954. I think therefore that the Chaunsat Jogini may date from the very foundation of the Chandel rule, or from the early part of the 9th century. The temple at Râhilya, near Mahoba, which was built by Râhila Varmma, about A.D. 900, is of sandstone; and I believe that all the granite temples must be older.

The next oldest building is most probably the small square temple of Brahmâ on the bank of the lake. It is built partly of granite and partly of sandstone, and is therefore most probably older than all the remaining temples, which are of sandstone only.

Khajuráha is described by Abu Rihán as the capital of the kingdom of *Jajáhuti*—a name which recalls the Chi-chi-to of the Chinese pilgrim Hwen Thsang. According to him Chi-chi-to was situated at 1,000 *li*, or 167 inches, to the north-east of Ujain, which is considerably under the real distance of about 250 miles. If, however, Hwen Thsang recorded his distances according to the number of *kos* between the two places, he must have allowed only 2 miles to each of the *chaurasi*, or 84 kos, distance between the two places. But as the kos of Bundelkhand and Malwa varies from 3 to 4 miles, the real distance would have been about 250 miles, which agrees almost exactly with the relative positions of Ujain and Khajuráha.

I have found the name of the province in two different inscriptions, one of the time of Kirtti Varma, and the other of the time of Paramárddi. In the former one, which I discovered at Mahoba, the name is written *Jejákhya* and *Jejabhukti*. The latter form at once recalls the name of *Tirabhukti*, which has long ago been shortened to *Tirhuti* and *Tirhut*. In the same way *Jejakabhuti* would have become Jejahuti, exactly as it is written by Abu Rihán. In the second inscription the name is given as *Jejakasukhti-desoyam*, which, by the common change of *s* to *h*, would have become *Jejákahuti* and *Jejáhuti*, as before.

It is not impossible that the name of the province may be hidden in Ptolemy's *Sandrabatis* or *Sandabatis*, and that Khajuráha or Khajurpur may be hidden in his *Kuraporina*, one of the towns of the district of *Sandrabatis*. The other towns of Empelathra and Nadu-bandagar might then be identified with Mahoba and Narwar or Nalapura, and perhaps *Tamasis*, by a slight change to *Tapasis*, might represent the hill of Kálanjar, the favourite resort of the *Tapaswis*, or ascetics. Kálanjar is said by Wilson to be " enumerated in the Vedas amongst the *Tapasiasthánas*, or spots adapted to practices of austere devotion." The name of *Tapasis* was therefore peculiarly appropriate to Kálanjar.

All the great temples now existing at Káhajuraha and other Chandel places would appear to have been built during the most flourishing period of the Chandel rule, that is, in the three centuries between the accession of Râhila Varmma about A.D. 900, and the conquest of Kâlanjar by the Muhammadans in A.D. 1203, just before the death of Paramârddi Deva.

In my first Report on Khajurâha (Vol. II, Archæological Survey) I gave a list of 24 temples which were still standing at Khajurâha, with a map showing their positions. During my late visit I sought for traces of other temples. I am afraid that most of the materials have been used up in the steps of the palace and tank built during the present century. The entrance to the Raja's garden is formed of the doorway of an old temple of large size, the clear opening being 7 feet 6 inches in height by 4 feet 8 inches in width. On the lintel there is a figure of the *Ardhanâri*, or Androgyne Siva, standing in the middle, with a figure of Siva over one jamb, and of Vishnu over the other jamb. At a short distance there is an eight-bracket capital, 2 feet $4\frac{1}{2}$ inches in diameter, and close by there is a colossal statue of Siva. On comparing the size of this bracket capital with those of the largest standing temples, it would appear that some much larger temple must once have stood near the site of the garden. The following are the dimensions of these capitals :—

		ft.	ins.	
Loose bracket capital	. .	2	4	diameter.[1]
Khandâriya capital	. .	1	10	,,
Ghantai capital	. .	1	8	,,
Chaturbhuj	. .	1	5	,,

The missing temple was probably an old one, as there are figures of the Ganges and Jumna with their symbols, the crocodile and the tortoise, on the jambs.

For the purpose of obtaining approximate dates for the existing temples I copied all the masons' marks and pilgrims' records on the walls and pillars. The former are presumably of the same dates as the temples themselves, while the latter must be later, although not necessarily much later.

---

[1] The fellow of this large capital is now lying in the court of the Jain temple.

I take the single names which are found on many of the
stones to be those of the masons who prepared them. In
a few instances this is absolutely certain, as the names are
upside down. Inside the Lakshmanji temple I found three
names thus inverted. In the Khandâriya temple I found the
word dâsân, or "architrave," engraved on the underside of
a beam. This also must have been a mason's mark.

In the accompanying plate I have given a few specimens
of these short records from all the principal temples. With
one or two exceptions they are much more roughly carved
than the large formal inscriptions which record the building
of the temples. One of the neatest is the name of Nemi
Chandra on a pillar of the Ghantai temple. Its letters are
quite equal to the best of the great inscription of Dhanga
Deva, dated in Samvat 1011, or A.D. 954. The following
account of these brief records will be sufficient to show that
none of the standing temples are of older date than the
great Jain temple of Ghantai.

B.—*Ghantai Temple.*

1. Nemi Chandra.   2. Swasti Sri Sâdhu Palna.

The second of these short records has already been published by Mr. V. A. Smith in the Journal of the Bengal
Asiatic Society for 1879, p. 287 and Plate XIV; but it had
not escaped my notice, as it was first brought to light by my
clearance of the temple in January 1875. At the same time
I found the other name of Nemi Chandra, which is not
noticed by Messrs. Smith and Black. I made an excavation
completely round the whole temple and cleared out the interior. My account of these operations will be found in
Volume X of the Archæological Survey. But, as this volume
was not published until 1880, Mr. Smith was not aware
of my labours, which must have afterwards facilitated the
measurements of his companion Mr. Black. A reference to
my Report also will show that I had long before established
the correctness of Mr. Fergusson's opinion that the Ghantai
was a Jain temple, by the discovery of numerous Jain figures
all round it, and of one at least *in situ* inside. As to the

date of the temple I am of opinion that the beautifully formed letters of the name of Nemi Chandra belong to the 10th
century, and that the other inscription is not earlier than
1150 A.D., or perhaps even later.

C.—*Colossal statue of Sántináth.*

This large statue is enshrined in a common-looking building made of old fragments and covered with whitewash, and
very dark inside. I got a copy of its inscription at the time
of my first visit in 1852. At my second visit in 1865 not a
single letter of the inscription was visible, as the whole statue
had been recently whitewashed. In the present year, 1884,
however, I have managed to get a fair impression after a long
time spent in cleaning the pedestal. The great figure is
14 feet high. I read the date as Samvat 1085, or A.D. 1028.
In the accompanying Plate, XX, I have given the portions of
this inscription which include the date and the name of the
statue. I read the whole line as follows :—

> Samvat 1085. Srimat Achârya putra Sri
> Thâkura Sri Deva dhara suta . Sri Sivi
> Sri Chandraya Devah Sri Santinâthasya
> pratimâ kâri.

Here we see that the name of the enshrined statue is
Sántinátha, and not *Setnáth*, as the people call it.

D.—*Statue of Sambhunáth.*

This is another single line inscription in small letters,
which is engraved on the pedestal of a black stone statue of
Shambhunâth, which is now lying in the courtyard of the Jain
temples. I have given the opening of the inscription containing the date and the name of the reigning king in Plate
XX. I read the whole as follows :—

> Aum! Samvat 1215 Mâgha Sudi 5 Srimân *Madana*
> *Varmma Deva* pravarddhamâna vijaya râjye ||
> Grahapati vanse Sreshthi *Dedu*, tat putra Pâhillah |
> Pâhillâ   .   .   .   pratimâ kâri tîta||
> tat putrâh Mahâgaṅa, Maha Chandrâ, Sani chandra
> Jina chandra Udya chandra, prabhriti, Sam
> bhavanâtham praṇamati nitya|| Mangala
> mahâsri|| Râpakâra Râma Deva.||

"In the Samvat year 1215 [A.D. 1158] on the 5th day of the waxing moon of Mâgha, during the prosperous and victorious reign of Srimân *Madana Varmma Deva*, the Sreshthi Dedu of the class of householders, together with his son Pâhilla   .   .   .   .   set up this statue. Then the sons, Mahaganâ Mahachandrâ, Sani chandrâ, Udaya-chandrâ, offered adoration to Sambhunâtha. May it be fortunate! Sculptor, Râma Deva."

E.—*Khandáriya Temple.*

The short inscription marked E I, which is carved on the under-side of one of the stone beams, is simply the word *dâsân*, or "architrave," and is, no doubt, a mason's mark contemporary with the building. The peculiar form of the attached vowels was common in the 10th century.

The inscription marked E 2, which is carved on one of the pillars, is of a later age, apparently about A.D. 1100. It seems to read as follows :—

Râjam minda samaye nasu. sama chârma vastrinam.

F.—*Chitr-gupt Temple.*

These three short records appear to be simply mason's names. They are all in early Kutila characters of the 10th century. No. 1 reads *Gharamvasa;* No. 2 *Subhavâ;* No. 3 *Nahinâ*, or perhaps *Dahina.*

G.—*Devi Jagadâmba Temple.*

The two records from this temple are also in early Kutila character. No. 1 reads *Jina-Deva*, and No. 2 reads *Devi-Juna.*

H.—*Viswanâth Temple.*

The single names found on the stones of this temple are very numerous. I noted about 20, but some of them were repetitions. Thus No. 2 I found on four different stones. I read it *Sri Dewân dûrgga.* No. 1 reads *Sri ganit,* and No. 3 *Sri Mihirata.* The names in this temple are peculiar in having the honorary prefix *Sri* attached to all of the early Kutila period of the 10th century.

J.—*Kunwar Math.*

There are two temples on the bank of the Kurar Nala, the large one being called simply *Kunwar Math*, or the

" Princes' Temple," and the smaller one being without name. The plinth, or basement, of the Kunwar Math, 6 feet in height, is of granite blocks, and the superstructure of sandstone. The Mandapa is covered by an overlapping dome, $18\frac{1}{2}$ feet in diameter, without the usual four pillars to support the weight. The name of Vâsalâ is found on several stones in both temples. On the wall of the smaller temple there is an inscription in two lines, which is apparently of later date than the temple itself. I read it as follows :—

> Samvat 1174 Jyeshṭa badi 3 Ṣanau likhitam ||
> Kayastha Jâktura Sri Gotha nityam pranamyati. ||

" In the Samvat year 1174 (A.D. 1117) on the 3rd of the waxing moon of Jyeshta, Saturday, this inscription was written. The Kâyastha, of Jâktura Sri Gotha, offered his adoration."

The date corresponds with Saturday, the 21st April 1117 A.D.

As the whole of this temple agrees very closely with that of the old temple at Râhilya, I think that it may be referred to the same date, that is, to the beginning of the 10th century.

K.—Statue of Shanmukha.

This inscription was found near a ruined temple on the western bank of the Khajur Sâgar. The two lines are engraved on the pedestal of a statue of Shanmukha, or Kârtikeya. I read them as follows :—

> Deva Sri Sasa Sinha—Bhaṭârka Srî Urddha.
> Sivah Achârjasya ||Sarvvpital odharah attambha.
> The characters belong to the Kutila alphabet.

18.—KHAJURÂHA INSCRIPTIONS.

The oldest inscriptions yet found at Khajurâha are a single specimen of the Buddhist creed, two short names on statues in the Chaunsat Jogini temple, and a record of three lines on the pedestal of a colossal statue of Hanumân, all of which appear to belong to the 9th century.

The Buddhist creed is very neatly engraved on the pedestal of a large seated statue. The characters are an early form

of Kutila similar to the oldest of the Magadha inscriptions
of the Pâla Rajas of the 9th century.

The two Chaunsat Jogini names are given in Plate XX,
No. 1. The first reads simply *Sri Maheswari*, and the other
Hinghulâja, which are the names of the goddess Durgâ, on
whom the sixty-four Joginis attend.

A.—The inscription on the pedestal of the colossal statue
of Hanumân is given in Plate XVI. It is the oldest *dated*
record now existing in Khajurâha. The figures of the date
are apparently those of the old notation in which each unit,
and each ten, has a separate symbol, while the hundreds are
formed by attaching a unit on the right side of the letter *s*,
which represents *sat*, or one hundred. In the Hanumân inscription the letter *s* has a cypher attached to it, which is the
same as that afterwards used for the day of the month, and
which I have formerly read as 9, thus making 900. The
other figure is similar to the old Gupta numeral for 40, thus
making the date Samvat 940, or A.D. 883. But the characters may, perhaps, be one or even two hundred years earlier,
making the date either Samvat 840 or 740, or A.D. 783 or 683.

There is a peculiarity about this inscription in the fact
that it is divided into two distinct parts by a blank space,
and further that the letters of the right half are smaller than
those of the left half. I infer, therefore, either that there are
two separate records, or that the right-hand half is a continuation of the left-hand half. I accordingly read the inscription as follows :—

1. Aum ! Golla Gâhila putrasya,
2. Samvatsare 940, Mâgha sudi 9,
3. Sri Hanumântam Gollâkah
   pranamati.

4. Gahilasya sutah Sri Mân
   Hanumân Pa-
5. vanâtmaja Sri Lukusaddhar-
   ma mâ-
6. lokya Gollâko prakritam.

As the date is uncertain, and no king's name is given, this
old record loses much of its importance. I cannot attempt
to translate it. But I understand that the statue was set up
by Golla, the son of Gâhila, in the Samvat year 940 (?) on the
9th (?) day of the waxing moon of Mâgha, when he paid his
adoration to the Gollak Hanumân. The name of *Hanumân*

Pavanâtmaja in the fourth and fifth lines seems to prove that the inscription consists of distinct parts, as I had supposed.

B.—*Plate XVI.*—The next oldest inscription at Khajurâha is unfortunately only a fragment of 13 imperfect lines. (See Plate XVI.) In the seventh line there is the name of *Sri Harsha Deva*, who was the father of Yaso Varmma, and the grandfather of Dhanga Deva. In the tenth line also there is another royal name, *Sri Kshiti Pâla Deva Nripati.* As his name does not occur in any of the genealogies, it seems probable that he may have been the eldest son of Harsha Deva, and that having died childless, he was succeeded by his younger brother Yaso Varmma; and accordingly his name was omitted in all the genealogical inscriptions. We know that Deva Varmma Deva, the eldest son of Vijaya Pâla, was treated in the same way. He actually succeeded his father, but as he was succeeded by his brother Kirtti Varmma, his name is omitted in all the genealogies.

This fragment was found to the north-east of the village, not far from the temple of Vâmana, to which it may have belonged.

C.—*Plate XVII.*—The oldest inscription at Khajurâha with a certain date is recorded on a very long slab now lying in the temple of Chaturbhûja. It consists of 28 lines of old Kutila characters, and gives the genealogy of the Chandel Rajas from Nannuka Deva down to Yaso Varmma and his son Dhanga Deva. The date is given in words as well as in figures; thus, *Samvatsare dasa-sata ekâdasa.*—Samvat 1011, or A.D. 954.

D.—*Plate XVI.*—These four short lines are carved on the pedestal of a statue now lying loose in the temple of Lakshmi Nâth. The characters are early Kutila. That the temple was most probably dedicated to Vishnu we learn, not only from its name of Lakshmi Nâth, or the lord of Lakshmi, but also from the name of *Garuda* in the first line of this inscription. The statue is recorded to have been set up by the sculptor Vena, the son of Bali Atamantai.

E.—*Plate XVI.*—This record is carved on the wall of the temple of Vâmana. The letters are all of the simple Kutila forms, but I am unable to make out any intelligible meaning from them.

F.—*Plate XVIII.*—The next inscription is that which was discovered by Burt in 1838. It is standing loose in the large temple of Viswanâth. It contains two dates. The earlier one, which I read as 1056, or A.D. 999, belongs to the main inscription which records the building of the temple by Raja Dhanga, his death at upwards of one hundred years of age, and the accession of his son Ganda Deva. If the date should be read as Samvat 1096, or A.D. 1039, the record would have been put up no less than 85 years after Dhanga's first inscription. This date would, besides, leave only eleven years, or from Samvat 1096 to 1107, between the reign of Ganda Deva and that of his great-grandson Deva Varmma Deva. As Râja Dhanga, according to other inscriptions, was certainly reigning in A.D. 954 and in 998, it seems almost certain that Ganda Deva must have succeeded him shortly after the latter date. I would therefore assign Ganda Deva to the period between A.D. 999 and 1025. We know that he was reigning in A.D. 1020, when he attacked the Raja of Kanauj, and also in the following year 1021, when he was himself attacked by Mahmud of Ghazni.

This inscription was published in the Journal of the Asiatic Society of Bengal for 1839, page 159; but the whole requires careful revision, as it abounds with mistakes, more especially in the names of the Chandel kings.

G.—*Plate XIX.*—The next inscription is on a large slab now standing loose in the entrance-hall of the temple of Viswanâth. It is dated in Samvat 1058, or A.D. 1001, and, so far as I can make it out, it does not mention the name of a single Chandel king, but refers to one Kokkala, who was perhaps a private person. There was, however, a Kalachuri prince of this name, Kokkala II, who, as the father of Ganggeya Deva, the contemporary of Abu Rihân, must certainly have been reigning at this very time. I cannot find any royal name in the inscription.

H This inscription has already been noted in my account of the smaller records given in Plate XVI, fig. C.

J.—*Plate XVI.*—This inscription is carved on the left door jamb of the Jain temple of Jina Nâth. It is dated, but the mason who cut the figures made a mistake in the hundreds, so that the date may be read either as Samvat 1011, or as Samvat 1111, the second figure being compounded of *o* and *1*. I formerly read it as 1011, but I have been induced to give up this date for 1111 for the following reason. In Samvat 1011 the week-day of *Vaisâkh Sudi* 7 was a Friday, and not a Monday. The true date is Samvat 1111, or A.D. 1054, in which year *Vaisâkh Sudi* 7 did fall on Monday, the 18th April. In the third line there is the name of Raja Dhanga, in whose reign the temple was most probably built. In the fourth line there is the name of the Jaina pontiff Jinanâth, or Jitanâth, to whom the temple was dedicated. Then comes the following list of gifts made to the garden by a member of the Pâhila-vansa during the time of Vâsava Chandra, the Mahârâja Guru or high priest. The following are the names of the gifts :—

1. Pâhila-vâtika, or the Pâhila garden.
2. Chandra-vâtika, or the Chandra garden.
3. Laghu-Chandra-vâtika, or the Little Chandra garden.
4. Sankara-vâtika, or the Sankara garden.
5. Pancha Itala-vâtika ?
6. Amra-vâtika, or the Mango garden.
7. Dhanga-vâri, or the Dhanga garden-house.

L—Is a small inscription of six lines carved on a pillar of one of the smaller corner shrines of the Lakhshminâth temple. The letters are much injured ; and, as no king is mentioned, the record is only valuable as showing that this corner chapel was most probably built in the year noted, or " Samvat 1161, Mâgha badi dwija, 2," or A.D. 1104. But the great temple of Lakshminâth must be at least a century older, as I found the name of *Sâhileh* in early Kutila letters on one of the square pillars of the Mahâ Mandapa, or central hall.

The inscription marked L I read as follows :—

> Swa (sti) Sri Bhaṭâraka
> Guṇa Devachâryyá Pra-
> bhâkara . . ja.
> Kâritam-Samvat
> 1161, Mâgha badi
> dwija 2.

From this the builder of the chapel would appear to have been the chief priest, Prabhâkara.

M.—*Plate XVIII.*—Last two lines of the great inscription of Ganda Deva. The translation given by Sutherland requires to be amended in the name of the characters used in the inscription. Sutherland reads *Kakudâkârâni*, whereas the inscription has *Kumudâkârâni*, that is, "lotus-like, or beautiful characters." With this correction the paragraph runs as follows :—

"The king Jaya Varmma Deva (like an elephant supporting the universe) re-wrote in clear letters the above verses, which had before been written in irregular letters (*Kírna*). These letters, in the *Kumudâ* form, that Gauda Kayastha, aided by the learned, inscribed by the hand of Jaya Pâla, that Kayastha, of untarnished lustre, the radiant moon of the king's race, who, the dispeller of gloom, had risen from the ocean of polished literature. Samvat 1173, Vaisâkh Sudi 3, Friday."

The week-day here given does not agree with the calculated day. The name certainly appears to be *Sukre*, or Friday ; but as the second letter may be read as *je*, it is possible that the original name was *Kuje* or Tuesday, and that the first letter was incorrectly engraved by the sculptor as *Su*. As the Hindu year Samvat 1173 began on Friday, 17th March 1116 A.D. the 3rd day of Vaisâkh sudi would have been the 18th April which was a *Tuesday* (Kuje) as proposed, and not Friday (*Sukre*) as appears to be recorded in the inscription.

N.—(See J.) *Plate XVI.*—I have already noticed this inscription in my account of the short temple records in Plate XVI.

O. P. Q. R. S.—These are short inscriptions on the court of the Jain temples.

O is dated in Samvat 1205, or A.D. 1148.

P is dated in Samvat 1212, or A.D. 1155. It is carved on the base of a statue of Viranâtha, and bears the name of the sculptor, Kumâra Sinha.

Q is dated in Samvat 1215, or A.D. 1158, during the reign of Madana Varmma. A copy of the date is given in Plate XVI, figure D.

R is dated in Samvat 1220, or A.D. 1163. It is engraved on the base of a statue of Ajitanâth.

S is dated in Samvat 1234, or A.D. 1177. It is engraved on a Jaina pedestal, and is the latest dated inscription found at Khajurâha.

19.—MANIYÂ GARH.

The large ruined fort of Maniyâgarh is situated on the left bank of the Kiyân or Ken River, rising immediately above the town of Râjgarh, on the high road between Chhatrpur and Panna. The hill is from 600 to 800 feet in height above the plain below. The fort derives its name from a small shrine of Manyâ Deva.

On the north face of the hill, about 200 feet below the crest, there is a terrace with a lingam of Mahâdeo, on which a small jet of water continuously falls from above. This is an object of worship, and an annual fair is held under the hill at Râjgarh on the Siva-râtri.

Mr. V. Smith quotes the bard Chand for a story of the Chandel Raja Kirat Singh having "hunted at Mainyâgarh with Singh, the Gond chieftain of Garha Mandala; and that afterwards, when war broke out, Kirat Singh was taken prisoner by the Gonds—an injury which was revenged by Alha in the reign of Parmâl."

This looks very like an interpolation of late date, as Kirat Singh was the contemporary of Sher Shah, while *Garha* certainly belonged to the powerful Kalachuri king Karna Deva, during the reign of Kirtti Varmma Chandel. We know also that Garha still belonged to the Kalachuri princes so late as Chedi Samvat 932, or A.D. 1181, and there seems good reason for believing that the kingdom of Dâhal, of which the capital was Tripura or Tewar, was still in the possession of the Kalachuris for a century later, or until the advent of the Bâghels into Rewa.

There is a shrine of Maniyâ Deva at Mahoba. The name is not Hindu, and the worship of Maniya Deva and Maniya Devi is believed to have been a cult of the aboriginal Bhars of Bundelkhand.

20.—MAHOBA INSCRIPTIONS.

As I have already given a detailed description of Mahoba and its antiquities, I will now confine my remarks to a few notes which were omitted in my previous account.

The Chandela kingdom is universally said to have been founded by Chandra Varmma, the son of Chandrama, or the moon, and the princess Hemâvati, the daughter of the Gahir-wâr Râja of Benares or of his purohit Hem Râj. The god informed the princess that her son would be born on the bank of the Karnâvati, or Kiyan River, the present Ken, and directed her to take him to Khajurâha, to offer him as a gift, and to perform the sacrifice of a *Bânda jâg*, to take away the reproach of her having become a mother without marriage.

Chandra Varmma is said to have been born on the 11th day of the waxing moon of Vaisâkh in Samvat 225.[1] When he grew up he built 85 temples,[2] and founded the fort of Kâlanjara. He then went to Mahoba, the place of Chandrama's "great festival" Mahotsava, and made it his capital.

According to the legend, Chandrama had promised Hemâvati that her posterity should continue to reign so long as they observed the four following conditions:—

1. Not to drink wine.
2. Not to put Brahmans to death.
3. Not to make improper connections.
4. To preserve the name of Varmma.

The unfortunate Raja Paramârddi Deva, who was first conquered by Prithi Râj Chauhân, and afterwards by the Muhammadans, is said to have broken all four of these conditions—

1. He drank wine.
2. He put Brahmans to death.
3. He cohabited with his own sister.
4. He did not bear the name of Varmma.

This account is firmly believed by all the people even at the present day, and the legend is probably as old as the time

---

[1] Other dates are given by different manuscripts, as Samvat 204, 661, and 662. See Archæological Survey, Vol. II, p. 446.

[2] These 85 temples are twice mentioned by the bard Chand, Vol. III, p. 85—"Asipânch prâsâd banal," and Vol. III, p. 52—"Pachâsi Math."

of Paramârddi himself, as all his successors bore the name of
Varmma.   In the bardic accounts his eldest son is named Bra-
mâdit, which I believe to be only a spoken form of *Varmmâ-
ditya*, or the " lord of the Varmmas," or Chandels.

Another legend which has also been handed down to the
present day tells how Paramârddis' general the Banâphar hero
Alha, when he quitted Mahoba, forbade any one from beating
a *nakâra* (kettle-drum) in the city for the future.   This in-
junction is still in force after a lapse of seven centuries !   The
general belief is that the ghosts of the old Chandel Rajas
still haunt their old capital, and would resent the beating of
a kettle-drum within their hearing.   Should any one do so,
the horse of the drum-beater would stumble and the rider be
killed, while the chief who ordered the drum to be beaten
would shortly meet with a violent death.   I was myself a
witness to the continuance of this old belief.   In February
1843, when I was residing at Mahoba, Bâkal Singh, the
brother of the Chhatrpur Raja, was obliged to go to Naogaon
to celebrate his daughter's marriage, as he did not dare to
have a wedding procession with music through the city which
the ghosts of the old Chandel Rajas were believed to haunt.

Mahoba was captured by Prithi Raja Chauhân in Samvat
1239, or A.D. 1182, as recorded in his inscription at Madanpur in the Lalitpur district.   But it could not have been annexed to the Delhi kingdom, as I found an inscription built
into the wall of the Mahoba fort with the name of Paramârddi
Deva and the date of Samvat 1240, or A.D. 1183.   There
are, however, no inscriptions of the Chandel kings of a later
date than Samvat 1240, either in Mahoba itself, or in any of
the old places in the Mahoba district.   At the close of Paramârddis' reign the city was permanently annexed to the
Muhammadan kingdom of Delhi.

The earliest inscription that has yet been found at Mahoba was discovered by myself in 1865, let into the wall of the
Dargâh of Pir Muhammad Shah.   It was thickly covered
with whitewash.   I was permitted to take the stone out of
the wall on condition that I restored it to its original position
after taking an impression of it.   I of course replaced it ; but

a few years later it was taken to Fatehpur in the Doab by the
Magistrate, and eventually found its way to the Allahabad
Museum, where I saw it in 1872, and I was thus enabled to get
fresh impressions. It is broken both on the right hand and at
the bottom, and the date is lost. It is written on a slab of
black basalt in the square characters called *Chitra-varna*, or
"ornamented letters." It consists of 17 imperfect lines, but
the characters are generally in good condition. It gives the
genealogy of the Chandel Rajas from Dhanga to Kirtti
Varmma. But just before the name of the later King I find the
name of the Kalachuri Râja Gânggeya Deva, who was reigning
over Tripura, or Chedi, in A.D. 1031, when Mahmud of Ghazni
besieged Kâlanjar. In the 13th line Kanyâkubja is mentioned. But the most interesting part of the record is the
mention of the name of the country as *Jejâ-bhukti* (line 6).
In a short inscription from Madanpur, which I have already
published, the name is given as *Jejâkasukti*. Both of these
forms would naturally be shortened to *Jejâ-huti*, just as *Tirabhukti* has become Tirhuti and Tirhut.

That this was the actual name of the country we learn
from two independent authorities of still older date. The
first is the Chinese pilgrim Hwen Thsang, who visited *Chi-
chi-to* in A.D. The second is Abu Rihân, the contemporary
of Mahmud of Ghazni. He calls it Jajahuti, which is the
form still preserved in the names of the Jajhaotya Brahmans
and Jajhaotiya Baniyas. Its application to both of these
classes shows that it was a geographical designation.

The second large inscription from Mahoba I found in 1843
in the fort wall placed upside down as a common building
stone. It is broken at top and at both ends, but the bottom
line is in good order, and contains the date of *Samvat 1240,
Ashâdha badi 9 Some* (A.D. 1183). It refers to the building
of a temple (*prâsâda*). The sculptor was Deva Raja, the
son of Soma Raja. I cannot find any king's name, but the
reigning Raja in Samvat 1240 was Paramârddi Deva.

A third broken inscription in the same square characters
consists of the remains of 16 lines. It seems to be nearly
perfect on the left hand and at bottom ; but both the top and

the right-hand portion are gone. The only part of the date now remaining is in the last line, where I read *Táksha Samvatsara*, which can only be *Raktáksha*, which was the 58th year of the 60-year cycle of Jupiter. This may be either A.D. 1141 or 1200. The stone-cutter was Deva Raja, the son of Soma Raja ; but I do not see any trace of a Raja's name. As Mahoba was lost to the Chandel princes after 12co A.D., the most probable date of the inscription is A.D. 1200, as will be seen from the next inscription, which was engraved by the same stone-cutter, named Deva Raja, the son of Soma Raja, in 1183 A.D. It certainly refers to the building of a temple, as I find that the word *prásáda* occurs twice (see lines 10 and 15).

I found also several short inscriptions on the pedestals of broken Jaina statues. Some of these are valuable, as they give both the date and the name of the reigning king at the time when the statue was set up. Some omit the king's name, but record the date, whilst others omit both.

The earliest of these short records that I have noted at Mahoba contains only a few words—

Samvat 1169, Phálguna Sudi 8 (A.D. 1112).

It most probably belongs to the time of Jaya Varmma Deva, who, we know, was reigning only four years later, in Samvat 1173.

A second fragment, dated in Samvat 1203, gives the name of the sculptor Lákhana.

A third inscription on the pedestal of a figure with a shell symbol (*Nemináth*) consists of two lines, of which the lower one reads as follows :—

Sri Mán Madana Varmma Deva rájye,
Sam 1211, Ashádha Sudi 3, Sanau (*shell*),
Deva Sri Neminátha—Rupákára Lákhana.

A fourth inscription with a goose symbol (*Sumatináth*) consists of one long line only. It opens with the date—

" Samvat 1213, Mágha Sudi 5 Guran."

No king is mentioned, and it ends with the name of the sculptor Rúkara (for Rupakára) Lákhana.

A fifth inscription with the elephant symbol (*Ajitanâth*) consists of two lines, giving the date and the name of the worshipper—

"Samvat 1220, Jyeshtha sudi 8 Ravau : Sadhu Deva Ga natasya putra Ratna Pâla pranamati nityam ||"

A sixth inscription gives the name of the same worshipper together with those of his wife and his four sons—

1. Sânggamya samâ tat putra sâdhu Sri Ratna Pâla | tasya Bhârya Sâdhâ | putra Kirtti Pâla |
2. tatha Ajaya Pâla | tatha Vasta Pâla | tatha Tribhuvana Pâla | pranamati nityam |
3. jita nâthayah ||

A seventh incomplete inscription belonging to the reign of Paramârddi Deva, consists of one long line—

Samvat 1224 Ashâdha sudi 2 Ravan || (Kâla njarâdhipoti Sri Mat Parâmârddi Devapâd—nâm pravardhamân a Kalyâna nijaya rajye.

21.—DAHI COPPER-PLATE.

About 1848 a copper-plate was obtained by Colonel Ellis from Dâhi, 4½ miles to the east of Bijâwar in Bundelkhand. I have not seen the plate itself, but Colonel Ellis kindly furnished me with the following account of it, in which two out of the four Rajas' names have certainly been misread. The first, which his Pandit reads as *Sri Kando Barm Deo*, must be *Sri Madana Varmma Deva*, as he was the father of Trailokya Deva, and the last, whose name was read Sri Sandin Barm Deo, must be Srimat Vira Varmma, as he was the son of the third king Bhoja Varmma, and was actually reigning in the very year in which the copper-plate grant was made.

The "abstract translation" which I received from Colonel Ellis is as follows :—

"Substance of a grant of land dated *Rab-din Bysâkh Sudi puno, Sambat 1337* (Sunday, A.D. 1280), written by Sri Harnâm Pandit, inscribed on copper, from Dâhi, a village 3 kos east of Bijâwar in Bundelkhand.

"Kando Barm Deo, a descendant of the line of Atri, was a great prince, mighty, like a second Chandrama. His son, Parmârd Deo, had issue Trilok Barm Deo, whose son, Sandin Barm Deo, was Raja of Kâlanjar. He was just, well versed in the Veds, and protected his people with the most tender anxiety.

"He assembled the Brahmans, Kayeths, Harkâras, cow-herds, goat-herds, orchard-keepers, and all other classes, high and low, and said, 'I have this day granted the lands and waters of the village Dahi, with its live and dead stock, rights and privileges, and everything belonging to it, past, future, and present, to the great grandson of Magana Brâhman, the grandson of Sava, the son of Chaonde, by name Balbhadra Mallaya, an illustrious chief of distinguished bravery, who has conquered the Rajas of Nalpur, Gopal-Madhuban, Hatta, Hâr-raj, Gopagiri, Sardhi, the Turks, and rulers from Kashmir. After bathing in water brought from sacred places of pilgrimage and performing worship to Bhagwân, Mahadeo, Suraj, and Bhovâni, holding the kus and Ganges water in hand, I make this grant for the benefit (s) to be accrued (? to accrue) to my mother's, my father's, and my own manes. My servants henceforward must have nothing to do with the village. The jangals, forests, graves, ponds, rivers, mines, hidden treasures, together with all privileges and rights of seignorage over the matmakers, banyas, siklegars, and other inhabitants within its boundaries, are included in the grant. Enjoy the gift without fear of molestation.' This is followed by the usual imprecations against the resumers of land and the advisers of resumption, &c."

Some time afterwards, in 1848, I saw an impression of the copper-plate inscription, from which I made a transliteration in Roman characters. The plate contained 30 lines of about 30 letters in each line. I then read the two doubtful names as Sri Yâdava Varmma Deva and Sri Sandhîra Varmma Deva. The change from Sandin of the Pandit's reading to Sandhîra shows that the last name was Vîra, as I have now suggested.

I cannot follow in my transcript all the names read by the Pandit. According to my reading the gift was made to one Mallâya of the Kâsyapa gotra, the great-grandson of Bhatta Mahattama Sinha, the grandson of Sîvâhada, and the son of Sri Chanda. This hero is said to have conquered the lord of Narwar ("Samarayugâparâjjtâ Nalapurapati") and the ruler of Mathura (Gopâla Madhuvankâdhipa), and Hariraja of Gwâlior (Gopagiri).

I copied the date as Samvat 1337, Samayâ Vaisâkha Sudi 15 Ravi-dine, which agrees with the Pandit's reading of "Rab-din Bysâkh Sudi puno Samvat 1337." But the 15th of Vaisâkh Sudi in Samvat 1337, or A.D. 1280, was Tuesday the 16th of April, and not Sunday.

In A.D. 1280 the fort of Gwâlior was in the possession of Balban, the Muhammadan king of Delhi.

I purpose to make enquiries for this copper-plate during the ensuing winter on my tour through Bundelkhand.

22.—GOBARI.

Gobari is a small village in the petty state of Mahiyar, 9 miles to the north-east of that town and 7 miles to the east-south-east of Uchahara. It possesses an inscribed slab, 27 inches high by 13 inches broad, with an inscription in large letters, containing a date and a king's name. I read portions of it as follows :—

1. Aum ! Swasti ! Samvat 1407,
2. Samaye Jyestha Su-
3. di panchami Bhaume Go-
4. bari grâme Mahârâ-
5. jâdhirâjâ Sri Vîra
6. Râja Deva râjye pratha-
7. ma pancha　.　.　11 mâna
8. Pan : Devadhara　.　.　.　gra.
9. me.

(The remainder is too much broken to be read.)

On the left side there is a single line, as follows :—

likhitam Sutradhâra Gopâla (?).

The date corresponds with Wednesday, 12th May A.D. 1350. The Raja may possibly be the same as the Chandel king Vira Varmma II ; but I think it much more probable that he may be the Baghel Raja Bhairava, who was reigning from A.D. 1335 to 1355.

23.—RAYPUR.

Raypur is a large village in the petty state of Kothi. about 20 miles to the north of the Satna railway station, and about 30 miles to the south-east of Kâlanjar. Here Colonel Ellis found a large black slab, with a long inscription, dated in Samvat 1408 and Sâke 1273, on Wednesday, the 11th Vaisâkh Sudi, during the reign of Sri Vira Deva Nripate. The date corresponds with Wednesday, 6th July 1351 A.D. It is within one year of that of the Gobari inscription last mentioned, and bears the name of the same Raja Vira Deva. From the proximity of Raypur to Kâlanjar one would expect to find the name of one of the Chandel princes in this record. But there is a barren and difficult range of hills between Kâlanjar and Raypur, whereas to the eastward the country is quite open to the valley of the Tons River, which flows through the heart of Rewa, or Baghelkhand. The existence also of another inscription of the same date, and bearing the same king's name at Gobari, which is within the Rewa territory, is very strongly in favour of both inscriptions to one of the Baghel Rajas. There is, however, no Vîra in the Baghel list, while there are two Rajas of that name amongst the Chandel kings. There are two inscriptions of Vira II Chandel in Ajaygarh Fort, both dated in Samvat 1372. or A.D. 1315. It is therefore quite possible that he may have been reigning in A.D. 1350-51. I have, accordingly, placed both the Gobari and Raypur inscriptions in the Chandel list for the present. I may note also that the Ajaygarh prince is called simply Vira Nripa, and not Vira Varmma. But if the Chandel dominions still extended to Gobari so late as A.D. 1350, the Bâghel rule must have been confined to the country to the south of the Son River with its capital at Bândhogarh.

24.—THE CHANDELA KINGDOM.

In two previous Reports I have given an account of the Chandela dynasty from all the materials then available. But later discoveries, including the inscriptions found during my late visit to Kâlanjar and Ajaygarh, the two great strongholds of the kingdom, now enable me to offer a much fuller and more complete abstract of their history. I feel conscious also that the wider reading and the more matured judgment which I now possess will justify me in making public all the information that I have now acquired.

The country held by the Chandel princes may be described as lying between the Dhasân River on the west and the Vindhya Mountains on the east, and extending from the Jumna

on the north to the sources of the Kiyân, or Ken River, on the
south.   The Kiyân River runs through the country from south
to north, dividing it into two nearly equal portions, with the
capital cities of Mahoba and Khajurâha in the western half
and the great forts of Kâlanjar and Ajaygarh in the eastern
half.   Within these limits it had an average length of about
120 miles with a breadth of 100 miles, and an area of more
than 12,000 square miles.   It, therefore, comprised about one-
half of the two British districts of Hamirpur and Banda, with
the whole of the Native States of Chirkhâri, Chhatarpur, and
Bijâwar to the west, and Jaitpur, Ajaygarh, and Panna on the
east.   In their most palmy days the Chandels pushed their
conquests to the Betwa River on the west, which added to
their dominions about 5,000 square miles more.[1]

The revenue of the first tract of 12,000 square miles is
now just 50 lakhs of rupees, while that of the second tract is
about 20 lakhs, the whole being about 70 lakhs.   During the
rule of the Chandels the revenue must certainly have been
less or, say, not more than 40 or 50 lakhs, or about half a
million pounds sterling.   But this was only during the most
prosperous period of the Chandel rule, when their dominions
attained their greatest extension.

It was at this time that Raja Ganda Chandel invaded
Kanauj to punish the Rahtor king for submitting to Mahmud
of Ghazni.   When Mahmud afterwards invaded his territory
the Chandel king is said to have brought into the field no
less than 36,000 cavalry and 45,000 infantry, supported by 640
elephants.   The numbers are, no doubt, much exaggerated;
but even if we reduced them by more than one-half, there
will still remain a force of 40,000 men, with 300 elephants,
which is just two-thirds of the strength of the Sikh army, as
it was left by Ranjit Singh, and greater than that of the
Gwalior army which opposed Lord Ellenborough.

According to the universal tradition of the country, which
is supported by all the chroniclers, the Chandels derive their

---

[1] Chanderi is generally supposed to have belonged to the Chandels from the
belief that it derived its name from them.   But the true derivation of the name
appears to have been from Chandragiri.

origin from Hemâvati, daughter of Hemrâj, the Brahman Purohit, or family-priest, of Indrajit, the Gahirwâr Raja of Benares[1]—

"Hemâvati was very beautiful, and one day when she went to bathe in the Râti Tâlâb, she was seen and embraced by *Chandramâ*, the god of the moon, as he was preparing to return to the skies. Hemâvati cursed him. 'Why do you curse me?' said Chandramâ. 'Your son will be lord of the earth, and from him will spring a thousand branches.' Hemâvati enquired—'How shall my dishonor be effaced when I am without a husband?' 'Fear not,' replied Chandramâ. 'Your son will be born on the bank of the Karnâvati River; then take him to Khajurâya, and offer him as a gift and perform a sacrifice. In Mahoba he will reign, and will become a great king. He will possess the philosopher's stone, and will turn iron into gold. On the hill of Kâlanjar he will build a fort. When your son is 16 years of age you must perform a Bhânda Jag to wipe away your disgrace, and then leave Benares to live at Kâlanjar.'"

According to this prophecy, Hemâvati's child, like another Chandramâ, was born on Monday, the 11th of the waxing moon of Vaisâkh, on the bank of the Karnâvati, the modern Kiyân, or Kane, River of the maps, and the Kainas of the Greeks. Then Chandramâ, attended by all the gods, performed a " great festival " (Mahotsava), when Vrihaspati wrote his horoscope, and the child was named Chandra Varmma. At 16 years of age he killed a tiger, when Chandramâ appeared again to him and presented him with the philosopher's stone, and taught him polity (*râjnit*). Then he built the Fort of Kâlanjar, after which he went to *Kharjurpur*, where he performed a sacrifice (*jag* or *yajnya*) to do away with his mother's shame, and built 85 temples. Then Chandravati Râni and all the other queens sat at the feet of Hemâvati, and her disgrace was wiped away. Lastly, he went to Mahotsava, or Mahoba, the place of Chandramâ's " great festival," which he made his capital.

But this popular tradition receives no support from the inscriptions. In the copper-plate record of Raja Dhanga Deva, the founder is said to be " of the great family of Sri Brahmendra Muni." In the stone inscription of Raja Ganda

[1] Archæological Survey Reports, Vol. II, pages 445 and 446.

Deva the kings are said to be of the Chandrâtreya line, which
agrees with the other statement, as Atri and Chandra were
the son and grandson of Brahmâ or Brahmendra.   But there
is no allusion whatever to Hemâvati, the Brahman maiden,
whose story is probably a pure fiction, invented to cover the
equivocal origin of the ancestors of the Chandels.

In the two long inscriptions at Khajurâha the earliest name
mentioned is that of Nannuka.   In Dhanga Deva's copper-
plate the earliest name is that of his own grandfather, Harsha
Deva, while in that of Deva Varmma Deva the earliest name
is that of Vidyâdhara Deva, the grandson of Dhanga.   The
following is the genealogy as derived from all sources :—

Chandela Rajas.

No.	Vik. S.	A.D.	Names.	
1	857	800	Nannuka Deva	......
2	882	825	Vâkpati	......
3	...	850	Vijaya	......
4	...	875	Râhila	......
5	...	900	Harsha Deva . . .	......
6	982	925	Yaso Varmma Deva . . .	......
7	1010	953	Dhanga Deva	Inscription, S. 1011 and 1055.
8	1056	999	Ganda Deva	Inscription, S. 1056.
9	1082	1025	Vidyâdhara Deva . . .	......
10	1097	1040	Vijaya Pâla Deva . . .	......
11	1107	1050	Deva Varmma Deva . . .	Copper-plate, S. 1107.
12	1120	1063	Kirtti Varmma Deva . .	Deogarh Rock, S. 11.
13	1155	1097	Hallakshana Varmma Deva	......
14	1 67	1100	Jaya Varmma Deva . .	Inscription, S. 1173.
15	1177	1120	Hallakshana Varmma Deva .	......
16	1179	1122	Prithvi Varmma Deva .	......
17	1186	1129	Madana Varmma Deva .	Inscription, S. 1186 to 1220.
18	1222	1165	Paramârddi Deva .	Inscription, S. 1224. Killed A.D. 1203.
19	1259	1203	Trailokya Varmma Deva .	Inscription, S. 1269-1297.
20	1297	1240	Vira Varmma I. . . .	Do. S. 1312 to 1337.
21	1309	1282?	Bhoja Varmma . . .	Do. S. 1345.
22	1357	1300	Vira Varmma II. . . .	Do. S. 1372.
23	1387	1330	Sasângka (bhupa) . . .	......
24	1403	1360	Bhilama Deva	......
25	1447	1390	Paramârddi	......
26	...	1420	......	......
27	...	1445	......	......
28	...	1470	......	......
29	...	1495	......	......
30	1577	1520	Kirat Singh . .	......
...	1602	1545	......	......
...	1627	1570	......	......

I now give a list of all the Chandel inscriptions at present known, as they form the authorities on which the above genealogy has been compiled—

Chandel Inscriptions.

No.	Place.	Letter.	Date. Vik.S.	Date. A. D.	King.		Lines.
1	Kâlanjar	P	...	400	?	Gupta character	3
2	Do.	Q	...	400	?	Ditto	1
3	Do.	L	...	600	?	At the Ganes Gate	16
4	Do.	K	...	800	?	Cell near Nilkanth	4
5	Khajurâha	...	...	800	?	Buddhist creed	...
6	Do.	A	940	883	?	Colossal statue of Hanumàn	3
7	Do.	B	...	900	Harsha Deva	Broken slab	13
8	Do.	C	1011	954	Dhanga Deva	Loose slab in temple	28
9	Do.	D	...	...	...		...
10	Do.	E	...	...	...	....	...
11	Nanyaura	...	1055	998	Dhanga Deva	Copper-plate, Bengal Asiatic Society's Journal, 1878	14
12	Khajurâh	F	1056	999	Ganda Deva	Loose slab in temple	32
13	Do.	G	1058	1001		Sri Kokala—loose slab	22
14	Do.	H	1085	1028		Colossal figure of Sântinâth	1
15	Nanyaura	...	1107	1050	Deva Varmma Deva	Copper-plate, Bengal Asiatic Society's Journal, 1878	19
16	Khajurâha	J	1111	1054		Left-door jamb, Jain Temple	11
17	Do.	K	1142	1085		Bull-symbol statue of Adinâth	...
18	Deogarh	...	1154	1097	Kirtti Varmma	On rock	8
19	Khajurâha	L	1161	1104		Corner temple of Lakshminâth	...
20	Mahoba	A	...	...	Kirtti Varmma	Idgâh wall—incomplete	17
21	Ajaygarh	P	...	...	Ditto	Rock outside gate	4
22	Mahoba	B	1169	1112	...	Fragment	1
23	Khajurâha	M	1173	1116	Jaya Varmma	Under Ganda's inscription No. 12	2
24	Do.	N	1174	1117		Kunwar Math, on Kurar Nala	2
25	Kâlanjar	A	1186	1129	Madana Varmma	......	8

Chandel Inscriptions—contd.

No.	Place.	Letter.	Vik. S.	A.D.	King.		Lines.
26	Kâlanjar . .	B	1187	1130	...	......	4
27	Do.	C	1188	1131	...	......	9
28	Augâsi . .	...	1188	1131	Madana Varmma	Copper-plate, Bengal Asiatic Society's Journal, 1878	19
29	Kâlanjar . .	D	1192	1135		Thakur Nrisingh, statue of Narsingh . . .	8
30	Do. .	E	1194	1137		Cave near Nilkanth .	7
31	Do. .	F	1195	1138		Rock to north of Nilkanth	21
32	Mahoba . .	C	1203	1146			...
33	Khajurâha .	O	1205	1148		......	...
34	Bârigarh . .	...	1207	1150		Pedestal of naked standing figure	...
35	Ajaygarh . .	A	1208	1151		......	18
36	Mahoba . .	D	1211	1154		Statue of Neminâth . .	2
37	Khajurâha .	P	1212	1155		Viranâth-Sculptor Kumâr Singh	...
38	Mahoba . .	E	1213	1156	Madana Varmma	Figure of Sumatinâth .	...
39	Khajurâha .	Q	1215	1158	Ditto . .	Figure of Sambhunâth .	...
40	Do. .	R	1220	1163		Statue of Ajitanâth .	...
41	Mahoba . .	F	1222	1165		...	...
42	Kâlanjar . .	G	1222	1165		Pavement of Nilkanth Temple . . .	2
43	Mhau . .	...	...	...	Madana Varmma	Asiatic Researches, Vol. XII .	...
44	Mahoba . .	G	1224	1167	Paramârddi Deva	On pedestal with figures .	1
45	Khajurâha .	S	1234	1177		Jain figure . . .	...
46	Ajaygarh . .	B	1237	1180	...	...	...
47	Madanpur . .	...	1239	1182	Paramârddi Deva	Small temple . . .	...
48	Mahoba . .	H	1240	1183	Ditto . .	Wall of fort . . .	...
49	Do. . .	J	...	...		Nearly square fragment .	...
50	Ajaygarh . .	C	1243	1186	...	...	8
51	Kâlanjar . .	H	1258	1201	Paramârddi Deva	Bengal Asiatic Society's Journal, Vol. XVII, p. 316	32
52	Bagrâri . .	...	...	...	Ditto . .	In 2 pieces, bank of lake .	24
53	Ajaygarh . .	D	1269	1212	Trailokya Varmma		6
54	Do. . .	E	1312	1255	Vira Varmma .	...	55

Chandel Inscriptions—contd.

No.	Place.	Letter.	Vik.S.	A.D.	King.		Lines.
			DATE.		King.		
55	Kâlanjar . .	J	...	...	Vira Varmma .	Yellow slab-circa, A.D. 1250	31
56	Ajaygarh .	F	1325	1268	...		...
57	Do. . .	G	1337	1280	Vira Varmma .	...	21
58	Dáhi	...	1337	1280	Ditto . .	Copper-plate, Colonel Ellis	30
59	Ajaygarh .	H	1345	1288	Bhoja Varmma .	Bengal Asiatic Society's Journal, 1837, page 885 .	...
60	Do.	I	...	...	...	Without date, long lines .	2
61	Do.	J	...	...	Bhoja Varmma .	Large letters, long inscription	15
62	Do.	K	1346	1289	Ditto . .	...	11
63	Do.	L	1349	1292		Over a female figure .	3
64	Do.	M	1311	1314		Upper round step of temple	2
65	Do.	N	1372	1315		Almost illegible from white-wash . . .	12
66	Do.	O	1372	1315	Vira Nripa .	Pillar of gateway . .	15
67	Kâlanjar . .	...	1372	1315	...		...
68	Gobari	...	1407	1350	Vira Raja Deva .	...	...
69	Raypur .	...	1408	1351	Ditto . .	and Sasângka Bhüpa .	...
70	Bachon .	...	1433	1376	Bhilama Deva .		...
71	Râsin	...	1466	1409	Paramârddi .	...	...
72	Kâlanjar . .	...	...	...	...	Outside the Lâl Darwâza .	16

Of the first three kings in the list, nothing whatever is related save the fact of their reigns.

To *No. 4 Râhila*, the chronicles assign the erection of a very fine temple, now in ruins, at the village of Râhilya, 2 miles to the south-west of Mahoba. As he was the great-grandfather of Dhanga Deva, his reign cannot be placed later than 75 years (or three generations) prior to the accession of Dhanga, or from 875 to 900 A.D.

Of *No. 5, Harsha Deva*, we learn that his wife was named Kaneshuka, and that their son was .

No. 6, Yaso Varmma Deva, whose wife was Narmmâ Devâ.— A great part of the earliest and longest of the Khajurâha inscriptions, dated in Samvat 1011, or A.D. 954, is taken up with an account of his reign. His son, Dhanga, is mentioned in line 25, and the date is given, both in words and in figures, in the 28th or last line.

No. 7.—Dhanga Deva is celebrated as the builder of a temple of Siva, in which was enshrined an emerald lingam, and also a stone image of the god. He is recorded to have lived more than 100 years (*jívitwa saradâm satam samadhikam*), when he drowned himself at the junction of the Ganges and Jumna Rivers. His copper-plate is dated in Samvat 1055, or A.D. 998; and as the great stone inscription at Khajurâha, which records his death, is dated in the following year, his son's accession may be placed in Samvat 1056, or A.D. 999.

No. 8.—Ganda Deva, the son of Dhanga, was the conqueror of Kanauj in A.D. 1020, and the opponent of Mahmud of Ghazni in 1021. He is called Nanda Deva and Beda Deva by the Muhammadan historians, both easy corruptions of Ganda in Persian characters. The mere omission of the *markaz*, or the substitution of a point, would have changed كنده *Ganda* into ننده *Nanda*, or even into بيده *Beda*. The beginning of Ganda's reign would appear to have been disturbed by an invasion of the Kalachuri King Kokkala, as there is an inscription of Sri Kokkala in one of the temples, dated in Samvat 1058, or A.D. 1001. It seems more probable, however, that Kokkala was only a private individual, as the inscription does not give him the title of king, but calls him simply *Srimat Kokkala.*

Nos. 9 and 10.—Of these two nothing is recorded.

No. 11.—Deva Varmma Deva is known only from a copper-plate inscription, translated by Mr. V. Smith.[1] It is dated in Samvat 1107, or A.D. 1050. He is called Kâlanjarâdhipati, or "Lord of Kâlanjar," and is expressly stated to be the son of No. 11, or Vijaya Pâla Deva. We learn also that his mother was named Bhuvana Devi.

No. 12.—Kirtti Varmma Deva was the brother of Deva Varmma. His reign was probably a long one, as we have his inscription from Deogarh dated in Samvat 1154, or A.D. 1097,

<hr>

[1] See Bengal Asiatic Society's Journal, 1878, page 82.

just 47 years later than his brother's copper-plate.[1] To him is
attributed the construction of the Kirat Sâgar at Mahoba, and
there are several broken inscriptions which bear his name, but
they are unfortunately without date. There are also gold
coins inscribed with his name *Srimad Kirtti Varmma Deva.*
Apparently Kirtti Varmma was one of the most powerful of
the Chandel kings. His territory extended to the south,
down to the great fort of Deogarh on the Betwa, to the south-
west of Lalitpur. At his court was performed the curious
drama, named *Prabodha Chandrodaya,* or " Rise of the Moon
of Intellect," composed by Krishna Misra. In the prologue
to this work he is represented as having been at war with the
powerful Karna (the Kalachuri Prince of Chedi) ; but the
enemies of the king having been destroyed, the administration
of government is entrusted to his celebrated ministers, and
having entered on the road of peace, he commanded the
manager to act the " Rise of the Moon of Intellect." Kirtti
Varmma was the contemporary of Bhoja of Malwa and of
Bhima Deva of Gujarât, as well as of Karna Kalachuri of
Dâhal or Chedi.

No. 13.—Hallakshana, or Sallakshana Varmma Deva, was
the son of Kirtti Varmma. In one inscription he is called
Sulakshana. To him is ascribed a great victory in Antarbed,
or the Doab of the Ganges and Jumna. He is called Hallakshana on his coins, of which I have specimens both in gold
and in copper.

No. 14, Jaya Varmma Deva.—The British Museum has
a silver coin of this prince from the Prinsep collection, and
I possess seven of his copper coins. He restored the long inscription in the temple of Siva, in which the emerald lingam had
been enshrined by Raja Dhanga. The original inscription,
which had been written in *Kirnakshara* characters, or " bent
letters," he restored in *Kumardâkarâni,* or " beautiful characters," in the Samvat year 1173, or A.D. 1116.

No. 15, Jaya, was succeeded by his brother *Hallakshana,*
or Sallakshana II., who could not have reigned for more than
a year or two.

---

[1] See Archæological Survey, Vol. X. p. 103.

No. 16, Prithvi Varmma.—Of him nothing is recorded; but I possess four of his copper coins. He was succeeded by his son,

No. 17, Madana Varmma Deva.—His reign was a long one, as we possess inscriptions of various dates, beginning with Samvat 1186, or A.D. 1129, down to 1220, or A.D. 1163. He made the beautiful lake of Madan Sâgar at Mahoba with its two temples. Of his coins I possess two large and four small specimens in gold, and one in copper. In one of the inscriptions it is said that " he in an instant defeated the King of Gurjara, as Krishna in former times defeated Kansa.[1] " During his reign the Chandel kingdom probably attained its greatest extent and prosperity.

No. 18, Paramârddi Deva, or Parmâl.—The annalists interpose a second Kirtti Varmma as the son and successor of Madana; but as I have found no other trace of him, I doubt their accuracy. Paramârddi, or Parmâl, or Parmâlik, was certainly on the throne in Samvat 1224, or A.D. 1116, or only four years later than the last of Madana Varmma's inscriptions. Paramârddi had a long and eventful reign. According to the annalists, he lost his kingdom because he was not a Varmma, as his predecessors had been. But the title of Varmma is first found in the inscriptions with Deva Varmma, the 12th Raja; and we now know that at least four of Paramârddi's successors bore the name of Varmma, so that the title did not die with him.

Early in his reign, or in Samvat 1239=A.D. 1172, Paramârddi was attacked and conquered by the famous Chauhân Prince Prithivi Raja, whose inscriptions at Madanpur I have already made known.[2] After his defeat the dominions of Paramârddi were limited by the Dhasân River on the west, and by the Bijâwar and Panna Hills on the south. But he still held Mahoba and Khajurâha to the west of the Kiyân or Ken River, and Kâlanjar and Ajaygarh to the east. A copper-plate inscription at Rewa, dated in Samvat 1297=A.D. 1240, with the name of Trailokya Varmma Deva, would seem to show

[1] Bengal Asiatic Society's Journal, 1848, page 319.
[2] Archæological Survey Reports, Vol. IX.

that the Chandel kingdom had been extended to the eastward by the defeat of the Kalachuris. His earliest inscription is dated in Samvat 1224, or A.D. 1167, and his latest in
Samvat 1240, or A.D. 1183. But we know that his reign
continued for 20 years longer, down to A.D. 1203, when
he was besieged in Kâlanjar by Kutb-ud-din Aibak. He
made arrangements for surrendering the fort, but was mur-
dered by his minister, who, after a few days' further defence,
was obliged to surrender by the failure of the water, on
27th April, A.D. 1203. The minister was killed and the
fortress was occupied by the Muhammadans, who desecrated
the temples and raised mosques in their places. But the
fortress was soon recovered by the Hindus, and probably
remained in their possession for some time.

No. 19.—Trailokya Varmma Deva was the son and successor of Paramârddi. There is an inscription of this Raja
in the fort of Ajaygarh, dated in Samvat 1269, or A.D. 1212.
When or how he recovered Kâlanjar is not known ; but he
was in full possession in A.H. 631, or A.D. 1233, when the
troops of Iltitmish, King of Delhi, under the command of
Nusrat-ud-din Tâyasi, invaded the territory of Kâlanjar for
the purpose of plunder. The country must have been rich,
as the invader returned with one hundred and twenty-five
lâkhs of some coin unnamed, but which was probably
dirhems.

No. 20.—Vira Varmma Deva I. was the son and successor of Trailokya. Of his reign there are three stone inscriptions, dated respectively in Samvat 1313, 1325, and 1337,
or A.D. 1256, 1268, and 1280. There was also a copper-
plate of his time, dated in Samvat 1337, which was in
the possession of Colonel R. R. Ellis, and which was lost
in the mutiny. His name was read as Sri Sandin Barm
Deo by Colonel Ellis' pandit, for which I guessed Sri
Sandhira Varmma Deva ;[1] but which I now see must have
been Sri Mad Vira Varmma Deva.

*No. 21.—*Vira was succeeded by his son Bhoja Varmma
Deva, of whom we possess a notice in a long inscription dated

---

[1] Archæological Survey, Vol. II, p. 455.

in Samvat 1345, or A.D. 1288.   This inscription records the genealogy of Nâna, the minister of the *Chandrâtreya* line, that is, of the Chandel princes.   He sent his horse to Bhoja Varmma, who is apparently "the newly-appointed royal Lakshmi," whom Nâna's father had supplicated (verse 27). The inscription itself is now in the Indian Museum in Calcutta.   It is written in the well-known square charac- ters of the later Chandel princes, which in this record are called *chitra-varna,* or ornamented letters.

There is a long inscription of Bhoja Varmma himself near the *Ashta Sakti* figures at the Terhauni Gate of the Ajaygarh Fort.   It is cut in the rock, and measures 7 feet by 2 feet 4 inches.   It contains 15 lines in large *chitra-varna* charac- ters.   The genealogy of the prince is given, beginning with Kirtti Varmma.

No. 22.—The successor of Bhoja Varmma was apparently a second Vira Varmma.   There are two inscriptions, dated in Samvat 1372, or A.D. 1315, in one of which I find the name Vira Nripa, and in a third inscription of apparently the same date a Vira Varmma is mentioned.

No. 23.—The name of Sasângka-bhûpa is found in an in- scription near Raypur, in the Koti District, 24 miles to the south-east of Kâlanjar.   The inscription has 23 lines, but it is much injured in the middle.   I have not seen it; but my information is derived from an impression taken by one of Colonel Ellis' servants.   In the 10th line I find the name of Sri Vira Raja Nripa, and in the 21st line the name of Sâsangka- bhûpa.   The date is given very fully as Samvat 1408 varshe Sake 1273, Ashadha sudi 11 Budhavâsare divasa, or Wednes- day, 6th July, A.D. 1351.   The absence of the name of Varmma might be supposed to show that Sasângka was not a Chandel. But in this very inscription the name of Vira Raja occurs without Varmma.   We know, also, that the name of Varmma was certainly discarded by the later Chandel princes, as the Raja of Kâlanjar who opposed Sher Shah was named Kirat Singh.

No. 24.—The name of Bhilama Deva Râja is found in a short inscription at Bachon, near the left bank of the Kiyân or

Ken River, 15 miles from Ajaygarh. There is no direct proof
that he was a Chandel prince, but the near vicinity of Bachon
to the great Chandel stronghold of Ajaygarh makes it almost
certain that it must have formed part of the Chandel dominions. The inscription is dated in Samvat 1433 and Sake
1298, both equivalent to A.D. 1376.

No. 25.—The name of Paramârddi-mahîpateh is found in
an inscription at Râsin, which is dated in Samvat 1466, or
A.D. 1409, on Saturday, the 7th of the waxing moon of
Chaitra, or Saturday, the 23rd March 1409. The reign of
Paramârddi II. may be assigned to the year 1390 to 1420
A.D.

Nos. 26, 27, 28, 29.—I have found no trace of the names
of the Râjas who must have reigned from A.D. 1420 to 1520.
During this period there would have been only four generations, but there may have been as many as six or eight
reigns.

No. 30.—Kirat Singh was the last actual Raja of Kâlanjar.
He was besieged by Sher Shah, and was put to death by
Islâm Shâh after the capture of the fort in A.D. 1545. He
was almost certainly the father of the famous Princess Durgâvati, the Queen of Dalapati, the Gond Raja of Garha Mandala, who reigned from A.D. 1530 to 1548. With Raja
Kirat Singh and his heroic daughter Durgâvati the Chandel
sovereignty came to an end, after a brilliant career of seven
centuries and a half, from A.D. 800 to 1545 and 1563.

The fort of Kâlanjar was acquired by Akbar in A.H. 977, or
A.D. 1569, and it remained in the hands of the Mughals until
the time of the great Bundela Chief Chhatra Sâl. It was
held by his descendants until A.D. 1812, when it was surrendered to the British Government.

The latest Khajurâha inscription is of Paramârddi Deva,
with the date of Samvat 1234, or A.D. 1177, in the early part of
his reign. When the Muhammadans invaded the country of
the Chandels, they at first made their head-quarters at
Kâlanjar; but after the Hindus had recovered the fortress the
Muhammadans retained Mahoba and the plain country to the
west of the Kiyân or Ken River, which included the old

religious capital of Khajurâha. It is no doubt on this account that no Hindu inscriptions are to be found either in Khajurâha, or Mahoba, after the Muhammadan conquest. There is a masjid in Mahoba, with an inscription of Tughlak Shah of Delhi ; and Khajurâha (or Kajarrâ) was visited by Ibu Batuta in A.H. 743, or A.D. 1342 during the reign of Muhammad. He mentions the temples and the jogis with matted hair, who were attended by numbers of Musalmans who were desirous to learn their secrets.

From the above abstract we learn that the Chandel rajas were in possession of the fortress of Kâlanjar for about four centuries, or from A.D. 800 to 1203, when the place was captured by Kutb-ud-din Aibak. It was soon re-captured by the Hindus, and must have remained in their possession for some time, as several attempts were shortly after made by the Muhammadans to re-take it. But the power of the Chandels was broken, and many of them left their country to seek safety and independence beyond the reach of the Moslem domination. Thus the present Chandel Rajas of Handur and Kahalur (near Simla) trace their descent from emigrants from Mahoba in the beginning of the 13th century of the Christian era. A large body also marched eastwards and sought refuge in the wild country near Bardhi, where the Son River breaks through the Kaimur and Vindhya ranges of hills. But the great body of the people still remained in their native country of Jejahuti with their capital of Ajaygarh. Their power seems to have gradually declined until the province was finally annexed to the Mughal empire by Akbar in A.H. 977, or A.D. 1569.

25.—MAP OF N.-W. INDIA BY PTOLEMY.

In attempting to identify the cities and peoples of ancient India mentioned by Pliny and Ptolemy, it is startling to find how very few names have been preserved to the present day. The names of the rivers have mostly remained unchanged, as the Ganges and the Jomanes (or Gangâ and Jamunâ), and even smaller streams at the Tamasis (Tamasa or Tons), the Cainas (Ken or Kiyân) and the Sonus (or Son). The great provinces of Indo-Scythia and the Kaspiræi were, no doubt, occupied by the Sakas and Kushâns. The territory of the latter, according to Ptolemy, included Modura, or Mathura, and their coins and inscriptions are still found there in considerable numbers. But to the east of the Kaspiræi we find the territories of Sandrabatis, the Bolingæ, and the Poruari, between the Ganges and *Vindius Mons*, or the Vindhya Mountains, with the Son River on the east ; while to the south are the Phullitæ, the Kondali, the Bettigi, the Adisathri, and the Soræ *Nomades*—not one of whom has yet been identified. I will now examine these names in succession, in the hope that I may be able to throw a few rays of light on this dark quarter of Indian geography.[1]

Sandrabatis.—This district is bounded on the west by the Kaspiræi, whose territory included Modura, or the holy city of Mathura of the present day. To the south lay the Vindhya Mountains, and to the east the Tamasis, or Tons River. With these landmarks I venture to guess that the province of Sandrabatis derived its name from the *Charmanvati*, or Chambal River, and that it comprised the whole of the country lying between the Chambal and the Tons Rivers, thus including the northern half of the present Gwalior territory, with the whole of Bundelkhand and a strip of Rewa.

The towns of Sandrabatis mentioned by Ptolemy are— 1, Tamasis; 2, Kuraporina; 3, Empalathra; and 4, Nadubandagar.

The first of these may, I think, be identified with the famous hill of Kâlanjar, which, before it was fortified, was well known as the favourite abode of *Tapaswis*, or " Ascetics." H. H. Wilson says that it is mentioned in the Vedas, and that it was one of the *Tapasya-sthânas*, or "spots adapted to practices of austere devotion." By a very slight change the Greek *Tamasis* may be read as *Tapasis*.

The second name, *Kuraporina*, as I have already suggested, may possibly be a corruption of Khajurapura by the simple elision of the letter j-, thus making Khurapura.[2] It was the

---

[1] See Plate XXIV for Ptolemy's Map of India, south of the Jumna.
[2] According to Vararuchi, the letter j might be elided.

capital of the country in the time of Abu-Rihân, and it still possesses the largest and finest collection of rich and stately temples in Northern India.

The third name, *Empalathra*, is a difficult one. I think that it may be Mahoba, of which the full name is Mahotsava-nagara.

The fourth name, *Nadubandagar*, is even more difficult. I think that it may be intended for Nalapura-dûrgga, or Narwar, as it stood on the high road leading from Modura to Kura-pornia, which agrees exactly with the position of Narwar. The fort is said to be as old as the time of Raja Nala, from whom it derived its name.

The district of the *Bolingæ* is placed to the east of Sandrabatis, and to the north of the Vindhya Mountains. It corresponds generally with the present state of Rewa, of which the earliest inhabitants are said to have been the Bâlands, or Bâlandas. They were first driven northward by the Kalachuris and afterwards by the Chandels, until they reached the Ganges. They have left their name in the town of Balwaniya, 35 miles to the south-south-east of Mirzapur. Mr. Carlleyle also suggests that Ptolemy's fort of Balanti-purgon, which I have identified with Bandho-garh, may have derived its name from the Bâlands. Bâlandi-garh would be the natural name for their capital, and Bândhôgarh would be a natural abbreviation of the name.

Only two towns are mentioned as belonging to the Bolingæ. They are named—1, Sagabaza, and 2, Bardaotis. The first seems to suit the position of Nâgodh, an old town belonging to the Parihâr Raja of Uchahara.

The second place, Bardaotis, I have already identified with Bharhut, where I discovered the remains of a grand Stûpa, surrounded with a richly carved railing representing many of the principal events in the life of Buddha, as well as a large number of the Jâtakas, or former births of Buddha. These sculptures are known to belong to the 2nd century before the Christian era, from the style of the characters used in their descriptive titles.[1]

---

[1] See my Stûpa of Bharhut for a discussion on the date.

To the south of the Bolingæ, Ptolemy places the *Poruari* with their three towns, named *Bridama, Tholobana,* and *Malaita.* The people I take to be the *Parihár* Rájputs, who have occupied this part of the country from a very early date. I have already mentioned the Parihár Raja of Uchahara, who traces his lineage up to a remote period. As the Parihárs are said to have been subjected by the Kalachuris, they were probably in possession of the country before the Kalachuri conquest of Kálanjar, and the establishment of the Chedi, or Kalachuri era, in 249 A.D.

The first town, *Bridama,* I would identify with Bilahari, an old town which possesses many ruins of the early Kalachuri princes. The second town, *Tholobona,* I would identify with *Bahuriband,* a very old town, with a number of Gupta temples in its neighbourhood. Perhaps the name may have been altered from Bolobana, which would be a very close approach to Bahuriband, or Boriband, as it is quickly pronounced.

The third town, Malaita, I would identify with *Multai,* an old town 30 miles to the north-east of Jabalpur, where some old copper-plate inscriptions have been found.

Still further to the south Ptolemy places the *Phullitæ* and the *Kondali,* whose country is described as *Pars Phullitarum.* Phullitæ I take to be a Greek name descriptive of the *Parna Savaras,* or "leaf-clad Savaras," one of the most powerful of the aboriginal races in the early centuries of the Christian era. Their only town was *Agara,* which may perhaps be identified with Ságar.

To the west of the Phullitæ were the Parapiotæ, with a single town, *Adisathra,* which I would identify with *Bidisa,* or Besnagar, one of the oldest towns to the north of the Narbadá. It is happily situated in the fork at the junction of the Besali and Betwa Rivers.

To the east of the Phullitæ and to the south of the *Poruari,* Ptolemy places the country of the *Adisathri* with their capital, named *Sageda Metropolis.* The Adisathri I would identify with the people of Chattisgarh. If this be correct, their capital must be looked for at Sirpur on the

Mahânadi River.   Their other town, named *Balanti-purgon,* is, most probably, the curious hill city described by the Chinese pilgrims Fa Hian and Hwen Thsang.   The latter calls it Po-lo-mo-lo-ki-li, or Paramala-giri, and says that its name meant the " black peak."   *Kili* or *giri* is certainly a hill, but the only word resembling *Polomolo,* with reference to blackness, is *bhramara,* or the great " black bee."   Another Chinese writer says that the word meant " coral beads," which would be Palâ-mâlâ, or coral necklace, in Sanscrit.   A third Chinese author says that the city was named *Pa-lai,* or " situated on a height." This would point to *bala,* or *balla,* which is the *Korku,* or *Kolian,* term for a hill : *male* also means a hill in several of the aboriginal dialects.   Any of these names might be identified with Ptolemy's *Balanti-purgon,* supposing that the term meant " a hill fort."   The position of the city described by the Chinese writers from hearsay has not yet been ascertained.

To the south of all these were the *Bettigi* on the west, and the *Sora Nomades* on the east.   The former I would identify with the people of *Vâkâtaka,* or *Bândak,* and the latter with the Savaras of South Chattisgarh.   The Rajas of Vâkâtaka were contemporary with the Guptas, and I have lately found an inscription of Prithivi Sena, one of their early kings, showing that their power once extended to Khutara, only 20 miles to the south-west of Nâgodh.

The *Soræ Nomades* I take to be the pure aboriginal race of *Savaras* or *Sauras,* and their chief town *Sora Arcati regia* must have been named after them.   They still extend from the Mahânadi down to the sea-coast of Ganjam.   I think that Sora may be identified with Savari-Nârâyan on the Mahânadi River.   It is a famous place of pilgrimage, and lies on the high road from Bilâspur to Jagannâth.   It is about 35 miles to the south-west of Bilâspur and 75 miles to the north-east of Raypur.   The people of the present day refer its name to the woman Savari, who is connected with the legendary history of Râma.   The term *Arcati regia* may perhaps refer to the temple of the sun (*arka*), which is apparently the oldest building now existing at Savari-Nârâyan.   The temple now holds a figure of Vishnu, but its original dedication to the Sun god is attested by a figure of the god being placed over the middle of the entrance doorway. There is a ruined site close to Ghâzipur, which is still called Suïri-ka-râj, which is said to have received its name from the Suïrs or Savaras, and which at once recalls the Savari or Suari-Nârâyan on the Mahânadi.

26.—NACHNA, OR KUTHARA.

The small village of Nachna is situated 2 miles to the west of the town of Ganj, which is 25 miles to the south-east of Panna, and 15 miles to the south-west of Nâgodh. The place lies in the southern extremity of the Ajaygarh territory, and it was from the Raja himself that I first heard of the ruined temples near Ganj. The little village of Nâchna stands on a clearing made by a party of twenty families of Kols in the beginning of the present century. The spot is covered with bricks, and there are many remains of brick buildings on the road from Ganj to Nâchna. The people say that Kûthara was a great city in former times, and that it was the capital of the king of the country. The site of Nâchna is still called Khâs Kûthara. In the early history of the Bundelas it is recorded that Sohan Pâl, the fourth in descent from Pancham, the founder of the family, captured *Kûtharagarh* about the middle of the 15th century.

Lakhura is the name of the ground outside the fort of Kûthara. It was called Lakhura, or Lakhâwara, because the Raja had planted there one lakh of mango trees, and had also fed one lakh of Brahmans. There is said to be a tunnel from the fort of Kûthara to the Satna or Gorena Nala, which flows past Nâchna, and joins the Kiyân or Ken River, 11 miles to the south-west of Ganj.

In the Atlas map of India the name of the village is erroneously written as *Narhua*, instead of Nâchna. The whole way from Ganj lies through jungle, chiefly of dhâk trees, from which the Kols collect gum for sale. There are many *pân* gardens near Ganj, which is a sure sign of an old Hindu city. The position in the entrance of a valley had the great advantage of offering a safe retreat into the recesses of the Vindhya Hills on the east, west, and south, in case of attack.

There are two temples still standing at Nâchna, one named after the goddess Pârvati, although at present it possesses no statue; the other named Chaturmukh Mahâdeva, after the colossal four-faced lingam, which is still enshrined inside.

The temple of Pârvati is one of the most curious and interesting shrines that I have seen. It is curious from the conventional imitation of rock-work on all the outer faces of its walls. It is especially interesting, as it seems to preserve the old fashion of the temples cut in the rock. The figures on the outer walls and on the doorway are all in the Gupta style of sculpture. The entrance doorway has the figures of the Ganges and Jumna standing on their respective symbols, the crocodile and tortoise. And, lastly, all the roofs are flat, like those of known Gupta temples at Sânchi, Eran, and Tigowa.

The Pârvati Temple is a building of two storeys. It is nearly square, 15 feet 9 inches by 15 inches in plan, with plain perpendicular walls. The lower storey is surrounded by a roofed cloister upwards of 5 feet wide, which is closed, except in front of the entrance door, by a wall, 3 feet thick. In front of the entrance there is an open, unroofed court, nearly 12 feet square, which is reached by a flight of steps, $4\frac{1}{2}$ feet in height.

The upper storey is quite plain both inside and outside. It was covered by a flat roof of apparently three slabs. These are still on the top of the walls, but are much tilted and out of position. The joints were covered as in the known Gupta temples. The doorway is on the west, and the chamber is lighted by two trellises, one in each side wall. These are formed simply by two plain loop holes, one on each side.

The doorway of the lower storey is very richly carved with human figures in pairs on each jamb, ending with small statues of the Ganges and Jumna. The figures are all of the Gupta period, and are much superior to all mediæval sculpture, both in the ease and gracefulness of their attitudes, as well as in the real beauty of the forms. The hair of the male figures is arranged in the same fashion as that of the Gupta kings on their coins, with rows of curls, like the wig of a judge. There are no obscene figures.

The sanctum is dimly lighted on each side by a stout trellis of simple square holes, which receives its light from another trellis in the cloister wall opposite.   In the middle of each of the outer faces there is a large trellis, with two horned lions and two men.   On one side the trellis has four small pillars, with three openings, each pillar being ornamented with a human figure.

The outer faces of the walls (excepting only the upper room) are carved to imitate rock-work.   A few figures are introduced, as well as a few lions or bears lying in holes or caves in the rock-work.

Inside there is a pedestal with a mortice hole for the reception of the tenon of a statue.   This has been pushed to one side by some treasure hunter who dug up the floor.

In the accompanying plates[1] I have given a plan and elevation of this curious temple, with a sketch of one of the pilasters, and two of the peculiar ornaments on the lintel of the doorway.   All these belong to the Gupta style, as shown in the temples at Eran and Udayagiri.   There is no inscription, and not even a single letter or mason's mark could be found on any of the stones.   But the Gupta style of the figures, the returns at the ends of the door lintel for the reception of statues, the prominence given to the figures of the Ganges and Jumna, all point to a very early period.   There is an inscription on a loose slab lying at Lakhuria which also certainly belongs to the Gupta period ; and as Lakhuria forms part of the old capital of *Kâthara*, the record most probably belongs to some one of the old buildings.   The inscription is written in the peculiar box-headed characters of the Vâkâtaka copperplates, which is also found in the Eran inscription of Samudra Gupta, and in the Udayagiri inscription of Chandra Gupta II. This peculiar character was, therefore, in use during the 3rd century of the Christian era.   But the inscription itself gives the name of one of the Vâkâtaka princes, Prithivi Sena, as suzerain, in conjunction with that of Vyâghra Deva, the local sovereign.   Now Vyâghra was the father of Jayanâth, whose inscriptions are dated in the years 174 and 177 of the Gupta

<hr />

[1] Plates XXV and XXVI.

era. Vyâghra therefore must have been reigning about 140 and 150 of the Gupta era, or about A.D. 300 according to my reckoning. He was, accordingly, a contemporary of Skanda Gupta. The temple may not be so old as the inscription; but, as it is undoubtedly of the Gupta period, it may perhaps be referred to about A.D. 400 with some degree of certainty.

The inscription, which is irregularly cut on a rough slab, consists of four lines on the face of the stone and two lines on the side or edge. But these two side lines are only a repetition of the inscription on the face. In the middle of the face there is a record as follows[1] :—

1. Vâkâṭakânam Mahâraja Sri
2. Prithivi Seṇa pâdânudyâto
3. Vyâghra Deva mâta pitro punyabhi (?)
4. Kritam-iti.

The side inscription is incomplete; but it was certainly only a repetition of the record on the face. The work which it refers to was done by Vyâghra Deva, the tributary of Sri Prithivi Sena, Mahâraja of Vâkâtaka.

The other temple, called Chaturmukh Mahâdeva, is quite different in style, although its doorway is similar to that of the Pârvati Temple. It is a square building, 11¾ feet inside and 16¾ feet outside. It has a tall spire, with slightly curved sides, and is now about 40 feet high. It stands on a raised platform, like that of the old temple at Deogarh. There are four broken figures of lions lying outside, each trampling on a bear. They probably flanked the staircases of the platform. In the middle of each side there is a stout stone lattice, surmounted by a couple of niches holding figures. There are also side niches; but these are now empty, with the exception of a standing figure of Brahmâ with four arms. All the figures are draped. Inside, there is a colossal lingam, 4 feet 8 inches in height, with a large head, with a most elaborate head-dress on each of the four faces. The heads are all perfect; and this is sufficient evidence to prove that the temple could never have been seen by the idol-breaking Muhammadans. In fact, the two temples occupy such a secluded position in a jungly

[1] See Plate XXVII.

valley, far from any main road, that they have hitherto escaped
the notice of English travellers.   The Chaturmukh Temple
must be considerably later than the other, and is probably not
older than 600 to 700 A.D.

27.—JASSO.

The town of Jasso is situated about half-way between Ganj
and Nâgodh, being 9 miles to the north-east of the former,
and 10 miles to the south-west of the latter.   It is now a
small independent state, with a yearly revenue of R30,000.
Jasso is said to have been called Hardi in former days, and
to have been a great city of the Jains.   It must certainly have
been a place of some consequence, as there are numerous
broken statues lying about, both Brahmanical and Jain, but
chiefly the latter.   At Dareda, to the south-west of Jasso, there
is a large stone set up under a pipal tree, which is now wor-
shipped as a lingam.   It is, in fact, a natural lingam, 5 feet in
height, and slightly bent and pointed towards the top.   On one
face there is a wheel, with the word *vangkatu* engraved above
in old Gupta letters.[1]   The wheel is similar to that on the old
inscription slab at Lakhuria, near Nachna, and may perhaps be
the cognizance of the old local chiefs of this district.

There is a very fine sheet of water at Jasso, with several
Sati pillars on its bank.   One of these, dated in Samvat 1396
[A.D. 1339], Jyeth badi 6, Thursday, bears several names of
a Thakur's family.

In Jasso itself there is a pretty little lingam temple, called
Kumhâra-math, or "Potter's Temple," because it was built by
a *kumhâr*, or potter.   It is 27 feet square outside, with an
entrance portico on the east, supported on four pillars.   On
the inner door step there is a single line of inscription of the
8th or 9th century, and in another place a part of the same
inscription is repeated.   It reads simply *Nehalasya Khandah.*
In another place, in modern Nâgari, there is a record of three
short lines, as follows :—

Râma Râma likhita-
sya Sri Pandita Mâ-
dhava Dâsa 96.

[1] See Plate XXVII.

This record cannot be more than two or three hundred years old.

28.—CHHOTA DEORI.

At different places, near the sources of the Kiyân or Ken River, there are some small ruined temples, which were once much freqented, but are now rarely visited.   The best known of these ruined buildings is at Chhota Deori, or the " Little Temple," where there is a famous pillar with an old inscription. This pillar is held in great veneration, and even awe, by the people of the neighbouring villages, who do not like to go near it.

The pillar is 7 feet 2 inches high and 1 foot square.   The inscription of 11 lines is near the top; in the middle there are two seated figures, male and female; and below there is a standing male figure.   The inscription is in old characters of the 6th or 7th century.   In the 1st line there is something like a date in three figures, preceded by a word which *may be* read as Samvat.   The unit figure of 6 seems certain.   At the end of the 1st line I read the name of Sangkaragana, and in the latter half of the 5th and beginning of the 6th line I read without any doubt words [1]—

Sri Sangkaragana Deva rájya.

"During the reign of the fortunate Sangkaragana Deva."

This is, no doubt, the name of the reigning king.   As the name is peculiar to the family of the Kalachuris of Chedi, I conclude that it must belong to one of them.   There is mention of a Budha Raja, the son of Sangkaragana, who was defeated by Mangalisa Chalukya about A.D. 550.   This date is, perhaps, too early for the characters of the inscription.

Chhota Deori is 16 miles to the west of the Jokahi railway station.

29.—MARHIA.

At a few miles to the west of Chhota Deori, near the village of Marhia, there is a small ruined temple only 7½ feet

[1] See Plate XXVIII.

square inside, and 12½ feet square outside. The lower walls
are still standing, but there is no inscription.

30.—BARGAON.

Bargaon is a large village to the north of the high road,
and just half-way between Damoh and the Jokahi station of
the Jabalpur Railway, or 26 miles to the west of Jokahi.
It is an old site of the Jainas, as shown by the remains of
their temples and sculptures. One temple is still standing to
a height of 21 feet above its basement. It is 13 feet square
inside, and 31 feet long by 26½ feet broad outside. The walls
are plain. It possesses a weather-worn inscription, 3 feet in
length by 13 inches in height, containing 12 lines of mediæval
characters. It is too much weather-worn to be readable. In
the 10th line I find the words *Kalachuri-nripa,* or "the Kalachuri King;" but this fact is only valuable as showing that
the district of Bargaon belonged to the Kalachuris of Chedi,
and not to the Chandels of Mahoba.

31.—SIMRA.

The village of Simra is situated 3 miles to the south of
the Jokahi and Damoh road. It stands 15 miles to the west
of Jokahi, and nearly opposite Marhia. On the bank of a
tank there is a slab with two lines of inscription as follows :—

Samvat 1355, Sake 1220.
Rau Daosat Singh * Patnika Nanna Devi.
"In the Samvat year 1355, and Sake year 1220 [or A.D. 1298],
Nanna Devi, the wife of Rau Daosat Singh (became Sati)."

During my long sojourn in India I have observed that
nearly all the Sati monuments are placed on the western bank
either of a stream or of a reservoir, with the face towards the
east.

32.—BESÂNI.

Besâni is situated on the old line of road leading down
from Kâlanjar and Ajaygarh, through Ganj and Kûthara and

Khopa to Bilhari and Jabalpur.   It is 13 miles to the north-
west of Jokahi.

On a loose broken slab, near the ruins of a temple, there
is an incomplete inscription of six lines, which I read as
follows :—

1. Samvat 958 prathama Ashâd*h*a Sudi 3
2. Sutradhâra Jama De grihita dramâ 30 ta Sri
3. *Nitad (r) amâ 10, Suja grihita dramâ 100
4. Prithiva vasiṇi grihita dra (mâ) 10 Râu (t).
5. *Kâ grihita dra (mâ) 1,000.
6. *   *   *   *   *   *

From the style of the characters the record cannot be
nearly so old as Vikramâditya Samvat 958, or A.D. 901.   I
conclude, therefore, that the era must be that of Kalachuri or
Chedi, which dates from A.D. 249.   This is confirmed by the
name of the month Prathama Ashâdha, which shows that
there was an intercalary month of that name in the year when
the slab was inscribed.   Now, this was actually the case in the
year 958 of the Chedi era, or 958 + 249 = 1207 A.D.   The
mention of the intercalary month in this year is particularly
valuable, as it proves that the tables of Hindu years with
their intercalary months, which I have prepared for publica-
tion, are absolutely correct for the long period of nearly 700
years.[1]   But my tables of intercalation are certainly correct
for even a longer period, as I find that the month of Srâvana
is recorded in an inscription as having been intercalary in the
Sake year 1091, or A.D. 1169.[2]

I have not yet made out this inscription satisfactorily.
The substance seems to record certain gifts of money (dramâs) by different individuals for some purpose not made out.
The work was most probably connected with the temple near
which the stone now lies.   But the sum of money must have
been small, as the dramâ (S. dramya) was a silver coin, the
representative of the Greek drachma, and weighed a little

---

[1] Book of Indian Eras.   Thacker & Co., Calcutta, 1884.
[2] Rice : Mysore Inscriptions, page 23.

over 60 grains. If the whole sum reached 300 dramâs, it would not have amounted to more than 100 rupees.

33.—BAGHELKHAND, OR REWA.

How or when the Bâghels obtained possession of the upper valleys of the Son and the Tons, they themselves know nothing. They say that they came from Gujarât, under Vyâghra Deva, either in Samvat 580 according to the Rewa chroniclers, or in Samvat 683 according to the Bâra chroniclers. Their first settlement was at Marpha, a large fort, 15 miles to the north-east of Kâlanjar. This statement receives some support from the existence of two large villages, named Bâghelwâri and Bagholan, within 12 or 13 miles of Marpha to the north and south. He is also said to have married the daughter of the Raja of Tirhâwan on the Paisuni River, 15 miles to the east-north-east of Marpha, and a few miles to the north of Chitrkut. The Bâghel chroniclers assert that Vyâghra succeeded in making himself master of most of the country lying between Kâlpi and Chunâr. His son, Karna Deva, added the valley of the Tons River, or Rewa proper, and at last obtained possession of the famous Fort of Bândhogarh by marrying the daughter of the Raja of Mandala.

The tract of country thus obtained forms the present state of Bâghelkhand. Previous to the conquest it is said to have been held by the Chandels, the Kalachuris (or Karchulis), the Chauhâns, the Sengars, and the Gonds. All these clans are still represented in Bâghelkhand by the Chandels of Bardi, the Karchulis of Raypur, the Chauhâns of Sidi, and the Sengars of Mhau and Naigarhi, while the Gonds have holdings in Singhwâra and other parts of the Râmnagar Tahsil.

From inscriptions discovered in the northern hills at Piâwan and Alha Ghât, we learn that the whole of the country above described formed part of the dominions of Gânggeya Deva, the Kalachuri Râja of Dâhal, in the beginning of the 11th century, and that it was still in the possession of his descendant, the Dahaliya Raja Nara Sinha Deva so late as Samvat 1216, or A.D. 1159—and Vijaya Sinha, his nephew,

was certainly in possession of the southern half of the territory, or the valley of the Son, so late as A.D. 1181.[1]

According to Tod, the Bâghels derive their name from
Bâgh Rao, the son of Sidh Rai Jay Sinh. Bâgh Rao, or Vyâ-
ghra Deva, therefore dates from the death of his father in
A.D. 1150. He was a contemporary of the Kalachuri Prince
Nara Sinha Deva, and his son Karna may have married his
daughter, as Nara Sinha must have been the ruler of Manda-
la, as well as of Tripura or Tewar. As it is quite certain that
the Bâghela Chief would not have married a daughter of any
Gond family, the Raja of Mandala could not have been a
Gond at that time.

Nara Sinha Deva was succeeded by his brother Jaya
Sinha Deva, who, according to the inscriptions, was a great
warrior. He was followed by his son Vijaya Sinha Deva, of
whom we have an inscription, dated in 932 of the Chedi Samvat, or A.D. 1181, at which time there was an heir apparent
named Ajaya Sinha Deva. As no later inscriptions of the
Kalachuri Prince have yet been found,[2] it seems probable
that their rule may have come to an untimely end some-
where about A.D. 1200. We know that the great fort of
Kâlanjar was captured by the Muhammadans under Kutb-ud-
din Aibek on 27th April 1203 A.D., when all the temples
were destroyed and mosques built on their sites. As the fort
was then occupied by the Muhammadans, I think it almost
certain that either they or the displaced Chandels must have
pushed their arms into the neighbouring territory of the Kalachuris. During the struggle for empire, and the consequent
weakness of the Delhi state, which followed the death of
Kutb-ud-din Aibek, the Chandel Raja of Kâlanjar recovered
possession of his fort, and with it the rule of most of his former territory. But the Delhi King towards the end of his
reign, when his authority had become firmly established, col-

[1] Since the above was written, I have obtained later inscriptions on copper,
which show that Vijaya Sinha Kalachuri was in possession in A.D 1196, and
Trailokya Varmma in A.D. 1240. Vyâghra's conquest must, therefore, be later
than A.D. 1240. If the Bâra chroniclers' date of Samvat 683 be referred to the
era of Harsha Vardhana, the date will be 683 × 606 = 1289 A.D.

[2] Except that of A.D. 1196, mentioned in the previous note.

lected a large force from Bâyâna, Kanauj, Gwalior, and other places, for a campaign against Kâlanjar and Jamu. This was in A.H. 632, or A.D. 1234.

"The army marched on 50 days from Gwalior, and great booty fell into its hands, so much that the imperial fifth amounted to nearly 22 lakhs.[1]"

The situation of Jamu has not been identified, and the name is very probably corrupt, but the distance of 50 days' march from Gwalior would tally with the position of the famous fort of Bândhogarh.

At a later date, in A.H. 645 or A.D. 1247, a second campaign against Kâlanjar was organized under the command of Ulugh Khan (afterwards the Emperor Balban). On this occasion the army advanced beyond Kâlanjar against a Râna, "over whom the Rais of Kâlanjar and Mâlwa had no authority." He bore the strange name of Dalaki-wa-malaki.

"He had numerous followers and ample wealth; he ruled wisely; his fortresses were strong and secure; in his territories the defiles were arduous, the mountains rugged, and the jungles many. No Muhammadan army had ever penetrated to his dwelling-place. When Ulugh Khan reached his abode, the Râna took such care for the safety of himself and his family that he kept quiet from the dawn till the time of evening prayer, and when it grew dark he fled to some more secure place. At day-break the Muhammadan army entered his abode, and then pursued him, but the accursed infidel had escaped into the lofty mountains to an inaccessible spot impossible to reach except by stratagem and the use of ropes and ladders. Ulugh Khan incited his soldiers to the attempt, and, under his able direction, they succeeded in taking the place. All the infidels' wives, dependants, and children, fell into the hands of the victors, with much cattle, many horses, and slaves. Indeed, the spoil that was secured exceeded all computation.[1]"

At first I thought that this powerful chief, who was independent of the Rajas of Kâlanjar and Mâlwa, must have been the Kalachuri Raja of Chedi or Dahal. The latter name also seemed to offer some similarity with Dalaki. But I have since found, amongst the early Bâghels, two Rajas in succession, named *Dalakeswar* and *Malakeswar*. These two names I take to be the originals of the Muhammadan author's

[1] H. M. Elliott's Muhammadan Historians, Vol. II, p. 366.

Dalaki-wa-Malaki. If this identification be admitted, then
the Bâghel dominion had already been firmly established as
early as A.D. 1247, and the "inaccessible" place in which
the Raja took refuge must have been the famous fort of Bândhogarh.

Ballâr Deo, the 12th prince and the 2nd Râja in succession after Dalakeswar and Malakeswar, is said by the chroniclers to have been a contemporary of Timur Shah, Emperor
of Delhi, and to have given him assistance when he was hard-
pressed, in return for which he received many honorary dis-
tinctions, along with the gift of the fort of Kâlanjar. As the
date of 1096 Samvat, or A.D. 1039, is assigned for this as-
tounding event, we have a good test of the utter worthless-
ness of the dates given by the chroniclers. Birbhân Deo, the
9th Râja, is said to have been a contemporary of Humâyun,
whose family received shelter in Bândhogarh, when he was
obliged to fly before Sher Shah. The chroniclers, in fact,
know nothing of the real history of their country. For instance, they attribute the foundation of Rewa, the present
capital, to Râja Vikramaditya, in A.D. 1618. But Rewa was
in the possession of Jalâl Khan, at the time of Sher Shah's
death, in A.D. 1545. The list of Râjas preserved by the
chroniclers is most probably correct, as the names of the
later princes have stood the test of comparison with the numerous notices of Muhammadan authors. For the following
list I am indebted to the kindness of Major Barr, the Political Agent, now in charge of the Rewa State during the minori-
ty of the Raja. I am also indebted to the Raja of Bâra for
a list of his ancestors from the foundation of the family under
Vyâghra Deva, the common progenitor of the two dynasties
of Rewa and Bâra. Each family gives a list of 31 princes,
from the death of Vyâghra in about A.D. 1150 to the present
time. In the Rewa list the 31st prince has passed away.
In the Bâra list the 31st Prince is still living. These figures
allow about 24 years to each generation, which is close to the
usual average of Eastern families.

I have restored the spelling of most of the names in the
following list, but a few still remain, of which I cannot even
guess the original form.

BAGHEL RAJAS.

No.	Samvat.	A. D.	Names.	
			Siddh Rai Jay Sinh.	
1	...	...	Vyâghra Deva.	
2	...	...	Karna Deva . .	(Kandhâru Deva in Bâra).
3	...	...	Sohâga Deva . .	Founded Sohâgpur.
4	...	...	Sâranga Deva.	
5	...	...	Bishâl Deva.	
6	...	...	Bhanâh Deva.	
7	...	...	Anîk Deva.	
8	...	...	Balân Deva.	
9	1297	1240	Dalakesar Deva .	⎰ Dalaki-wa-Malaki, A. D. 1246,
10	...	...	Malakesar Deva .	⎱ of Minhâj (Tabakât-i-Naseri).
11	1357	1300	Bariâr Deva.	
12	1387	1330	Ballâr Deva.	
13	1417	1360	Singh Deoji Sidhi.	
14	1447	1390	Bhairava Deva.	
15	1447	1420	Narhar Deva.	
16	1497	1450	Bhîra Deva . .	Bhid, invaded by Sikander Lodi, A.D. 1494.
17	1552	1495	Sâlivâhana Deva.	
18	1577	1520	Vîra Sinha Deva .	— ? Founded Birsinghpur in N. Rewa.
19	1597	1540	Virabhâna .	— Humâyun's family received shelter.
20	1611	1554	Râja Râma Deva .	Copper-plate Râja Râma Chandra. S. 965 = A.D. 1557.
21	1648	1591	Virabhadra.	
22	1649	1592	Vikramâditya .	Founded city of Rewa.
23	1658	1601	Duryodhana.	
24	1677	1620	Amara Sinha .	Reigning in 1625 and 1634.
25	1702	1645	Anûpa Sinha .	Attacked by Pahâr Singh Bundela in A.D. 1650.
26	1727	1670	Bhana Sinha.	
27	1752	1695	Anirudha Sinha.	
28	1782	1725	Abdhut Singh .	Six months old at father's death.
29	1832	1775	Ajita Sinha.	
30	1866	1809	Jaya Sinha Deva.	
31	1882	1825	Bishnâth Singh.	
32	1911	1854	Raghurâj Singh.	
33	1937	1880	Bankatesh Raman.	

I have already quoted the Muhammadan account of the invasion of the territories of Dalaki-wa-Malaki by Ulugh Khan in A.D. 1247, during the reign of Nâsir-ud-din Mahmud I. This was followed, about 50 years later, by a second attack under Ala-ud-din Muhammad Khalji, who, according to Abul Fazl, besieged Bândhogarh in vain.[1]

Our first detailed notice of Bâghel history is in the early part of the reign of Sikandar Lodi, A.H. 897 = A.D. 1492,

[1] Ain-i-Akbari, p. 367, note.

when Rai Bhid (or Bhira of the list), Râja of Bhata, whose
territories extended to Kantit on the Ganges near Mirzapur,
had seized Mubârak Khan, Governor of Jaunpur. Mubârak
was soon after released, and the king proceeded to Kantit,
when " Rai Bhid came out to meet him and proffered his
allegiance, for which the Sultan confirmed him in the possession of Kantit.[1] " But the Rai, being suspicious of treachery,
afterwards fled ; and in A.H. 900 = 1494-95 A.D. Sikandar
invaded his country for the purpose of chastising him. At
Khân Ghâti, or *Gungauni,* he was opposed by Bir Singh
Deo, one of the Raja's sons. The name of the place seems
corrupt, and I think that it should be *Kathauli,* which is still
the principal ghât leading over the Vindhyan Range from
Allahabad to the south. Bir Singh was defeated, and the
king advanced against Bândhogarh. " Raja *Bhid* fled towards
Sirguja, but died on the road.[2] " The king penetrated as far as
Phâphund (20 miles to the north of Bândhogarh), and then
retired under the plea of want of provisions. As the new
Raja shortly afterwards supported Sikandar against Husen
Shah of Jaunpur, it seems probable that the king may have
bought his assistance by his withdrawal of the besieging
army

A few years later (Ferishta says A.H. 904, A.D. 1498-99),
Sikandar again invaded Bhata in person to revenge himself
on Sâlivâhan for the refusal of his daughter in marriage.

" He destroyed all signs of cultivation. His most valiant soldiers
showed their courage at the fort of Bândhu, the strongest castle of
that district, and Sultân Sikandar having utterly devastated and
ruined the whole of that territory, went back to Jaunpur.[3] "

The successor of Sâlivâhan was Bir Singh Deo, or Vira
Sinha Deva, who may have been the son of Bhira Deva, who
opposed Sikandar on his first invasion of Bhata. Bir Singh

---

[1] See Niâmatullah in H.M. Elliott's Muhammadan Historians, Vol. V p. 94.
Sikandar then marched to Arail and *Bayâk*—according to Dowson, or *Biak*
according to Dorn. For both of these names read *Payôg,* the common Hindu
form of Prayâg, the modern Allahabad. Its position near Arail should have led
to its identification.

[2] H. M. Elliott's Muhammadan Historians, by Dowson, Vol. V, p. 95.

[3] H. M. Elliott's Muhammadan Historians, by Dowson, Vol. IV, p. 469.

Deo was followed by Birbhân, who, according to the chroniclers, gave asylum to the family of Humâyun, when he was
chased out of India by Sher Shâh. I first heard of this story
at Asni on the Ganges just two years ago, as I have related
in my account of that place, as follows [1] :—

" The people of Asni also have a strange story about Akbar.
They say that, when Sher Shâh defeated Humâyun, the latter fled
to the west, leaving a Begam named Choli in Delhi, who was captured by the conqueror. Shortly afterwards Sher Shâh, being pleased
with some verses of a bard named Narhar, told him to ask a boon.
The bard accordingly asked that Choli Begam might be given to him,
which the king granted. Narhar carried off Choli to Bândhogarh,
in Rewa, where, soon after, she gave birth to Akbar. When he
was twelve years of age, the boy Akbar asked Birbhân, the Bâghel
Raja of Rewa, to let him have some soldiers, so that he might go up
to Delhi and recover his kingdom from Sher Shâh. The Raja gave
the troops, and Akbar advanced against Delhi, while Humâyun
returned from Ghazni. Sher Shâh was then dead and Islâm Shâh
was defeated by Akbar, who thus recovered the kingdom of his
father."

This story has found general acceptance amongst the
people, in spite of the explicit statement of the Muhammadan
historians that Sher Shâh treated Humâyun's queen in the
most chivalrous manner. Thus Abbâs Khan, the author of
the Târikh-i-Sher Shâhi, says :—

" Masnad Ali Haibat Khan told me, Abbâs Khan, the author of
this book, that he was at Sher Khan's side, when the Emperor
Humâyun's queen, with other noble ladies and a crowd of women,
came out from behind the *parda*. As soon as Sher Khan's eyes fell
upon them, he alighted off his horse, and showed them every respect,
and consoled them."

The popular story, however, is likely to survive, as it has
been related in a *kabit* by *Ajbes*, the Bhat of the Raja of
Rewa. Some, indeed, say that the verse finds favour owing
to the wretched pun on the name of Akbar, to whom Raja
Birbhân of Rewa is said to have been an *Akhe-bar* or *Akshaya-
bar*, " the imperishable banian tree," which is the name of the
famous tree of Prayâg.

[1] See Archæological Survey, Vol. XVII, p. 101.

These are the verses—

" Dilli kê jitêk Sardâr, Mansabdâr,
Raja Rao, Umrao, sabhi ko nipât bhao
Begam bichâri bahi kitahu na pâî thâh,
Bândhogarh, gâṛo gûṛ tâko pachh pât bhao,
Sher Shâh salil praleye ko baṛo Ajbes.
Bûrat Humâyun kê mahâ hi utpât bhao,
Balhîn bâlak, Akabar bachâi-ve ko,
Birbhân bhûpati, Akhebar ko pât bhao."

" In Delhi all the Sardârs and the Mansabdârs,
' The Rajas, the Raos, and the Umraos, were distracted :
' The Begam, helpless, found no place of refuge,
' Till the stronghold of Bândhogarh became her protector.
' Then Sher Shâh's power prevailed, says Ajbes.
' Though Humâyun escaped drowning, he was in great distress,
' And the boy Akbar was saved solely
' Through Birbhân becoming his *Akhebar*."

No. 20.—The son and successor of Birbhân was Raja
Râma Chandra Deva, of whom we have numerous notices in
the reign of Akbar.   He is generally called Râm Chand by the
Muhammadan authors ; but he is named Râma Chandra Deva
in the lists, and also in a copper-plate inscription which I saw
at Karra on the Ganges two years ago.   The record is dated
in " Samvat 965," which can only be intended for the Hijra
reckoning.   The date will, therefore, be A.D. 1557-58, or the
third year of the reign of " *Akbar Sâh Gâji.*"

Râma Chandra had already succeeded to the throne before
Akbar, as he is mentioned as having given asylum to Ibrahim,
the son of Sikandar Sur, in A.H. 962, or A.D. 1555.   As he
died in the 37th year of Akbar = A.H. 1000, or A.D. 1592, his
reign may be fixed at about 37 years, or from A.D. 1555 to
1592.   The following is Blochmann's brief account of the
career of Râm Chand and his successors as gathered from the
Muhammadan historians [1] :—

" Râm Chand was Raja of Bhat'h (or Bhattah, as the Maâsir spells
it).   Among the three great Rajas of Hindustân whom Bâbar mentions in his memoir, the Raja of Bhat'h is third.

" Râm Chand was the patron of the renowned musician and singer
Tânsen.   His fame had reached Akbar ; and in the 7th year, the

---

[1] Ain Akbari, by Blochmann, p. 406.

Emperor sent Jaláluddin Qûrchi to Bhat'h to induce Tânsen to come
to Agra. Râm Chand, feeling himself powerless to refuse Akbar's
request, sent his favourite with his musical instruments and many
presents to Agra, and the first time that Tânsen performed at Court,
the Emperor made him a present of two lakhs of rupees. Tânsen
remained with Akbar. Most of his compositions are written in
Akbar's name, and his melodies are even now a-days everywhere
repeated by the people of Hindustân.

"When Açaf Khân led his expedition to Gaḍha, he came in contact with Râm Chand; but by timely submission the Raja became 'a
servant' of Akbar. In the 14th year, Râm Chand lost Fort Kâlanjar.
He sent his son, Bîrbhadr, to court, but from distrust would not pay
his respects personally. In the 28th year, therefore, when Akbar was
at Shâhâbad, he ordered a corps to march to Bhat'h; but Birbhadr,
through the influence of several courtiers, prevailed upon the Emperor
to send a grandeé to his father and to convey him to court. Raja
Birbhadr and Zain Kokah were selected for this office, and Râm
Chand came at last to court, where he was well received.

"Râma Chandra was succeeded by Virabhadra or Birbhadr, who
on his way from court to Bhath fell from his palanquin and died
soon after, in the 38th year, or A.H. 1001 = 1593 A.D.

"Birbhadr had married a daughter of Rai Singh, son of Kalyân
Mall, the Rathor Raja of Bikaner. Akbar interceded for their young
children and prevented the widow from burning herself.

"Virabhadra's sudden death led to disturbances in Bândhu, of
which Bikramâjit, a young relative of Râm Chand, had taken possession.[1] The history of the family is thus continued by Blochmann—
Akbar therefore sent Ismâil Qulikhân to Bândhu, to convey Bikramâjit
to court (41st year), their intentions being to prevent Bândhu from
being conquered. But Akbar would not yield; he dismissed
Bikramâjit, and after a siege of eight months and several days
Bândhu was conquered (42nd year).[1]

"In the 47th year, Duryodhan, a grandson of Râm Chand, was
made Raja of Bândhu. In the 21st year of Jahangir's reign, Amar
Singh, another grandson of Ram Chand, acknowledged himself a
vassal of Delhi. In the 8th year of Shahjahân, when Abdula Khan
Bahâdur marched against the refractory Zamindâr of Ratanpur, Amar
Singh brought about a peaceful submission. Amar Singh was suc-
ceeded by his son Anûp Singh. In the 24th year, when Raja Pahâr
Singh Bandela, Jagîrdâr of Chauragadh, attacked Anûp Singh, because
he had afforded shelter to Dairâm, a zamindâr of Chauragadh, Anûp
Singh, with his whole family, withdrew from Rewa (which, after the

---

[1] Ain Akbari; by Blochmann, p. 407.

destruction of Bândhu, had been family seat) to the hills. In the 30th year, however, Sayyed Calâbat Khan, Governor of Ilahâbâd, conducted him to court, where Anûp turned Muhammadan. He was made commander of 3,000 infantry, 2,000 horse, and was appointed to Bândhu and the surrounding districts."

With Anûp Singh our Muhammadan authors fail us, and we are reduced to the scanty records of the chroniclers. According to them, Abdut Singh, the 28th Raja, was only six months old at his father's death, about A.D. 1725. His country was accordingly soon after invaded by Hridaya, or Hirde Sâh, the Raja of Panna, who succeeded his father Chhatr Sâl in 1718 A.D. The invasion probably took place about A.D. 1730, when the capital was occupied by Hirde Sâh, while the Raja fled to Partâbgarh. His reign was a long one, probably from 1725 to 1775 A.D.

He was succeeded by his son Ajit Singh, who was followed in A.D. 1809 by Jaya Sinha Deva. "It was during his rule that British influence was established in Bâghelkhand, and the first formal treaty between the British Government and Rewa was made with Jaya Sinha Deva in 1812 A.D."

Jayanâth was succeeded by his son Bishen Nâth, who abdicated in 1854 in favour of his son the late Raja Raghurâj Singh, who died in 1880.

34.—PIÂWAN.

The Tons River, with its tributaries, has long been known for the number of its water-falls and the wild beauty of its scenery. The falls are found from 20 to 30 miles to the north and north-east of Rewa, where the river rushes down the Vindhya Hills to join the Ganges near Panâsa. All the principal falls are considered holy by the Hindus, and pilgrimages are still made to them by devout people. One of these holy spots lies in a small valley, called Piâwan, 6 miles to the south-east of Kathaula, and 25 miles to the north-north-east of Rewa.

Piâwan, or Payâwan, means simply the "drinking-place." The spot is a small valley about 800 feet wide and half a mile in length, with precipitous rocks on both sides, about

200 feet high.   At the western end a small stream falls over
the cliff, and the rock below, on which the water falls, has been
formed into an *Argha* for the reception of a lingam, or phallic
symbol of Siva.   A view of this Argha has been given by my
assistant, Mr. Garrick, who first discovered the place.   He has
described it under the name of *Jhirna*, or the "water-fall."
The name given to me was received from the people, who
grazed their herds in the neighbouring hills, and who knew it
only as the *Piâwan*, or "watering-place."   The Argha is
14 inches in diameter.

On the upper face of the Argha there is an inscription
of six lines in boldly carved letters, which are unfortunately
much weather-worn.   Mr. Garrick made a large photograph
of the inscription, and my servants made several impressions
of it on paper.   The inscription is a valuable one, as it is the
only record yet found of the Kalachuri Prince Gânggeya
Deva, the contemporary of Mahmud of " Ghazni.   He is
mentioned by name by Abu Rihân, as *Gângeo*, of *Dâhal*, of
which the capital was *Pituri*, or, more correctly, Gânggeya
Deva of Dâhal, of which the capital was Tripuri, now Tewar,
near Jabalpur.[1]   The inscription is especially valuable, as
showing that the dominions of the Kalachuri kings of Chedi
extended so far north as the Vindhya Hills, only 50 miles from
Allahabad.   The letters are much defaced, as people are constantly walking over the face of the rock.   I read the text as
follows :—

> 1. Sri mad Gânggeya Deva Mahârajadhirâ—
> 2.—ja parameswara bha * maha mandale—
> 3. swara * naka Sri Dhâhala mahâbha * * *
> 4. sahitam Maheswara De * *
> 5. Asangga pranamati.
> 6. Samvat 789————* * Sri Dhâhalamiti.

The date consists of three figures, which I read as above,
789, of the Chedi era, equivalent to 249 + 789=1038 A.D.
The name of Dâhala is twice given, but both times as
Dhâhala.

---

[1] Reinand; Fragments, pp. 85—106, and Elliott's Muhammadan Historians,
Vol. I, page 56.

35.—ALHA GHAT.

Alha Ghât is one of the natural passes of the Vindhya Hills, by which the Tons River finds its way from the table-land of Rewa to the plain of the Ganges. From Allahabad to Chaukhandi at the foot of the Ginja Hill the distance is only 45 miles to the south-west. From Chaukhandi there is a clear view of the open valley of the Tons between the hills to Koni and Rupaoli on the left bank of the river. At Rupaoli the road crosses to the right bank, from whence begins the ascent by the Alha Ghât to Sirnol on the table-land, 22 miles to the north of Rewa. The distance is called 12 kos.

About one mile-and-a-half from the river there is a large cave, 110 feet in length, with a breadth of from 8 to 10 feet, and a height varying from 22 to 50 feet in the middle. At the main entrance it is 10 feet broad; but it has two other entrances on the right hand, each about 30 feet long, one by a passage varying from 3 feet to 2 feet in width, and the other varying from 6 feet to 3 feet. In the further corner of the cave there is a small pool into which water is constantly dripping. The cave has, of course, been in frequent use by ascetics; but no traces, either of inscriptions or of paintings, could be found on the walls.

About 100 yards from the cave there is a very large block of stone on which there are three inscriptions. The best preserved of these consists of seven lines, and contains the name of the Dâhaliya Raja Narasinha Deva with the Samvat date of 1216, or A.D. 1159. The second inscription has fourteen lines, but it is too much injured to be deciphered. I can read the following words :—

      1. Srimukho nâma Samvatsara   . (Srava)—
      2. na sudi   .   .   .   . Mahârajadhira—
      3. ja .   .   .   .   . Brahmâ Deva râjye
      4. Ran.

As *Srimukha* is the name of the 7th year of the 60-year cycle of Jupiter, the exact date of the inscription might easily be obtained, if we only knew something about Brahmâ

Deva Raja. One of the sons of Paramârddi Deva Chandel, named Brahmâditya, is said to have fallen in the defence of Mahoba. If the inscription belonged to him the date might be A.D. 1209, which was the *Srimukha* Samvatsar, or the 7th year of the Jovian cycle in Northern India. There may have been a Kalachuri prince of this name, but we know nothing of the Kalachuris after Vijaya Sinha Deva in A.D. 1197. The presence of Nara Sinha Deva's inscription makes it highly probable that the other records on the same stone belong to the Kalachuri kings.

The third inscription consists of only four lines in bad order. There is no date and no Raja's name. The first line reads—

> Rajâputra Sri Sosharma Devah Râ Râma Deva.

"The king's son Sri Sosharma Deva, (and) the Rá(ut) Râm Deva."

Râ is the conventional abbreviation for Râüt, just as Thâ is for Thâkur.

Near the foot of the Ghât there is a Sati Pillar with an inscription in large letters dated in Samvat (13)72 and Sake 1237, Aswina Sudi 10 Budha dine (A.D. 1315).

I now return to the first inscription of Nara Sinha Deva, of which nearly every letter is certain—see Plate XXVIII. I read the text as follows :—

1. Samvat 1216 Bhâdra sudi pratipada Ravau‖ Dâhâliyan Mahârâjâ
2. dhiraja Sri Nara Singha Deva Vijaya râjye‖ Pipala—mahâ—
3. rânak Sri Jalhana putra rânak Sri kkihulasya Kali-juga
4. Dharmmârtha khata Khandika Ghâta bandhan Margrateti-mika Deva Karâ
5. pita iti‖ Dharmartha kâma moksha sadhana‖ Kausâmbi nikâsa Ran—
6. ti Anâmajâti udharitah‖ Thakur Sri Kamalâdhara likhita
7. sutradhâra Kamalâ Sinhah some | Kokâsam‖ Pâlhana Jalhana.

36.—KEVATI-KUND.

Kevati-kûnd is a famous pool near the junction of the Mahâ River, with the Tons, 22 miles to the north-north-east

of Rewa, 9 miles to the south-east of the Alha Ghât, and
12 miles to the north-west of the junction of the two high
roads leading from Allahabad and Mirzapur to Rewa.   Kewati-
sthâna is one of the holy places of the Tons circle.   In the
Atlas map, No. 89, the name is written *Keonti*, but it is
always pronounced *Kevati*, and it is so spelt in the oldest
of the four Sati inscriptions found on the spot.   The Kûnd
is a small pool into which the waters of the Mahânadi fall
from a cliff 336 feet in height.   The Kûnd is well known
throughout Northern India, and is much frequented by
pilgrims.   Mr. Macaulay Markham describes it as " almost
quite circular," and as hemmed in by perfectly perpendicular
rocks on each side.[1]   The water then flows "from over
2 miles through a canon of perpendicular rocks," keeping the
full height almost the whole way.   "On one side of the
beetling crag is a fine old native fort, and on projecting crags,
on the edge of the fall, are picturesque Hindu temples.
Altogether it is a lovely spot."

In a cave close by Mr. Markham discovered an old Pali
inscription of about 200 B.C.   It has been read as follows by
Dr. Hoernle—

Hârîtîputenam Sonakena kârîtâ pukharinî.

"The pool (cave) caused to be made by Sonaka, the son of Hâriti."

The slabs on which the Sati inscriptions are engraved are
simple monumental pillars, as each of them has the figure
of a soldier armed with sword and shield in the attitude
of fighting.

The oldest of the four inscriptions marked A consists
of five short lines, and is dated in the Samvat year 1390, on
Bhadra badi 4, *Şanau dine*, or Saturday, the 31st July, A.D.
1333.   The text reads as follows :—[2]

A. 1. Aum ! Kevati-sthâna râje Si=
     2. dhi kâritam yogai sataji Dadhi=
     3. gauni milam Jujhitam-Samvat.
     4. Samvat 1390 Samaye, Bhadra
     5. sya badi 4, sanau dine.

[1] Journal of Bengal Asiatic Society, 1880, p. 121.
[2] See Plate XXIX—A.

Jujhitam is a term generally used for soldiers who have fallen in battle. This confirms the conclusion drawn from the figure of the fighting soldier.

The inscription marked B consists of six lines which I read as follows (see Plate XXIX) :—

1. Aum! Samvat 1397 Samaye Mâgha sudi 4 Soma dine‖ tasmin Kâleva=
2. rattammâne Samvatsara‖ Lukasthâne Mahâraja Sri HAMIRA DEVA râjye‖ Baori grâme Râ (u)
3. Sri Jai Singha Deva bhula mane‖tasya mânya Rau Lohareswa Ran Drona para‖ Kathau=
4. li-sthâna Mahârajadhirâja Sri Mahâraja *Devakasya* Pâdimayura grâmati=
5. â got‖ tasya judyanevarstiti‖ asya vantwâri-hetita‖ Sutradhâri Holi . .
6. rupakâra Gâdhita‖Shangharo likhiti.

"In the Samvat year 1397, on Monday, the 4th of the waxing moon of Mâgha (Monday, 22nd January 1341), in that year, during the reign of Mahâraja *Hamira Deva* of Lukasthâna, .   . Rau Jai Singh Deva of Baorigrâma, .   . Ram Lohareswa, Rau Drona .   . of Kathaulisthana Maharâjadhirâja Sri Mahârâja Devaka, &c."?

The date falls in the reign of Muhammad Tughlak of Delhi. Neither of the Rajas' names occurs in the list of the Bâghel kings of Rewa. Hamira Deva might have been a petty Raja of Lukasthâna; but the higher title given to the second Chief Devaka certainly denotes a king of higher rank than an ordinary raja.

The inscription marked C consists of seven lines, which I read as follows :—

1. Aum! Samvat 1397 Samaye, Mâgha sudi 4, soma dine‖ tásmin Kaleva-
2. rattammâne Samvatsara ‖ Lukasthâne Mahârâja Sri Hamira Devarâ
3. jye Baori grâme Ra (u) Jaya—Singha Deva râjya | tazamanya.
4. Rau Loharasura | Rau Râmpâr Kathaulisthâna Mahârâja Sri .
5. Mahârâja Dendakasya Ghâdi Mayura Grâmahi âgat tasya
6. judhana varttini | asya sutra . . mâjara sâhita 3 ma sutra-
7. dhâ(ra) Nudi Devam hetitâ ‖ Suvakâra Hâli, Rupakâra, Phitam.

Here the fight is referred to distinctly in the beginning of the 6th line by the word *judhan*.

The inscription marked D consists of six lines, which I read as follows :—

1. Samvat 1397 varshe Mâgha sudi 4 somadine tasmin Kale-
2. varttamâna Samvatsara || Lukasthâne Mahârâja Sri Hamira De-
3. va râjye || Baorigrâma Rau Sri Jai Singh Deva. mâna ta-
4. sya manya Rau Vijaidhara sute Rau Yaso Kathaulisthâna Mahâ-
5. râjâdhirâja Sri Mahârâja Devakasya Ghâdikapura grâma-
6. hi agat | tasya judhya . ve tritâ || Rau Duleharita.

In the three inscriptions marked B, C, and D, we have the names of one Mahârâjâdhirâja Sri Mahâraja Devaka, of one Mahâraja Sri Hamira Deva, and of several Râüts. There are also three holy places mentioned as Kevati-sthâna, Kathaula-sthâna, and Luka-sthâna.

The names of two villages, Baodigrama and Mayuragrâma, occur in all three ; but I have not been able to identify them. The three holy places, or *sthânas*, still exist. Kevati-sthâna is now known as Kevati-kund ; Kathaula-sthâna is now the large village of Kathaula, near the Mamani Ghât ; and Luka-sthâna is the large village of Lûk, on a low hill on the right bank of the Tons River near its exit from the hills.

Of the two Rajas I can find nothing certain. The foundation of Hamirpur on the Jumna is attributed to a Raja Hamira ; but his date is uncertain. From the date of Samvat 1397 = A.D. 1340, I should be inclined to conclude that the great fight, in which the Râüts fell, must have been between the Chandels and the Bâghels. In A.D. 1240 the Chandels were in possession of the country, and, so late as A.D. 1315, it seems probable that they still held the northwestern portion of the Rewa territory under their King Vira Varmma II. I hope to have an opportunity of examining these inscriptions more leisurely during the ensuing cold season.

37.—GINJA HILL.

The Ginja Hill is an isolated mountain, about 800 feet in height, which stands out prominently in the plain close to the exit of the Tons River from the Vindhya Hills. It is 11 miles to the south of the Bargarh railway station, and 40 miles to the south-west of Allahabad. It is 1,326 feet in total height above the sea; and is similar in appearance to many of the hills about Kâlanjar and Ajaygarh. The hill is said to be 3 kos, or 9 miles, in circumference at the base. The top of it is a narrow ridge of perpendicular rock about 200 feet in height, while the lower part is a steep slope all round, thickly covered with jungle. It is said to belong to the Bâra Pargana of the Allahabad District; but in all our maps it is assigned to the Native State of Rewa.

At rather more than half-way up the ascent there is a large reservoir of water about 200 feet round. Up to this point the ascent is tolerably easy, but above the tank it becomes very steep and difficult, and is much impeded by thorny jungle. On the south face of the top the scarped rock overhangs very considerably, and forms a large open hall, or rock shelter, about 100 feet long by 40 or 50 feet broad, and of irregular height, varying from 20 to 25 feet. It is closed at both ends by rough walls; but the whole of the front is open. In the middle of the rock at the back there is an inscription in red paint with some rude drawings of men and animals. The characters of the inscription are of the earliest Gupta forms; but the opening is worded in the well-known style of all the shorter Indo-Scythian inscriptions.

The letters were traced on oiled paper, and the accompanying plate gives a very faithful copy of all the better preserved portion of the inscription. I read it as follows :—

1. Mahârâjasya Sri Bhimasenasya sam (vatsare) . 52 Gimha pakshe 4 divasa 12 etaya-

2. purvayam Siddhi Sri triṣe ṣatasy puna *Gija ka* lika bhâta.

"(In the reign) " of Mahârâja Sri Bhima Sena in the Samvat year (52), in the 4th fortnight of the hot season, the 12th day, on that date
*   *   *

The date may be explained in two different ways, either with reference to the era of the Seleukidæ, which would appear to have been in use with the Indo-Scythians, or with reference to the era of the Guptas. In the former case it must be taken as the year 452 of the era, the hundreds being omitted, and would correspond with 140 A.D., in the middle of the reign of the Indo-Scythian King Huvishka. In the latter case it would correspond with the year 166 + 52 = A.D. 221, according to my reckoning of the Gupta era. The Indo-Scythian style of the inscription, with its fortnights and seasons, is in favour of the earlier date. But the forms of the letters seem to me to be more in accordance with those of Samudra Gupta's inscriptions. The difference in date of 81 years is not great. But the style of recording the date agrees so exactly with that used by the Indo-Scythian Princes, Kanishka, Huvishka, and Vasu Deva, that I feel constrained to assign the record to the earlier period.

To the right and left of the inscription there are several very rudely drawn figures of men and animals sketched in outline in red paint. Their age is doubtful, as they have no connection with the inscription.

38.—KATKÂ OBELISK.

On the west bank of the Tons River, opposite the village of Katkâ, and close to the railway bridge, there is a very curious sculptured obelisk. From its position on the west bank of the river, and facing the east, it may be a Sati monument; but there is nothing about the sculptures on the four faces that is peculiar to the known Sati pillars of later times. The obelisk is 3½ feet high, with two long faces of 20 inches and two short faces of 12 inches. The upper part above the four sculptures slopes backwards like the roof of a Dravidian temple, with three knobs on the top of the ridge.

The principal sculpture represents a Raja on horseback with his umbrella-bearer behind him, very much after the fashion of the Gupta gold coins. On the opposite face there is a four-armed figure of Bhainsâsuri Devi; with one hand she holds a leg of the buffalo, and in two other hands a sword

and shield. On one of the short sides there is a seated figure
holding a cup in his right hand; and on the fourth side there
is figure of Ganeṣa.

There is no inscription on the obelisk; but the sculptures
and ornaments have so much in common with those of the
Gupta period that I have no hesitation in assigning this curious
monument to a very early date, not later than the 3rd or 4th
century of the Christian era.

39.—HALIYA.

The town of Haliya is situated on the north or right bank
of the Adh, or Adhwa River, as it is more usually called, 31
miles to the south-west of Mirzapur and 13 miles to the south
of Lâlganj. On the bank of the river, on a high point above
the road, there is a large flat slab, 7 feet 8 inches high by 4 feet
6 inches broad, with two long inscriptions in English and
Hindi, describing the capture of the fort of Bhopâri on the
Son River on 18th April, A.D. 1811, by a regiment of Native Infantry. Both inscriptions are rather roughly cut.

The English inscription is as follows :—

"Under the auspices
of Lord Minto, Governor
General of India, and General Hewett,
Commander-in-Chief and Vice-President,
a passage was made through the *Kirahe Pass*,
of vast height, 2 miles in extent,
into *Burdee* for 18-pounders, &c., &c.,
by Lieutenant-Colonel James Tetley, Commanding
the 2nd Battalion, 21st Regiment, Native Infantry,
aided by the great exertions
of his gallant and willing corps,
the following of whom fell courageously
assaulting *Babarrah Ghurry in Burdee*,
April A.D. 1811 :—
Which is now destroyed,
and levelled with the ground—
Golaub Sing Naick, Sepoys Cassee Deen,
Pheeroo Sing, Jysook, Deenah, Boodie,
Incha, Byjenaut, Goorauge Sing, Poornu,
Bahâder Cawn, Golundauze,
Panchoo, Gun Lascar,

Soane, Head Bullockman.

Tilloock Sing, Sepoy of the same corps, killed at *Bissore Gaut.*

February 18th.—I Jemadar, 2 Havildars, 2 Naicks, &c. 30 Sepoys defending the post against 300 Banditti, beating them off."

The Hindi inscription, which consists of 25 lines, is rather fuller than the English one, as it mentions that no batteries were made, and that the guns were brought up close to the gate, but that the fort did not fall then, as the *kiladar,* or governor, made his escape. The Hindi text is given in the accompanying plate.[1] The following is an English transcript of this curious record, which, from its homely language, I judge to have been the composition of some of the sepoys themselves :—

1. Batâl 2 Rejmant 21 Karnal Tetali Sâheb Bahâdu-
2. r *Kiâri ka* Ghâṭâ banwayâ, Lât Manda (Minto)
3. Sâheb ke hukum se, Jarnai Hêwaṭ Sâheb ke
4. hukum se, path kaṭâï ke bagali patâi ke, wâ pâ-
5. thar se wâ maṭi se, bhar Ghâta duï kos ka tha au (?)
6. Sipâhi apanî khusi se, au kuchh log Mirjâpur se
7. mangâyâ thâ, Ghâta duï kos ka lambâ thâ athâ-
8. ra pani ke lejâne mâphak bana, au (?) Ghâta bahut
9. uchâ thâ, Sipâhi apani khusi se banâya baṛi mehan-
10. t se, au BARDI ke rasta . au Tarîkh 18 Sani 1811
11. mahina Abarel *Garhi Bhopâri* mâ larâï huâ, leken
12. murchâ nahi lagâ thâ, au Top chhapani dui thâ kilâ
13. te, pandarâ kadam par darwâja ke sâmane, au Dîwâl
14. nagîch thâ au(r) Sipâhi kilâ ke nagich pahuncha, le-
15. kan kilâ us wakht nahi chhuṭa Sâm ke kilâdâr bhâ-
16. gi gayâ Bhopâri garhi Ghâti ke girâi ke barâbar kiyâ bâgi-
17. cha katâi ke bâhar phenk diâ indârâ (*wells*) girâ diâ. Jûjhâ
18. Nâik Gulab Singh ; Sipâhi Jaisukh, wa Pheru, wa Kâsi din,
19. wa Dina Singh, wa Budhaï, wa Ichha Râm, wa Gajrâj Singh, wa Baij-
20. nâth, wa Puran, Nâik 1, Sipâhi 9 ; Golandâz Bahâdur Khan
21. Khalasi Pânchu wa Bulakmân ka Chaudhari Sôn *Garhi Bhopâri* wa Ta
22. duâ, wa joki, tino Gaḍi me gadahâ kahar phirâ. Bhoswal ke thâ
23. na Lochan Singh ke sâth gârd thâ jemadâr I.H.2., S. 30 târi-
24. k 18 larâi huâ ‖ Dâke par larâi mârâ jo tin so log Dâka
25. ayâ thâ, so bhâgi ga (yâ) Sipâhi Tilok Singh *Ghâṭa Bhaiswal.*

[1] See Plate **XXXI**.

The following translation will show the differences between the two versions—

"The 2nd Battalion of the 21st Regiment, under Colonel Tetley Sâheb Bahâdur, made the Kiâri-ka-Ghât, by order of Lord Minto (and) by order of General Hewett Sâheb. They cut a road and built up the side with stones and with earth, making the Ghât for two kos in length. The sepoys worked of their own accord, and some workmen were got from Mirzapur. The Ghât, 2 kos in length, was made passable for 18-pounders. The Ghât was very lofty, and the sepoys made it of their own free-will with great labour towards Bardi. On the 18th day in the year 1811, in the month of April, the fort of Bhopâr was attacked ; but batteries were not made, and two 6-pounders were taken up in front of the gate within 15 paces, and the sipahis went up to the wall, but the fort did not then surrender. In the evening the kiladâr fled. The walls of Fort Bhopâri were thrown down and levelled, the trees were cut and thrown outside, and the wells were destroyed. Killed—Naick Golâb Singh ; Sepoys Jai Sukh, Pheru, Kâsi Din, Dina Singh, Budhai, Ichha Râm, Gajrâj Singh, Baijnâth and Puran ; Naick 1, Sepoys 9, Artilleryman Bahâdur Khan, Khalâsi Pânchu ; Head Bullockman Son.

"The forts of Bhopâri, Tadu, and Joki, were all three levelled by ploughs drawn by asses.[1]

"In Bhosâwal Thana with Lochan Singh there was a guard of 1 Jemadar, 2 Havildars, 2 Naicks, and 30 Sepoys. The Dâkas (*dakoits*) were beaten off, and all the 300 who came there ran away. Killed Tilok Singh at Ghâta Bhaisâwal."

Both inscriptions conclude with a list of the names of the sepoys who were killed. Mention is made at the end of the defence of Bissore Ghât by a party of 35 sepoys against 300 banditti (in Hindi *Dâka*), in which one sepoy was killed.

As I was unable to find any account of this gallant exploit in our histories, I applied to Major Barr, the Political Agent, now in charge of the Rewa State, who kindly furnished me with the following note on the subject :—

"The story of the capture by assault of the Bobarry ghurry in Burdee is well known at Rewa. Bobarry, or Bhopâri, was a stronghold of the Chandels of Bardi, who in 1811 were not entirely under

---

[1] The position of *Joki* is shown in the map, 4 miles to the west of *Bhopari*. The third fort, named Tadua, is most probably *Tendua*, to the south of the Son River, only 5 miles to the south-south-east of Bhopari. The Rani is still living there.

the Rewa Râj. Their subjection was afterwards completed. Fouj-dâr Singh was the Thâkur of the clan, and lived in the fort, where he harboured an offender from the neighbouring British district of Mirzapur. Our demand for his surrender was refused, and a regi-ment of Native Infantry was therefore sent against the place. Foujdâr Singh opened fire on the troops, and, in consequence, the fort was taken by assault after a very tough fight. Foujdâr Singh seems to have escaped from the fort, as the Chauhâns afterwards gave him the village of Râmdit, where his descendants, Siwai Lâl Singh and Hira Lâl Singh, are now living."

Haliya has lost most of its importance since the new road by the Katra Pass from Mirzapur to Rewa was completed. The old road to the south passed through Haliya *via* Dibhor and the Kerahi Pass. In the Gazetteer of the Mirzapur Dis-trict, the following account of the erection of the inscription slabs is given by the compiler [1]:—

"This monument was erected to commemorate a little expedition undertaken at the instance of Lallu Nâik, a well-known merchant of Mirzapur, to punish the marauders of Rewa, who used to plunder the rich convoys of merchandise which passed between Mirzapur and the Dakhin. This was before the construction of the Dakhin road and the Katra Pass, when the route lay *via* Hallia and the Kerâi and Dibhor Ghâts. This same Lallu Nâik constructed along the latter route a number of fine masonry tanks, which still, in their ruin, testify to the importance of the trade it once possessed. He was a power-ful and wealthy man, and seems to have used his riches well. His house has decayed along with the city, and only the name remains. His grandson, Râi Durga Prasâd, died in comparative obscurity some years ago, and only a few female relatives remain to represent the family—a striking example, if one were needed, of the instability of oriental fortunes."

Lallu Nâik is the same person who is mentioned in my account of Dibhor as Lâlla Mor. His name was Mor, and he was the Nâik or Chief of the Banjâra community of Mirza-pur.

40.—DIBHOR.

In reply to my repeated enquiries about ancient buildings, I had often been told of a temple and large tank at Dibhor,

---

[1] North-Western Provinces Gazetteer, Art. Mirzapur, Vol. XIV, p. 194.

in a narrow valley of the Vindhya Hills, 12 miles to the south
of Haliya and 43 miles to the south-south-west of Mirzapur.
I accordingly visited the place, and was much disappointed
to find a small temple of the modern Mirzâpur type, only 10
feet 9 inches square. The tank, however, is a very fine one,
being 430 feet in length from north to south and 352 feet in
breadth, with steps all round.

There is a long inscription of 22 lines of raised letters in
the verandah of the temple, describing its erection by Srimân Nayak Mân Mor in the Samvat year 1881, on Wednesday, the 5th of the waxing moon of Phâlgun, or Wednesday,
the 23rd February 1825 A.D. Mân Mor was the head of the
Banjâra merchants of Mirzâpur. The date is also given in
the year *Manmatha*, of the 60-year cycle of Jupiter, which
corresponds with 1881 Samvat.

Dibhor itself is a small hamlet of a few houses belonging
to the attendants of the temple. There is a pathway through
a gap in the hills to the east, which joins the road running
southward to Bardi on the Son River. The place is a regular
cul-de-sac, and is extremely hot. I suppose that the vagrant
instinct of the old Banjâra preferred a jungle site. No doubt
he got the ground cheap ; and from this vantage point he was
able to supply Mirzâpur with both wood and charcoal. This
trade still continues ; but, as no young trees are ever planted,
the jungle is gradually being cleared away, and both wood
and charcoal are becoming dearer.

41.—ADESAR HILL.

Adesar is a lofty, flat-topped hill, some 700 or 800 feet
in height. It stands on the left, or east, side of the road
leading from Mirzâpur through Haliya and Dibhor into Rewa.
It is said that there are several caves in the precipitous sandstone cliff near the top of the hill, but the lower slopes are
so densely covered with jungle that none of the Kol population ever attempt to ascend it. It is believed, however,
that one of the Bijaypur Rajas managed to reach one of the
caves by means of ladders, and that he found an image of the
goddess Devi.

The Adesar Hill seems to be similar in its formation to the hill forts of Kâlanjar and Ajaygarh, the lower three-fourths being comparatively easy slopes of granite, thickly covered with jungle, and the upper fourth being a bare bluff of sandstone. The hill itself is an isolated offshoot of the Kaimur Range, immediately facing the most easterly peaks of the Vindhya Range on the opposite bank of the Adhwâ River. It is possible that there may have been some connection originally between the name of the river and that of the hill. The latter was probably named after the former, as the "hill of the Adhwâ River," which, after the adoption of the lingam stone by the Brahmans, would naturally have been changed to the Hill of Adesar.

42.—TURA.

Tura is the name of a perennial spring near the top of the hill, 2½ miles to the north-east of Dibhor, and close to the Rewa village of South Lohâri. Close by the spring there is a rude stone cell that was formerly occupied by a *Sâdhu*, or holy man. There are several fine trees near the cell, which are visible from Dibhor. The people call the cell a cave, but it is simply an irregularly shaped room built of rough stones. It is only 6 feet long by 4 feet broad, covered with a flat roof. Formerly there was a second room, 6 feet square on the east side, but it has now fallen in. The cave, or cell, is approached by a flight of steps on the east side. The spring flows out from beneath the cave, and its course is marked by a green track right down to the foot of the hill. There was no inscription in the cave.

43.—AHUGI.

Ahugi is an old village situated on the road between Haliya and Dibhor, at the point where it divides into two branches, one going direct to Dibhor and Bhopâri, and the other to the east of the Adesar Hill, to Bardi on the Son River. The houses of the village are scattered along both banks of the Adh, or Adhwâ River, which here flows in a deep channel with plenty of water. In the Atlas sheet, No. 89, of the map of India the name is written once as Onji (apparently a mistake for Ougi), and again as Ahogee Kd., the abbreviation standing for the Persian word *Khurd*, or " Little." [1]

Its favourable situation amongst fine old trees on the banks of a running stream must have led at an early date to the selection of Ahugi as a halting-ground for the Banjára merchants, and afterwards to its occupation by the Brahmans as a pleasant site for their temples. There are, however, no temples now standing, but there are many ruins of stone temples both to the north and to the west of the village, besides numerous statues.

On a low mound to the west of the village, there are the ruins of a temple of Siva, of which the sill, one jamb, and the lintel of the entrance to the sanctum still remain on the ground. The lintel has a figure of Siva, four-armed, seated in the middle, with Brahma to his right and Vishnu to his left. There is a single pilaster, 5 feet 5 inches in height, and a standing statue of Surya, 3 feet 2 inches high, with Aruna on the pedestal, and five horses.

To the north of the village there are the remains of at least three different temples.

No. 1 is a small lingam temple facing the west, the interior being only 3 feet 9 inches by 3 feet, while the walls are formed of single upright slabs only 4½ inches thick.

No. 2 is also a small lingam temple, but its entrance is to the east. The interior is only 4½ feet by 4¼ feet, and the walls are formed of single slabs containing figures in panels. I recognized Ganesa, Bhainsásuri Devi, and a four-armed female, who was probably intended for Durgá.

No. 3 is similar to the east, but it is much more broken.

On a long, flat slab of No. 2 temple I found a few letters, which were sufficient to show that the temples belonged to the mediæval period of about 1000 A.D.

---

[1] This is one of the absurdities which still disfigure the sheets of the Atlas of India. Thus, we find everywhere the scarcely known Persian terms *Kalán* and *Buzurg*, for " great," and *Khurd*, for " small," instead of the universally known vernacular terms *bará* and *chota*, for " big and little."

44.—BARDI and BHOPÂRI.

The fort of Bardi is situated on a rocky ridge to the south or right bank of the Gopat River, just above its junction with the Son. It is 213 feet long and 138 feet broad, with walls 4 feet thick at top, and octagonal towers at the four angles. The entrance gate on the north side is 10 feet 8 inches high, but only 3 feet 4 inches wide.

Bardi was captured by the Rewa Raja in Samvat 1876, or A.D. 1819. Before that time the Chandel chiefs who held the fort are said to have sacrificed a man, or some human being, every year to the goddess of Bardi.

Bhopâri is on the northern bank of the Son River, 10 miles to the west of Bardi, and the same distance south-south-west from Dibhor in a direct line. By the Kirâhi Pass the actual road distance is nearly double, and the descent from the top of the Kaimur Range towards the Son is both steep and bad.

45.—DURGA-KHO.

In a former report I have given a short notice of the inscriptions engraved on the face of the wall in the cave of Durga-kho, near Chunar. Durgâ kund is a perennial pool, or reservoir, situated about half a mile up a narrow ravine to the south-south-west of the Railway Station at Chunar. The mouth of the ravine is 1 mile from the station. On the north side of the ravine stands the temple of Kamâksha Devi, and just below it a small old temple without name. The ravine, or Jhirna Nala, is spanned by a bridge which leads to a row of three *dâlâns*, or cloisters, formed by building against the face of the rock. Against the back wall there is a low platform or seat, 15 inches high and 16 inches broad, which was probably intended for the reception of statues.

Sculptured on the rock there are several figures of lions, horses, and elephants in outline. The face of the rock is 5 feet 3 inches high, above which the required height was obtained by building up. The beams and pillars of the present arcade are quite new. The whole back wall is literally covered with short inscriptions of all ages from the Gupta period downwards. Several of these I have already published; but, as my last visit was a more leisurely one, I was able to examine the writings with more attention. I have accordingly given in the accompanying plate[1] some of the previous ones over again, along with several new ones. I read them as follows:—

1. Vishnu.
2. Isâna Shatapasa (a mistake for Khatapasa).
3. Samavidaivikântâ.
4. Prasṭa satadhinarchilaka Chandra.
5. Jaya Samudra.
6. Sri Bharkarasta.
7. Bhagwaloka chirnattakudra.
8. Garga datta.
9. Prachaṇḍa Prithivekah.
10. Jambu Dâsa.
11. Yaṣalokacha.
12. Sujam bhara.
13. Ujala.
14. Uja.
15. Heṇṇa ha ˙˙ va, or Meṇṇa ma ˙˙ toa.
16. Bhârosaviniya.
17. Sri Bhoja Deva.
18. Sri Bhoja Devabhavira.
19. Bhadra Viloka.
20. Vashana Chilaka.
21. Dhâra kâhṇada.
22. Govinda.
23. Chhedi Bhagat kâ dwari.

There is nothing amongst these records of any interest, except perhaps the juxtaposition of the names of Chandra and Samudra in Nos. 4 and 5. As they are in old Gupta characters, similar to those used upon the coins, it is possible that the names may refer to the two kings, Chandra Gupta and his son Samudra Gupta.

Most of the names appear to be those of the quarrymen or stone-cutters who occupied the rock shelter, which has been turned into a long arcade.

[1] See Plate XXXII.

46.—BHUILI.

In a former report I have described the remains at Bhuili, and I only visited it on the present occasion, because it happened to be in my way from Durgâ-kho. A few new objects were discovered, of which the only one of any interest was an old Muhammadan inscription of 5 double lines let into the lower wall of a masjid in Dakhin Tola. Unfortunately it is much injured, but I was able to read in the 2nd line—

Sultán bin Sultán Shah Mubárak ánk Kutbi.
and in the 5th line *Sabamiah* (or 700).

The inscription therefore belongs to the time of Kutb-ud-din Mubârak Khilji, who reigned from A.H. 716 to 720.

At the same place also there were three Hindu pillars and a bracket capital.

In the hill to the south there is a cave dargâh of *Makhdum Sâhib Chirâgh Hind.* It is whitewashed inside, and no inscriptions were visible. It is only a small room of 8 feet by 6 feet, and 6 feet high.

There is also a rock shelter called *Chilam marfia*, 15 feet by 12 feet, and $6\frac{1}{4}$ feet high. Near it there is a curious natural monolith, $5\frac{1}{2}$ feet in height, or with its base and pinnacle $9\frac{1}{2}$ feet. It is reckoned a curiosity, as the shaft is considerably curved.

47.—SEOPUR.

Seopur is $1\frac{1}{2}$ mile to the west of Kantit near Mirzapur. In former days it possessed a very large temple, of which the ruins now lie scattered about. The present temple of Râmeswar Nâth contains many large capitals, and there are numerous broken sculptures and other remains in the neighbourhood. The most striking thing is a life-size female figure seated on a throne with a child in her lap. The sculpture is 5 feet 2 inches high by 3 feet 8 inches broad, and 1 foot 8 inches deep. The face is gone, but a small figure of Buddha still remains on the top of the head. The right arm is broken at the elbow, and the left arm supports the child. The left knee is bent, and the leg is resting on the ground at

the foot of the throne.   At the back of the figure there is a
large tree with foliage and flowers.   At the foot of the throne
under the left leg there is a lion.   I believe the statue to be a
representation of Shashti, the goddess of Fecundity.   There
are 7 attendants on each side, 2 flying, and 5 standing.
The statue is now called *Sangkaṭa Devi*, very probably for
Sangkaṭa-haraṇi Devi, "the remover of misfortune."

48.—KÂLPI.

The old town of Kâlpi stands on a bluff cliff of clay overhanging the Jumna.   The fort occupies the highest position,
and commands the passage of the river.   It has walls only on
the three land sides, the river front being inaccessible.   To the
westward there are many old tombs and mosques, now in ruins.
There are no inscriptions on any of them, and only a few
names are now remembered.   At the north-west corner there
is a piece of ground called *Prabhâvati Mandi*, or the "splendid
market-place," where old coins are found in the rainy season.
It is said that *ata* (or flour) mixed with water cannot be cooked
on this spot, and that dead bodies cannot be burned there.

Kâlpi was the birth-place of Mohes-dâs, a poor Brahman,
who afterwards became famous as Raja Bir-bar, or Bir-bal,
the companion of Akbar.

Kâlpi also was the residence of the holy Shekh Burhân,
who died at 100 years of age in A.H. 970, or A.D. 1562-63.
He is said to have lived on milk and sweetmeats only.   He
was buried in his cell, the site of which is not now known.

According to Ferishta the fort of Kâlpi was built by Vasu
Deva, Raja of Kanauj, the contemporary of Bahrâm Gor.   But
the people of the place know nothing of this doubtful chief,
and attribute the building of Kâlpi to an ancient Raja, named
Kalib Deva.   The earliest mention that I have found of Kâlpi
is the notice of its capture by Kutb-ud-din Aibeq in A.H. 593
=A.D. 1196.   It was afterwards joined to Mahoba and
placed under an imperial governor from Delhi.   During the
troubled times which followed the invasion of Timur, Kâlpi
and Mahoba became independent under Muhammad Khan,
the son of Malikzâda Firoz, who took the title of king.   In

A.H. 937 Kâlpi was attacked by Ibrâhim Shah of Jaunpur, who retired on the advance of Mubârak Shah of Delhi, to whom the governor, Kadir Khan, had made urgent appeals for aid. In the following year, A.H. 938 or A.D. 1434-35, during the war between Delhi and Jaunpur, Kâlpi fell into the hands of Hushang Shah of Malwa. Before A.H. 847 or A.D. 1443 the new governor of Kâlpi, named Nasir Khan, the son of Kâdir Khan, still acknowledged fealty to Malwa. But the place was shortly afterwards attacked by Mahmud of Jaunpur, who sacked the town, and compelled Nasir Khan to fly to Chanderi.

After the conquest of Jaunpur, Kâlpi fell into the hands of Bahlol Lodi of Delhi, who appointed Kutb Khan Lodi to be the governor. During the reign of Sikandar Lodi, his son Jalâl Khan became ruler of the eastern provinces, including Kâlpi and Jaunpur. He was afterwards dispossessed by his brother Ibrahim Lodi, who put him to death.

Kâlpi was successively occupied by Bâber and his son Humâyun, by Sher Shah and his relatives, Ibrâhim Sur, Sikandar Sur, and Muhammad Adil; and, lastly, by Akbar, by whom it was permanently attached to the Mughal empire of Delhi. Here he had a mint for copper coins.

The principal remains at Kâlpi are the tombs of Madâr Sâhib, of Ghafûr Zanjâni, of Chol Bibi (a square enclosed by trellises), of Bahâdur Shâhid, and the great enclosure called Chaurâsi Gumbaz, or "eighty-four domes." There is a large statue of a lion at another tomb, which is assigned to a barber. The lion is said to have been turned into stone when struck by the holy saint Madâr Sâhib.

The only remarkable building at Kâlpi is the Chaurâsi Gumbaz. It is said to be the tomb of Lodi Shâh Bâdshâh, and some people even assign to it Sikandar Lodi. But we know that he died near Agra, and that his body was carried to Delhi to be buried. The Chaurâsi Gumbaz is built of blocks of kankar laid in lime mortar. All the ornamentation is in stucco, with flowered borders and bands. Altogether, the style corresponds very closely with that of the Lodi period, and I think, therefore, that the people are right in their attribution of it to a Lodi prince.

The building itself is only remarkable for its size, being 125 feet square outside, and about 80 feet high—seven narrow arched openings, divided by thick square piers. The whole building is divided, something like a chess-board, into eight lines of piers, and seven lines of open spaces, thus forming 64 piers, all connected by twice 49 arches, with the 49 intervening spaces covered by flat roofs. In the middle there are four piers omitted, and the square space thus obtained is covered by a lofty dome which rises about 60 feet above the flat-terraced roof of the main body of the building. There are four small domes covering the four corner intersections, and there is a small domed turret over each of the sloping towers at the outer corners. But the appearance of the great central dome rising for about 40 feet or more cylindrical neck above the terraced roof is extremely bold and imposing. The meagre appearance of this domed tower might easily have been softened by the addition of a second storey rising from the next inner line of piers to within a few feet of the spring of the dome.

The piers vary from 6 feet 2 inches to 8 feet 8 inches square, and the arches from $6\frac{1}{2}$ feet to $9\frac{1}{2}$ feet span. Altogether the building is very solid, and is likely to last for a long time. No one could explain why the tomb was called Chaurâsi Gumbaz, or "the eighty-four domes." There are only 40 intersecting spaces in the roof, after deducting intersections in the middle which are covered by the main dome. These, with the four corner turrets and the great dome, make only 45 possible domes, so that the name of *Chaurâsi Gumbaz* is decidedly incorrect. The original name may have been *Châlisi Gumbaz*, or the "forty domes," which would have been strictly correct, as well as in accordance with a favourite Hindu number.

The present town of Kâlpi occupies a site to the south-east of the original old town and the great mass of ruined tombs and masjids.

49.—SULTÂNPUR.

I have given a description of Sultânpur, in the Jâlandhar Doâb, in my report of my last tour in the Panjâb (see

Archæological Survey, Vol. XIV, p. 55), where I have shown
that it corresponds in position with the Tamasa-vana monastery of Hwen Thsang.   The people of the place, however, say
that it was named after Sultân Khân Pathân, a brother of
Haibat Khân, in the time of the Pathân kings.   There was
a Haibat Khân in the time of Sikandar Lodi, who gave his
name to the old town of Patti, to the west of the Biâs River,
nearly opposite to Sultânpur.   Since my visit a short inscription has been found outside the serai, dated in A.H. 970
(*Sabain-wa-tisamiah*), which records the building of a mosque
by Abdullah, son of Shamsuddin, son of Jamâl Ansâri, the
humblest of mankind.

50.—CHINI.

I have described the lofty mound of Chini in my last
Panjâb Report, Volume XIV, page 53, of the Archæological
Survey.   I then identified it with the *Chinapati* of the pilgrim
Hwen Thsang, who notes that the Chinese hostages were kept
there by Kanishka during the winter months.

During the present year the mound has been dug into by
a contractor for bricks.   During the excavations a very old
statue of Vishnu was brought to light.   The contractor claim-
ed it as part of his property, but the villagers put in a counter-
claim for the figure as that of their village deity.   I have
hitherto failed in getting a photograph of this interesting piece
of sculpture.

51.—CHAMBA.

The small Hindu state of Chamba is situated in the alpine
Panjâb, and embraces all the country lying on the River Râvi
and its tributaries, from their sources to the point where their
collected waters pierce the outer range of hills.   About one-
third of the territory forming the Chamba District of Lâhul
lies on the Chenâb River and its tributary the Bhâga.   But
this is a poor country with a very small population.

The capital, named Champapuri, or Chamba, stands on
the northern bank of the river, in the south-western corner of
the territory, at an elevation of rather more than 3,000 feet
above the sea.   On all sides it is surrounded by lofty ranges

of mountains, rising to 16,000 feet in height on the south, towards Kangra, and 18,000 and 20,000 feet in the north-east, towards the valley of the Upper Chenâb. On the north-west side the mountain range is less lofty, although several of the peaks reach 16,000 feet.

The original capital of the country was at Barmâwar, on the Budhil River, about 60 miles nearly due east from the town of Chamba by the road, but only 32 miles distant in a direct line. Barmâwar is upwards of 7,000 feet above the sea, and possesses several old temples, both of stone and wcod. These I have already described in a previous volume.[1] All the earlier Rajas bore the name of Varmma, and the inscriptions on the pedestals of the statues give the names of Meru Varmma, and his three predecessors with the same title.

The change of capital from Barmâwar to Chamba is assigned to Sâla Varmma, who was defeated and killed by Ananta Varmma of Kashmir in A.D. 1060. In the inscriptions this Chamba King is called Sâlivâhana, of which Sâla is only a common contraction. He built the famous temple of Lakshmi Narâyan, which is by far the most popular of all the temples now standing at Chamba. His son was Soma Varmma Deva, of whom there is a copper-plate grant now existing at Chamba. This document is attested both by his own signature and by that of his son Asata Deva. Kalasa, the son of Ananta of Kashmir, married Asata's sister, named Vappikâ, who became the mother of Harsha Deva, the next king of Kashmir.

There are four inscriptions now existing at Chamba, of which three are engraved on copper-plates, and one on a stone slab.

The oldest is that mentioned above. The copper-plate is 17¼ inches long and 12 inches broad. There are 29 lines written direct, with 1 line to right, and another at top upside down, and a third on the left hand, or altogether 32 lines. There are two dates noted in it, namely, the first year, *Samvatsare prathame*, on Friday of the 3rd of the waxing moon, Vaisâkh. The second date is Samvat 11 Bhâdrapada, Sudi

---

[1] Archæological Survey, Vol. XIV, p. 109.

13th, on Some, or Monday. These dates correspond with
the Christian years A.D. 1060 and 1070. In the former
year Raja Sâla was killed by Ananta, and was succeeded by
his son Soma Varmma Deva. In the latter year Raja Soma
was still reigning, but his son Asata had then grown up, and
the grant was accordingly attested by him as heir apparent
as well as by his father. Raja Kalasa, of Kashmir, married
Asata's sister.

The second inscription is also on copper. It has 17 lines
quite perfect, but I can find no date. The Raja's name is Bhaṭa
Varmma, son of Mânikya Varmma Deva. Both names are
found in the list of the Rajas of Chamba; the latter being
spelt Bodha.

The third inscription is engraved on a stone slab, which
is now lying under a very large Toon tree, on the side wall of
a Chabutara, or platform, besides a tank. It consists of 10
lines, but is only remarkable for the precise way in which its
date is recorded. The words are Sri Mân nripati Vikramâditya Samvatsara 1717, Sri Sâlivahara Sake 1583, Sri Ṣâstri
Samvatsare 37, that is—

in the Vikrama Samvat year	.	. 1717	= A.D.	1660
in the Salivâhana Saka ,,	.	. 1583	= ,,	1661
in the Sâstri Samvatsara ,,	.	. 37	= ,,	[16]61

Here we meet with the Lok-Kâl, or Sapt Rishi-Kâl, under
the name of Ṣâstri Samvatsara, or *Sâstri era.* The week-day
Budhavâsare, or Wednesday, shows that the year corre-
sponded with A.D. 1661. The era of the seven Rishis might
appropriately be called the holy Samvat, or divine era.

The fourth inscription is engraved in 23 lines on a copper-
plate. It is quite modern; but, as it gives the Ṣâstri Samvatsara, it is of some value. It bears two different dates as
follows :—

line 7, Vikramâditya Samvat 1917, Sâstri Samvatsare	. 36
line 8, do. do. 1915, do.	. . 34
lines 18-19, do. do. 1917, do.	. . 36

Here the Vikramâditya dates are correct, as they give A.D.
1858 and 1860; while the Ṣâstri Samvat gives the same, *viz.,*

1824+34 = 1858, and 1824+36 = 1860 A.D. The seal also bears the two dates of " Samvat 34 and 36," but without the corresponding years of the Vikramâditya, I have given a full account of the Sapt Rishi-Kâl or Lok-Kâl in my " Book of Indian Eras."

PART II.

REPORT OF A TOUR IN REWA, BUNDELKHAND, MALWA, AND GWALIOR,

IN

1884-85.

REPORT OF A TOUR IN REWA, BUNDELKHAND, MALWA, AND GWALIOR, IN 1884-85.

PART II.

1.—KEVATI-KUND, or KEONTI.

The falls of the Tamasa, or Tons River, have long been famous. The river rises in the small state of Mahiyar, 50 miles to the south-west of Rewa, and, after a course of 130 miles, measured in a direct line, falls into the Ganges, between Allahabad and Benares. None of the falls are on the main stream, but on its larger tributaries just above their junction with it. The following are the names of the principal falls :—

Fall.	Stream.	Height.	Distance from Rewa.
		Feet.	
1 Piâwan	Piâwan Nala	115	23 miles N.
2 Damdo	Damdo Nala	?	24 ,, N.
3 Pûrwa	Small stream	240	17 ,, N.
4 Chachai	Behar Nadi	368	20 ,, N. N.-E.
5 Kevati	Mahâ Nadi	331	21 ,, N.-E.
6 Bilohi	Odda Nadi	464	36 ,, E. N.-E.

The *Piâwan fall* has been described by both Mr. Garrick and myself. It possesses an inscription of Gânggeya Deva, the Kalachuri Raja of Chedi or Dâhal, dated in the Chedi Samvat 789, or A.D. 1030. The inscription is carved on the Argha of a lingam.

The *Kevati-Kund* is the most famous of all the Tons waterfalls, partly perhaps for its easier accessibility, but chiefly, I believe, for the romantic beauty of its scenery. The Mahâ Nadi River pours over the sheer rock in one unbroken fall of 331 feet into a deep blue pool, and continues its course for some miles between the beetling cliffs of the narrow ravine.   On the east the cliff is crowned by a fort and some small temples, below which, at 130 paces, there are two long ledges, protected by the overhanging rocks, which form the shelters now known as caves.   The larger one is 200 feet long and 43 feet broad, but only 3 feet in height at the back, and it appears to have been partly quarried out.   The other shelter, now known as the Mahâdeva cave, is partly artificial, being closed on the outer side by built walls, 7 feet in height. It is 36½ feet long by 33 feet broad, and 7 feet high, diminishing to 3 feet at the back.   Inside there are a few lingams, from which it derives its name of the Mahâdeva cave.   On the rock outside there are two Buddhist stûpas carved in outline.   These prove the Buddhist origin of the cave, which is confirmed by the following inscription on the roof of the cave, carved in letters of the 2nd century B.C.   The inscription was found by Mr. Macaulay Markham, and the following reading of it has been published by Dr. Höernle :—

Hariti putenam Sonakena kâritâ pukharini.

"The pool (cave) caused to be made by Saunaka, the son of Haritî."[1]

The cave is rather difficult of access, but one is well repaid for the trouble by the fine view of the waterfall and of the blue pool below which the cave commands.

In the open rock-shelter there are numerous figures of animals sketched in red ochre, such as antelopes, bârasinghas, and elephants, with floriated letters in white.   One man told me that the proper name of the pool was *Dharmâtma*, but the place is named in all the inscriptions as *Kevati-sthân*, and is more generally known as *Keönti-Kund*.

One mile from the waterfall, on the high ground near the village of Keönti, there is a row of four Sati pillars called *Panch Bhaya*, or "the Five Brothers."   Only four are now

[1] Indian Antiquary, Vol. IX, p. 121.

standing ; but there is a gap showing where the missing pillar once stood. Two other pillars, standing a little way off, are called *Nand-bhau.* All bear representations of armed soldiers in the act of fighting, with inscriptions beneath. The northern pillar is dated in Samvat 1390, but all the others are seven years later, and bear the same date of Samvat 1397, on Monday, the 4th day of the waxing moon of Mâgha (Monday, the 22nd January, A.D. 1341). The people say that these were five brothers who all fell on the same day. From the existing inscriptions it is certain that three of them fell on the same day ; but one of them fell upwards of seven years earlier, on Saturday the 31st July A.D. 1333; or, if the Samvat date be read as 1340, he must have fallen fifty-seven years earlier.

In the three later inscriptions, dated in Samvat 1397, there is mention of Mahârâjâ Hamira Deva, of Luka-sthân, and of Mahârâjâdhirâja Devaka, of Kathauli-sthân. I conclude, therefore, in spite of their royal titles, that these two Rajas were only the petty chiefs of the two neighbouring towns of Luka-sthân and Kathauli-sthân, which still exist; and that the fight commemorated by the pillars was only a quarrel about their contiguous boundaries. The men who fell are all designated as Raus, or zamindars. Both Luka and Kathauli will be found in the accompanying map, Plate 1. Of Baori-grâm, which is mentioned in all these inscriptions, I could not get any information. Kathauli is a large village on the table-land near the Mamani pass, 30 miles to the west of north from Rewa. Lûk is a large village on the right bank of the Tons River, near where it leaves the hills, 27 miles to the east of north from Rewa. The distance between the two places is not more than 12 miles in a direct line.

2.—REWA, or BAGHELKHAND.

The city of Rewa, the present capital of Bâghelkhand, is of comparatively modern date, as it was founded by Raja Vikramâditya Baghel, after the fort of Bandhogarh had fallen into the hands of the Muhammadans during the reign of Akbar, about 1595 A.D. The only objects of any interest about the city are a very fine Toran gateway, and some sculptures, all of which were brought very recently from the ruins of the old city of Gûrgi Masâun, 12 miles to the east of Rewa.

The Toran gateway has been set up in front of the palace. A view of it has been given by my assistant Mr. Garrick. [1] The clear span between the bases of the two pillars is 10½ feet, and between the shafts 1 foot more. It is one of the richest and largest temple gateways that I have seen. Its original position at Gûrgi is still pointed out by the people.

Of the four sculptures which were brought from Gûrgi, one is undoubtedly Buddhist, and the others Brahmanical.

I.—The Buddhist sculpture is a seated figure of Padma-pâni, half life-size. One hand rests on the knee, which is raised up, while the other, holding a lotus flower, lies in the lap. On the back is engraved the Buddhist creed in three lines of well-cut characters of about the 10th century.

Ye dharma hetu prabhavâ hetun teshân Tathâgato
hyavâdatteshân cha yo nirodha evam vâdi
Mahâsramanah.

II.—A standing figure of Vishnu.

III.—A seated figure of a four-armed goddess, on the pedestal of which is engraved her name in an inscription of two lines.

Sri Hasti-vâhini Devih‖
Sâhârana pâda pankaja—

The statue derives its name from a small figure of an elephant, *hasti*, which forms the end of the pedestal. [2]

IV.—A bas-relief, 4 feet high, Siva and Pârvati, seated at top, his foot resting on a bull, and her foot on a lion. In the middle are two male figures seated and attended by women. Below, there are two tall swordsmen with shields, fighting two small men, armed with bows and arrows. I have a suspicion that this may be a Sati monument. [3] But I cannot even guess why the two swordsmen on the left are

[1] Archæological Survey of India, Vol. XIX, p. 80, and Plate XIX.
[2] See Plate XXXVI, for a picture of this Goddess from a photograph.
[3] See Plate XXXVII, for this battle-scene, taken from a photograph.

represented as giants of just twice the height of all the other figures. It is possible that they may be intended for fabulous monsters, as one of them has been shot through the body with an arrow, and I think also through the left thigh. Under this view the scene might represent the fight between Râma-chandra and the giant Kûmbhakarna.

The Rewa Durbar is in possession of several copper-plate inscriptions, of which only four are old. These I will refer to as A, B, C, and D.

A is engraved on a single plate, and is dated in Samvat 926, on Thursday, in Bhâdrapada, the 4th of the waxing moon, or A.D. 1175, as I take the Samvat date to be recorded in the Kalachuri era of Chedi, which starts from A.D. 249-50. The week-day, however, according to this reckoning does not agree with the day stated in the inscription. The characters of the inscription are of much too late a date for the Vikrama Samvat 926, or A.D. 869, and, as the Raja Jaya Sinha Deva Kalachuri is known to have been living in A.D. 1177, when the Rewa territory actually belonged to his family, I have no hesitation in assigning the inscription to him. But there is another difficulty in this record which begins with the name and titles of—

Parama bhaṭâraka Mahârajâdhirâja Parameswara
Sri Vâma Deva—

followed by the term *pâdânudhyâto*, or "bowing to whose feet," after which we have the name and titles of the reigning king as follows:—

Parama bhaṭâraka Mahârâjadhirâja parameswara parama
Mâheswara Trikalingâdhipati nij bhujo parjitâswapati,
gajapati, narapati Rajatrayâdhipati.
Sri Maj Jaya Sinha Deva vijayarâjye.||

Now, we know that Jaya Sinha Deva was the son of Gaya Karna Deva, and the younger brother of Nara Sinha Deva. Who then was Vâma Deva? In the Bharhut inscription the very same titles are given to Nara Sinha Deva, who is also said to have bowed to the feet (pâdânudhyata) of Vàma Deva. Either Vâma must be taken as another name of Gaya Karna, or as that of the original founder of the family. At first I

thought that Vâma might have been intended for Siva himself, and this would seem to be the truth, as in the next inscription, B., Jaya Sinha's son Vijaya also bows down to the
feet of Vâma Deva.

The inscription goes on to say that during the time of
Kîrtti Varmma the Kaurava Mahâranak of Kakareḍi nagari,
the village of Ahir-pâr-grama was given to two Brahmans
on the anniversary of the death ceremony of Rânak Balarâja at Pindârchansthan.

Kakareḍi, or Kakareṛi, is a large place on the table-land
at the head of the principal Pass, the Mamani Ghât, leading
to the west towards Bânda and Kâlanjar and Mahoba.

B.—This inscription is engraved on one plate. It records
a grant made in the Samvat year 1253, on Friday, the 7th of
the waxing moon of Mârgasirsha, during the reign of Vijaya
Deva. The donor is Salakhana Varmma Deva, the grandson
of Kîrtti Varmma Deva, of Inscription A, and the chief of
Kakareḍi. The date is twenty-one years later than A, taking
the Samvat to be that of Vikramâditya, which agrees with the
relationship of Salakhana Varmma as grandson of Kîrtti
Varmma of Kakaredi, as well as with that of Vijaya Deva as
son of Jaya Sinha Deva, the paramount lord of that country.

By my calculation the week day comes out Thursday,
instead of Friday, as stated on the plate.

The inscription records the gift of the village of Nauagra-
ma, in the district of Kakareḍi-sthâna to certain Brahmans
of the Kausika gotra by name, and ends with the usual
denouncement of the resumers of land, who will suffer for
60,000 years in hell.

C.—This inscription is engraved on two sheets of copper
with a short postscript on the back of the second sheet, giving
the names of the donees, with the measure of the land which
each of them received.

The grant of the village of Rehi is dated in Kârtika of
the Samvat year 1297, or A.D. 1240, and was made by
Kumâra Pâla Deva, the Mahâranak of Kakareḍi, to six Brahmans of the Kaundinya gotra, named Sânge, Suhaṛ, Mahâ-
datta, Pem Singh, Soma Biro, and Sâmanta, of whom the

first four received 3 biswas each, and the last two only one biswa each.

The date is given in words, as well as in figures, as follows :—

Saptanavatyâdhike dwâdaṣa ṣata Samvatsare, Ankepi 1297.

A great part of the record is taken up with the praises of the city (*Nagari*) of Kakaredi, which is said to possess many high temples and white-washed houses, with tanks, wells, and baolis, hills and caves, gardens and big trees, learned men and beautiful women ;—such is Kakaredi, the city of the Kaurava race !

The donor is Kumâra Pala Deva, the Mahârânak or chief of Kakaredi, under the paramount sovereign Trailokya Varmma Deva, whose titles are exactly the same as those of Jaya Sinha Deva and Vijaya Deva, in the two preceding inscriptions A and B. As he is also called a worshipper (pâdâ-nudhyâta) of Vâma Deva, it is certain that the god Siva must be intended, and not one of his ancestors.

But the change in the name of the king is remarkable, as there can be little doubt that Trailokya Varmma Deva is the Chandel prince of Kâlanjar, who was actually reigning at the date of the inscription. He succeeded his father Paramârddi Deva in A.D. 1203, when the Muhammadans captured Kâlanjar. The only other inscription of Trailokya that I have got was found in the fort of Ajaygarh. It is dated in Samvat 1269, or A.D. 1212, when it is probable that Ajaya-garh was still his capital. But, as I have shown in my notice of the Chandel kingdom, he was in full possession of Kâlan-jar in A.H. 631, or A.D. 1233, when the troops of Iltitmish, king of Delhi, invaded that territory for the sake of plunder. His father Paramârddi had lost Mahoba to Prithirâj ; but from the present inscription it would appear that the power of the Chandel princes was but little broken when they extended their dominion to the east, by the conquest of the Rewa territory, which they must have wrested from the Kalachuris during the reign of Trailokya himself. The Chandelas still hold possessions in the eastern portion of the Rewa territory, and they are even more numerous in the districts of Mirzapur and Jaunpur to the north, to which they must have retired before the increasing power of the Bâghels.

D.—This inscription is engraved on three smaller plates. The paramount sovereign is named Trailokya Malla, but, as the Samvat date of 1298 is only one year later than that of the last inscription, C., there can be little doubt that the two records refer to the same king. The reigning chief of Kakareḍi is here named Prithiraja, the son of Salakshana Varmma, and therefore a brother of Kumâra Pala Deva of the previous inscription, C.

The grant gives a similar glowing description of the city of Kakareḍi-nagari as in C., with the genealogy of the donor from the Kaurava chief Châhila downwards. The gift of the village of Barbarâ to certain Brahmans of the Sândilya gotra was made in the month of Mâgha in Samvat 1298, or A.D. 1241. The names of the donees are the same as in C., with the exception of the last, namely—

Râüt Sânge	.	.	.	.	2 biswas of land.
Râüt Suhar	.	.	.	.	4 do. do.
Râüt Mahâdatta	.	.	.	3 do. do.
Râüt Sâmant	.	.	.	8 do. do.
Râüt Kirtu Yuvarâj Singh	.	3 do. do.
TOTAL	.	.	20 biswas.

The family of the Mahârânaks, or chiefs of Kakareḍi, as derived from these four inscriptions, is as follows, with their approximate dates :—

A. D. 1050.—Châhila.
   ,,   1075.—Durjaya.
   ,,   1100.—Bhoja Varmma Deva.
   ,,   1125.—Jaya Varmma Deva.
   ,,   1150.—Vatsa Raja, or Balarâja Deva.
   ,,   1175.—Kirtti Varmma } brothers.
   ,,   1196.—Salakhana
   ,,   1220.—Harirâja (1240)
            Nâhara Varmma } Sons of Salakhana.
   ,,   1241.—Prithvi Raja Deva

3.—GURGI-MASÂUN.

The ruins of Gûrgi-Masaun are situated 12 miles to the east of Rewa, on an open plain, near the sources of the Mahâ Nadi River, which, at 20 miles to the north, forms the famous waterfall of Kevati-Kund.

The remains consist of a large fort called Rehuta, to the east of the village of Silchat, and a large mound 1 mile to the south-west, covered with ruined temples. The actual villages of Gûrgi and Masâun lie 1 mile to the west. On the south-east, upwards of 1 mile distant, flows the Bichia Nadi, the principal feeder of the Bihar River, which forms the great waterfall of Chachai, 368 feet in height. To the south-west of the mound of ruined temples, and more than a mile distant, there is a solitary hill called Goragad, crowned with a modern temple.[1] To the south and east, about 8 miles, the view is bounded by the Kaimur range of hills, which divides the valley of the Tons from that of the Son. In every direction the eye falls upon numerous large tanks, which form a characteristic feature of this part of Rewa. The country is generally well wooded and well cultivated.

All old Hindu cities are remarkable for the number of their *Pân-bâris*, or "Pân gardens." Mahâsthân, the old capital of North Bengal, is literally surrounded by them, and many still exist around Kanauj. The Pân gardens of Gûrgi are famous, and the cities of Allahabad and Benares are said to be chiefly supplied from this source. In fact, the shortest and most frequented route leading from Gûrgi to the north, past the Kevati-Kûnd, descends from the Vindhya Hills by the Panyâri or Panwâri Pass, on which I met numerous bullocks, laden with packs of Pân leaves, going to the Bargarh station of the Allahabad and Jabalpur Railway.

The fort of Rehuta is unanimously ascribed to Raja Karan Dahariya, who is supposed to have been a Bhar chief. But his very title of Dahariya shows that he must have been the famous Karna Deva, the Kalachuri Raja of Dâhal or

---

[1] See Plate XXXV, for a map of these ruins.

Chedi. His father, Gânggeya Deva, is known to have possessed the Rewa territory, as we have an inscription bearing his name, carved on the Argha at the foot of the Piâwan waterfall, in which he is called the Dahaliya Raja. Another inscription of Nara Sinha Deva still exists in the Alha Ghât, between the Piâwan and Kevati-Kûnd waterfalls, in which the Kalachuri Raja also takes the title of Dahaliya. It is certain, therefore, that the territory of Rewa belonged to the Kalachuri Raja Karna Deva of Dâhal, and to him we must assign the building of the fort of Rehuta. His reign extended from A.D. 1040 to 1080. Some of the temples may, perhaps, be older, as the few inscriptions which I obtained agree better in their characters with those of the earlier Kalachuri Rajas Lakshmana and Kokalla.

The fort of Rehuta, or Rehunta, or Gûrgi-Masâun, as it is usually called, is irregular in shape, as the east and west sides slope inwards from the south to the north, thus shortening the northern face by about 1,400 feet. The four faces are irregular ; the east and west faces being much intended and the north and south faces being of unequal length. I make the measurements as follows :—

					Feet.
North face	.	.	.	.	1,980
South ,,	.	.	.	.	3,432
West ,,	.	.	.	.	3,168
East ,,	.	.	.	.	3,234
TOTAL			.		11,814 circuit.

It is difficult to measure the faces exactly, but the circuit may be taken at 12,000 feet, or 2½ miles. According to Mr. Garrick's measurement the circuit is 452 feet greater than I make it.

The outline of the fort is well defined by the stone walls, which are still standing on all sides. They are between 10 and 11 feet thick, and were probably 20 feet in height, as they still reach 15 feet in many places. The remains of the ditch are still quite distinct, from 40 to 50 feet broad and 5 feet deep.

There are no towers or bastions now visible, although I thought that I could trace the basement of a circular tower at the south-west corner.

In the interior there are numerous stone wells, all square in form, and many mounds of stone ruins, from which the wrought stones have been removed. Every mound shows numerous broken statues, all belonging to the Brahmanical faith, excepting one near the south gate. Here there are many broken Jain statues, both seated and standing, and all naked. There is a curious two-faced lion. The head is turned at right angles to the body, so that on both sides the spectator has the lion facing him.

Everywhere the temples have been thrown down, and the cut stones removed, leaving masses of shapeless rough stones forming irregular mounds, more or less covered with jungle. There are two clumps of bamboo jungle, both of which are filled with stones and broken statues.

All sorts of absurd tales are told about Raja Karna Dahariya. It is said that he took no land rent, but only some of the iron tools of the cultivators, which he turned into gold. When the *Pádshah* heard this, he invaded the country, when the Raja entered the ground and disappeared.

There is a still more absurd story about the great number of the inhabitants of Gûrgi. A camel, laden with vermilion, on entering the town was stopped by the women, every one of whom dipped her finger in the pigment to make a red streak down the parting of her hair. The Raja fined each of them one cowrie, and the number of cowries is said to have been equal to one year's revenue. As 5,000 cowries are only equal to one rupee, the revenue must have been very small.

The great mound of temple ruins, called *Gurgaj*, is about 1,200 feet square, and from 10 to 15 feet in height. It is a mere confused mass of rough stones, the whole of the squared stones having been carried away to Rewa within the last twenty years by the Dewân of the late Mahârâjâ. The sites of two large temples are now marked by deep pits and the overturned colossal figures which were once enshrined inside.

On the east side of the mound there is a colossal figure of a four-armed goddess, 9 feet 3 inches high and 4 feet 7 inches broad, seated on a lion. The right leg hangs down, but the left leg is drawn up and rests on the lion. This figure is called Devi, and is, no doubt, intended for the goddess Durgâ, whose *vâhan* is a lion.

On the north-west of the mound there is a still larger sculpture of Hara-Gauri, or Siva and Pârvati, lying on its face above a deep hole. The slab is 12 feet 8 inches long by 5 feet 3 inches broad. At the foot is the bull Nandi. The figures are partly cut clear. The great Toran gateway in front of the Raja's palace at Rewa is said to have stood in front of this temple facing the east. If the temples which occupied this mound bore any proportion to the size of the colossal figures which they enshrined, they must have been of considerable size,—certainly not less than 100 feet in height. I could not ascertain whether the temples had *completely* fallen down when the stones were removed, but all the people agreed that they were in ruins. No traces of any inscription, in fact not even a single letter, could be found on this site.

Inside the fort, and under several trees to the north of the village of Silchat, there are numerous statues of all sizes, more or less broken. There are only a few Buddhist figures, but the Jain and Brahmanical figures are numerous. The following list gives the names of such as I could recognize :—

1. Colossal figure of Hanumân.
2. Statue broken at waist, horse below ; on its pedestal is inscribed—

    "*Sri Lakshmi Devi Bhatâraka*
    Bhagini pranamati."
    "Sri Lakshmi Devi, the king's sister offers adoration."

3. Standing Vishnu, 3 feet high, with Brahmâ and Siva to right and left, small.
4. Bhainsâsuri Devi, half-life size,
5. Four-armed female, bull on pedestal.
6. Broken 8-armed female, half-life size.
7. Kâli Devi, skeleton goddess.
8. Three-headed male with four arms, and canopied by a three-snake-hood.

9. Eight-armed figure of Ganesa.
10. Slab, with three snakes, middle one very stout.

There are many other figures, but none of any interest, as there are no inscriptions on them, and they are all more or less broken. The Jaina figures are numerous in the fort, but they are of the usual well-known types, and are not inscribed. The whole of the Gûrgi sculptures are of the same style and age as the two specimens in Plates XXXVI and XXXVII, which were brought from Gûrji to Rewa. From the alphabetical characters of their inscriptions they must belong to the period of Kalachuri rule in the 10th and 11th centuries.

Of the early history of Rewa prior to the occupation of the Bâghels, who still hold the country, nothing whatever is known. Several existing inscriptions, however, show that it must have formed part of the dominions of the Kalachuri kings of Chedi for at least two centuries before the conquest of the Bâghelas. I have already mentioned the inscriptions of Gânggeya Deva and Narasinha Deva at the Piâwan waterfall and the Alha Ghât; but there is a third inscription, and a very long one, in a very fine temple at Chandrehe, close to the Son River, and only 20 miles to the south-east of Rewa, which must certainly have been set up by the Kalachuris of Chedi, as it is dated in Samvat 724. As the characters are those of the 10th century, the date must be recorded in the Chedi era, or A.D. 249+724=A.D. 973, and the inscription must, therefore, belong to the time of Lakshmana, the founder of the Lakshman Sâgar at Bilhari, who reigned from about 950 to 975, or somewhat later.

But it seems highly probable that the Kalachuris must have occupied the country of Rewa for several centuries prior to A.D. 950, as the Kalachuri princes of Southern India claim to have conquered Kâlanjara before they occupied Dahala or Chedi. The tradition is thus given by Mr. Rice from a stone inscription at Harihara, dated about 1160[1] :—

"A Brahmani girl (ilâmara putri), having paid worship to Siva, seated on a hide, in order to obtain the fulfilment of her desires,

---

[1] Mysore Inscriptions, by Lewis Rice, p. 64.

she had a dream, in which Siva himself embraced her, and she conceived a portion of his glory. Having thus conceived, when nine months were accomplished, it happened that she bore a son named Krishna, possessed of great beauty, of surpassing courage, bearing all the marks of fortune, famous in all learning.

" He slew in Kâlanjara an evil spirit of a king, who was a cannibal and followed the occupation of a barber, thus obtaining great fame among all people. Placing him between the teeth of Yama, this king Krishna, by the might of his arms, took possession of the government of his kingdom, and reducing the nine-lakh (*country of*) *Dahala mandala* to obedience to his word, ruled in peace, an ornament of the Kalachuri kula. "

According to this account the progenitor of the race, named Krishna, captured Kâlanjara before he occupied Dahala. He must, therefore, have crossed from Rewa; and, as the initial point of the Chedi, or Kalachuri era, is A.D. 249, it seems probable that this year may, perhaps, mark the date of the capture of Kâlanjara. In this case the Kalachuris must have held the territory of Rewa for nearly one thousand years.

The old name of the country, as given by the Muhammadan historians, is *Bhath*, or *Bhath-ghora*, and sometimes *Pattah Ghorâ-ghât* Blochmann calls it *Bandah* Rewa. In the Maâsir it is spelt Bhattah.[1] It seems not impossible that Bhath-ghora and Ghora-ghât may have some connection with *Gurgaj* and *Gurgi.* The name of Bhath is quite unknown at the present day, and I think it not impossible that it may have originated with some early Muhammadan corruption of the name of Bandho-garh.

The earliest mention that I have found of the name of *Bhati-ghor* is in the Tabakât-i-Nâsiri of Minhâj, under date A.H. 641, or A.D. 1243-44, when Malik Timur Khan-i-kirâ is recorded to have several times plundered the territory of *Bhati-ghor* and extorted tribute. The name is also written *Bhati-ghora* and *Bhath-ghorah*.[2]

4.—BAIJNÂTH.

Eight miles to the west of Rewa, and about 1 mile to the north of the road leading to Sutna, stands the small village of

[1] See Blochmann's Ain Akbari, pp., 122—355 and 406.
[2] Raverty's Tabakât-i-Nâsiri, p. 743.

Baijnâth, which once possessed some five or six temples, of which only one is now standing. This temple was complete until the middle of the last rainy season, when, during the month of Ashâdha, the mandapa fell down. The shrine was dedicated to Mahâdeva as Vaidyanâtha or Baijnâth, who is represented by a lingam inside. The temple consisted of a *mandapa*, or hall, 18 feet square, to the east, supported on sixteen pillars, leading through a small *antarâla*, or ante-chamber, to a sanctum, 14½ feet square outside. The whole building was only 33½ feet by 14½ feet. The entrance to the sanctum is richly carved, with the usual figures of the Ganges and Jumna on the crocodile and tortoise. A figure of the bull Nandi occupies the entrance.

Lying round about there are numerous carved stones and pieces of sculpture. But the most interesting of the remains is a colossal figure of the Ganges, 7 feet 3 inches high and 4 feet 1 inch broad, which is known by the name of *Madâwar*. It has four arms, and on the pedestal, quite detached from the figure, there is a crocodile, 2 feet 3½ inches long.

Close by there is a large lion, and in a rude hut there is a figure of Durgâ seated on a lion, now called Kâli, to whom goats are regularly sacrificed every Monday and Thursday, as well as on other uncertain days. During my stay of one day at Baijnâth no less than ten goats were sacrificed. They were brought at different times by small parties of men and women, accompanied by music. The goats were beheaded on the spot. The heads remained as the perquisite of the executioner, a Kol of the village of Baijnâth. The bodies were carried off by the sacrificers.

I recognized several other sculptures, amongst which were :—

Siva, with a canopy of seven snake-hoods, 4 feet 1 inch by 2 feet 4 inches.

Vishna, with lotus, of same size as Siva.

An annual fair is held at Baijnâth on the *Râm-navami* of Chaitra, or 9th day of the waxing moon. It is attended by thousands of people from all the surrounding country. The people of this part of the country are mostly Kols.

5.—RAYPUR-KOTHI.

Raypur is an old village in the small Bâghel state of Kothi, 14 miles to the north-west of Sutna, and the same distance to the north-east of Nâgodh. About 1850 there existed here a stone inscription, $3\frac{1}{4}$ feet long by $2\frac{1}{2}$ feet high, which was broken in two pieces. I had a rough copy of the inscription which had been taken by one of Colonel Ellis's servants. During my last tour I sent a servant of my own to get a fresh copy, but the stone was gone, and he was informed that it had been taken to Nâgodh, where Colonel Ellis resided before the Mutiny in 1857. My servant then proceeded to Nâgodh, where, after much enquiry, he learned that the stone had been taken to Sutna. He continued his journey to Sutna, where he found that only one portion of the inscription was now in existence. Of this he made a copy, which on examination I found to be the right-hand portion of the Raypur stone, comprising about one-third only of the original record.

The inscription is dated in Samvat 1408, and Sake 1273 (or A.D. 1351), Ashâdha sudi 11 Budhavâsare, or Wednesday. In the 2nd line I find the name of *Nripa Sâlivâhana*, or "king Salivâhan," and in the 10th line *Sri Vira Râja Nripa*. In the 21st line also there is the name of *Sasângka bhûpa*, or "king Sasânka." This record most probably refers to one of the Bâghel Rajas of Rewa. There is a Sati pillar at *Gobari*, 28 miles to the west-south-west of Rewa, which certainly belongs to the same king. He is called Sri Vira Râja Deva, and the monument is dated in Samvat 1407, or A.D. 1350, just one year earlier than the Raypur inscription. I think it probable that both records belong to the Bâghel Raja Bhairava Deva (as his name is written in the chronicles), who reigned from A.D. 1335 to 1355. I have referred to this inscription in my previous Report, *ante* page 76.

6.—KIYÂN, OR KEN RIVER.

On looking over the old maps of the country about the sources of the Ken River, I found so many notes of "ruined temples" that I determined to explore the whole country lying between Jukahi on the Jabalpur Railway and Saugor, a distance of about 120 miles. This tract includes all the main branches of the Ken, or Kiyân River, which, beginning on the east, are named as follows :—

1. The *Aloni* River rises to the south of the Sati Pahâr, near Bilhari. It is a fine, clear, rapid stream, about knee-deep, and 25 feet broad. It joins the Ken 8 miles to the north-west of the Jukahi railway station.

2. The *Ken*, or *Kiyân* River, rises to the north of the Sati Pahâr, 12 miles to the north-west of Bilhari. It flows generally down a rocky bed; and about 10 miles from its source passes between two groups of temples at Chhoti Deori and Simra. Still further to the north-east are the old villages of Suror and Paraini, which still possess some remains of antiquity.

3. The *Pâtna* River rises in the Kaimur range at Bahuriband, 20 miles to the south-west of Bilhari. It is a fine stream, and near its banks are the extensive ruins of Bargaon and Nând-Chând.

4. The *Biarme*, or *Bermi* River, rises in the Vindhya Hills 50 miles to the south-east of Saugor. It is a large river, 200 feet broad and $2\frac{1}{2}$ feet deep. Near its left bank is a famous group of Jaina temples at Kundalpur, with a few old Brahmanical shrines.

5. The *Bewas* River rises 30 miles to the south-east of Saugor. It is a much larger stream than the Ken, which it joins 12 miles to the north of Damoh, after a course of 80 miles.

6. The *Sonar* River rises in the Vindhya Hills, 30 miles to the south of Saugor, and joins the Ken, 50 miles to the north-east of Damoh. At Garha Kota it is a fine, clear, rapid stream.

7. The *Kopra* River rises 30 miles to the south-west of Damoh, and joins the Sonar, 16 miles to the north of Damoh.

After the junction of all these tributaries the Ken River becomes a fine stream, little, if at all, inferior to the Betwa. It flows through the middle of the Chandel country, having Mahoba and Khajurâha on the west, and Kâlanjar and Ajaygarh on the east.

7.—PARAINI.

Paraini is an old village on the right bank of the Ken River, 11 miles to the west of the Jukahi railway station. There are the ruins of several temples on the bank of a tank to the north of the village. The principal object is the statue of a boar, 5 feet 3 inches long, with a snake of seven hoods raising itself in front, and two human figures, male and female, to the right.

8.—SUROR.

Suror is a good-sized village, 2½ miles from Paraini, on the left bank of the Ken River. Here there is an old Sati Pillar, with a curious inscription, giving the name of the Muhammadan king. It consists of five lines, which I read as follows :—

1. Samvat 1385 samaye 1 Jyeshtha sudi 4 Sanau | Suraudi
2. Sâthâne 1 Suratrân Mahamuda Mojdin râjye || Sri Ajitamâ
3. Deva bhujyamâne | Brahmana anwayapam |

There is a difficulty about the name and title of the Muhammadan king. The date of Samvat 1385 is equal to A.D. 1328, which was near the beginning of the reign of Muhammad Tughlak. I would, however, hazard a guess from the title of Mojdin, that the writer's intention was to refer to Muizuddin Muhammad bin Sâm, the founder of the Muhammadan empire of Delhi, and that the name of the actual reigning king was unknown at the sources of the Ken River in the beginning of the 14th century of the Christian era.

9.—CHHOTI DEORI.

Chhoti Deori, or "the small temple," is the name of an extensive group of small temples, from thirty to forty in number, buried in dense jungle on the left bank of the Ken River, 5 miles to the west of Paraini. All of the temples faced the east, and were most probably lingam shrines. I saw four arghas and 1 lingam *in situ*, but I was unable to trace the plan of any of the temples owing to the thick covering of prickly pear bushes. The name of Chhoti Deori has reference to the greater temples at Simra, on the opposite side of the Ken River.

There is one inscribed pillar at Chhoti Deori which I have already brought to notice in my last year's report. It is inscribed about the middle of a square pillar of 13 inches each side. It gives the name of Raja Sankaragana, which is, I believe, quite peculiar to the Kalachuri line of princes. I can find no one to read the inscription, as the language is declared not to be Sanskrit. The characters are distinct enough, and are decidedly of an early date—perhaps as early as the 7th century.

10.—SIMRA.

The large village of Simra stands on the right bank of the Ken River, near the northern end of the Sati Pahar, about 10 miles from Marwâra and the Katni station of the Jabalpur Railway. To the east of the village there are the ruins of four temples, one large and three small. On the embankment of the Bara Tâl, or Great Tank, there are the remains of a fifth temple, with a lingam and two broken figures of Vishnu and Hanumân. Here also is a large slab, with a man and woman standing sculptured on it, and the following inscription—

Samvat 1355, Sake 1220,
Râm Dausat Singh patnika.

"*In Samvat 1355, Sake 1220, Râm Dausat Singh's wife.*"

This is clearly a sati monument, dated in A.D. 1298, in memory of the wife of Râm Dausat Singh.

In the village there are squared stones lying in heaps. These are said to have been collected some twenty years ago by a Railway Saheb, who came from Marwâra to obtain stones for the bridge over the Katni River near Marwâra. An old woman stated that she remembered the great temple standing. The Saheb is said to have got his foot hurt, or his leg broken, and so left the stones lying where they now are !

From the style of carving the temples would appear to have been of the same age as those of Bilahri, or of the 10th century. The following figures belonged to the large temple, and must have formed a belt of sculpture round the walls outside. They are all from 2 feet 6 inches to 2 feet 8 inches in height—(1) four-armed Vishnu ; (2) godâdhar Vishnu ; (3)

Hara-Gowri; (4) four-armed Brahmâ standing; (5) eight-armed Durgâ; (6) Vishnu sitting on Garuda; (7) Ganesa.

11.—RITHI.

The village of Rithi is situated near the head of the Ken River, at the junction of the two roads from Jukahi and Mar-wâra to Damoh. It is 18 miles to the north-west of Marwâra. To the east of the village there is a long heap of cut and carved stones, the remains of some ten or twelve temples. Only one statue is now left; but there are numerous pieces of flat roofing slabs, with lotus flowers, and some eight or ten pieces of amalaka pinnacles.

The group of temples near the large tank is called *Barâh-Deoka sthân*, and there is an old statue of the Varâha incarnation of Vishnu trampling on a Nâga.

In the village there are the jambs and lintel of a richly carved doorway, with Vishnu seated on Garuda in the middle of the lintel, and a figure of the Ganges on her crocodile on the right jamb.

A portion of a roofing slab has been used as a Sati pillar, 5 feet 6 inches in height. In the upper panel there is a figure of Siva with four arms, and below are two men fighting. One is armed with bow and arrow and attended by a horse. The other is about to throw a spear.

The source of the Ken River itself does not appear to be considered holy, as there are no shrines established there.

12.—NÂND-CHÂND.

Nând-Chând is a small village, situated on an island, formed by the junction of two branches of the Kundo Nala with the Pâtna River, one of the principal tributaries of the Ken, or Kiyân River. On the bank of the Pâtna River there are some fine Hindu remains, consisting of a ruined temple and a Toran gateway, with numerous statues. The place is 8 miles to the north of the high road leading from the Jabalpur Railway to Damoh, being 25 miles to the west north-west of Marwâra, and 40 miles to the east-north-east of Damoh.

A great melâ, or fair, is held here annually on the Sivarâtri or Phâlguna badi 14, and another on the Basant of Mâgh.

The remains at Nând-Chând are the following:—

1. Ruined temple of Martangesar or Mritangeswara, "the Lord of the dead," a name of Siva, with a large lingam still standing *in situ*. The lingam is 6 feet 8 inches high and 2 feet 1½ inches in diameter. At 222 feet 9 inches to the east there is a lofty Toran, or gateway, with a colossal statue on each side· These figures are 8 feet 6 inches high. They face one another at a distance of 20 feet 9 inches apart, and 17½ feet from the gateway inside the enclosure. Each had a halo round the head, and rests one arm on the head of a male figure, 5 feet 4 inches in height.

2. To the south of the gateway lie two broken octagonal pillars of large size, 1 foot 11 inches diameter at bottom, and a very curious capital, 1 foot 11 inches broad. These may have formed another gateway.*

3. Close by, on the south, there are the ruins of several small temples—one lintel 3 feet 7½ inches, with two pillars of portico 5 feet 4 inches high.

4. At a short distance to the south-east, on the western bank of a tank (about 150′ × 100′), there is a long row of small ruined temples, not less than ten or twelve, with about a dozen statues, nearly all of the same dimensions, averaging 4′ × 2′. Apparently these temples contained the Ashta-sakti and several lingams, besides a figure of Ganesa and one of Vishnu, a Siva with ten arms and a Hara-Gauri.

5. To the north-west of the tank there are the remains of a stone temple with lingam.

6. To the north-east, on the bank of the Pâtna River, there are the remains of two temples, one of which was a lingam shrine.

Not a single inscription could be found on any of the statues.

The style of the architecture seems old—perhaps as old as 700 A.D. And, if so, the name of Sri Karna Deva cannot be of the same age, as the letters are as late as 1000 or 1100 A.D.

The gateway, or Toran, consists of two pillars, each 1 foot

* See Plate XLI for a sketch of one of these pillars.

6 inches square and 14 feet 6 inches high. They stand 7 feet aqart, and support an architrave, 1 foot 7 inches in depth. The total height is 16 feet 1 inch as it now stands. The people unanimously described it as lofty enough for an elephant to pass under it, which is quite correct, as its clear height of 14½ feet would be amply sufficient for an elephant with a rider on its back. The Toran stands 222¾ feet to the east of the temple ; and at 22 feet to the west of it there are two colossal statues, each 8½ feet high, and 20¾ feet apart, one to the right, and the other to the left, of the path leading to the temple. Apparently there has been a raised courtyard all round the temple extending as far as the Toran on the east, and surrounded by a brick wall.*

The pillars of the Toran are square for the lower 3 feet, and slightly moulded above. They are without capitals. The architrave is ornamented with five bee-hive-shaped bosses.

At a short distance from the Toran there are two broken octagonal pillars with heavy capitals of a rather early date, similar to those at Eran and Udayagiri. They are lying quite loose and detached, and there is nothing to show what they belonged to. Perhaps they formed part of the portico of one of the temples on the bank of the neighbouring tank.

To the south-east of the Toran, on the western bank of a large tank, there is a long row of small ruined temples, the walls of which were mostly made of single upright slabs. The following statues were found amongst the ruins :—

1.	Siva, with 10 arms			4′ 9″	×	2′ 0″
2.	Hara-Gauri			3 7	×	2 1
3.	Three-headed goddess, 4 arms			3 11	×	1 9
4.	Goddess on peacock, 2 arms			4 1	×	2 0
5.	Standing goddess, 4 arms			3 11	×	2 1
6.	Four-armed goddess with child, seated on elephant			4 0	×	2 0
7.	Nara-Sinha, 4 arms			3 8	×	2 2
8.	Four-armed goddess, with bull			3 11	×	2 0
9.	Ganesa, 4 arms			3 6	×	2 0
10.	Goddess, with 2 arms, sitting with child, 7-hooded canopy			2 8	+ 1	6

* See Plate XL for a sketch of this Toran gateway.

Each of these had a small slab temple, 2 feet 8 inches broad, and the same in depth inside. I traced eight distinct temples ; but there must have been several more, chiefly very small ones. One of these, which I was able to measure, was found to be only 3 feet 1 inch by 2 feet 4 inches outside, and 2 feet 7½ inches by 1 foot 2½ inches inside. It was 2 feet 7½ inches high.

Only one inscription could be found after a diligent search of two days. It was carved on a large flat slab, which was perhaps a side wall of one of the small temples. The characters may belong to the 9th or 10th century. I read it as *Sri Karna Deva.* If this is intended for the great Kalachuri king of Chedi, the date must lie between A.D. 1040 and 1080 ; but the style of the temple is apparently much earlier.

13.—BARGAON.

Bargaon is a large village of 500 houses. It is situated on the high road leading from the Jabalpur Railway to Damoh and Saugor. It is 8 miles to the south-west of Nând-Chând, and only 2 miles from the right bank of the Pâtna River. It possesses a large number of ruined temples, both Brahmanical and Jain. I counted no less than thirty-five, all of which have been determined by actual survey ; but several must have escaped observation, as I found it very difficult to distinguish each separate small temple amongst the great mass of ruins. Many of them are extremely small, and are only to be discovered by the square flat slabs which once formed their roofs.

The greater number of the Bargaon temples are mere confused heaps of stones. Many of the smaller ones can still be measured ; but the larger ones are generally inaccessible. In several instances some portions of the doorways have been found, and in one instance the outer entrance of the great temple to the west is still standing, with a figure of Garuda carved in the middle of the lintel. This temple must, therefore, have been dedicated to Vishnu.

The temple of Somnâth, in the village, is quite different, both in style and plan, from all the other shrines at Bargaon.

They are of the usual type, with pillared mandapas and sculptured walls; but Somnâth has no pillars, and its walls are quite plain, with the exception of a single string moulding, and the edges of the flat roof. Its construction is also quite different, as its walls are perpendicular, and the stones are fastened together with iron cramps instead of being laid upon the top of one another without fastenings of any kind, like a house of cards. Unfortunately the villagers found out that these iron cramps have a value, however small, and they have accordingly cut them out with chisels from all the courses within their reach. All the upper courses above 6 feet are still in perfect preservation. Its stability has been farther ensured by the massiveness of the three stones covering the entrance, one above the other. The lowest, which forms the sculptured architrave, is 14 feet 4 inches long by 3 feet 7 inches high, and 3 feet 4 inches thick and contains 170 cubic feet. The other two are equally long, but not so high. These three stones are marked AB, CD, and EF, in the elevation given in Plate XXXVIII.

The roof, as seen at present, is a low pyramid of steps, of which the uppermost stone is the square slab that forms the top of the ceiling. But, as all these stones are rough at the sides, it is certain that they must have been hidden by the dressed stones which formed the outer faces of the walls. The roof must, therefore, have been flat outside, like those of the Gupta temples. This seems highly probable, as I found two flat slabs lying on the ground to the north and north-west, which, from their sculptured edges, must have formed part of the outer course of roofing stones.

I have given a sketch of one of these stones, Plate XXXIX.

In the plan and elevation also will be seen a string course which still exists at 13½ feet above the plinth, or a few feet below the upper edge of the roofing slabs. This also is a peculiarity common to all the Gupta temples that I have seen. The temples of Sânchi, Udayagiri, Tigowa, Deogarh, and Pathaora, all have this string course at a few feet below the roof.

I searched diligently for other stones which might have

formed part of the outer roof, but could not find even a single fragment. Had the roof been a pyramidal spire, many of the carved stones would have been still there, as they would have been useless for common village-work. But, on the other hand, the stones of all flat roofs would have been at once available for all kinds of purposes, for the walls, for pavements, or for seats. I conclude that the villagers got upon the flat roof, cut out the iron cramps of the outer layers (the holes still exist in the two sculptured roofing stones already described), and then threw the slabs down. All the middle stones were too massive to be easily moved, and these still remain *in situ.*

Inside, the roof is formed by cutting off the corners of the sanctum by three successive overlaps until the fourth opening could be spanned by a single square slab, which must be about 10 or 11 feet square. The lower surface of this slab is carved with a large lotus flower. It is 23 feet 4 inches above the floor of the temple.

The lingam of Somnâth is 2 feet 2 inches in diameter, and 4 feet in height. It stands on a square pedestal, 6 feet 3 inches each side.

Outside, the temple is 34 feet by 24½ feet, and the sanctum inside is 13 feet 5 inches by 12 feet 7 inches.

A very diligent search was made for inscriptions for two days, but the only result was one very long record too much injured to be read, except in a few places : see A of Plate* and a short line on a pillar reading *Sri Bhâsam Bodha tapaswi.* The large inscription is 5 feet long and 1 foot 2 inches high. A third inscription was found by a barber, standing on end and half sunk in the ground. It is 3 feet long and 1 foot broad. The upper part, or left end above ground, had been used as a sharpening stone for so long a time that a great part is now worn away. It is incomplete also at the right end. The characters are similar to those in use in the 9th and 10th centuries. In the 1st line I can read the words *Vigraha Chedi*, and in the 10th line *Kalachuri Nripa.* It is certain, therefore, that the record belongs to the Kalachuri kings of Chedi.

* Plate XXXIX—A, B, and C.

Many of the stones of the Somnâth temple also possess masons' marks of about the same age as the great inscription, but they appear to be simply the names of workmen, such as Chhitara, Bhote.

A few miles to the north of Bargaon at Nayakhera I found a slab 5 feet long and 2¼ feet broad, covered with round "cup-marks," from 1 inch to 3½ inches in diameter, to which the boys of the village were still adding fresh ones. I counted 136 marks. The whole of these cup-marks were said to have been made by the boys. In fact, I saw a boy making one during the course of the day, and several of them looked very fresh.

14.—KUNDALPUR.

The famous Jain temples of Kundalpur are situated on the northern end of a range of low hills, on the left bank of the Bearmi River, 20 miles to the north-east of Damoh.

There was formerly held here a very grand melâ, which is said to have lasted for the greater part of the month of Chaitra. The Deputy Commissioner, owing to the constant mortality that attended these meetings from the heat and great crowds, got the leading men to agree to hold the melâ some time in Mâgh, during the cold season. The proposal was accepted, and an agreement was signed; but when the time came for holding the melâ, the people stayed away, and no melâ has now been held for thirteen or fourteen years.

The Jain temples are all square blocks, with dome-roofs and pinnacles at the corners. They are all whitewashed, and look very like Muhammadan tombs.

The principal temple contains a colossal image of Mahâ-vira or Vardhamâna, and is known generally as Bardhmân. The pedestal is 4 feet high, and the figure is 12 × 11 feet, seated, with lions on pedestal.

There is an inscription of twenty-four lines of the time of Mahârâja-dhirâjâ Sri Chhatra Sâla, dated in Samvat 1757, Mâgh badi 15 Somavâsare (Monday 31st December A.D. 1700). In the 4th line I find the name of Sri Vardhamâna and in the 8th line the terms Jina Mârga and Jinadharma. The temple is 16 feet square inside. On a small temple in the courtyard there is a short inscription in large letters of two lines, as follows :—

> Samvat 1501 varshc Paush sudi 2.
> Gurau dine vâ Sri Guru Nâkîni sahî.

The week-day by calculation is Saturday, and not Thursday, as stated.

There are, altogether, 50 Jaina temples, of which 20 are on the hill, and 30 at the foot near the Vardhamâna Talao. A new temple, No. 51, is now building.

After some search two old Brahmanical temples were found at the foot of the hill near the Vardhamâna talao. They are both of the single slab and flat-roof pattern, and are, of course, small. Both face the north. One of them is empty, but the other still holds a standing figure of Vishnu.

These temples are similar to the flat-roofed shrines of Udayagiri, Sânchi, and Tigowa, and possess the same peculiarity of a band of moulding running round the body of the building at the level of the roof of the portico. The pillars of the portico are indented at the angles, and the plinth is surmounted by a simple and bold moulding, but the walls are quite plain.

The larger temple is only 13 feet long by 7 feet broad, and the other is a few inches less. They are weather-stained and mouldy, and look very old ; but there is nothing to show their exact age. They probably belong to the later Gupta period, about 600 A.D., but the figure of Vishnu does not appear to be so old—see Plate XLII for a plan and elevation of the larger temple. The slab walls are 9 inches thick in both temples, and the roofs are formed of two large slabs, one covering the sanctum, and the other the portico. The construction is simple and durable. Temples of this kind would, in fact, last for ages, if not attacked by violence, or the roots of trees. This is cleary shown by the great numbers of these small slab temples which still exist in Gwalior and Malwa, as well as in Bundelkhand and Rewa.

15.—HINDORIA.

Hindoria is a large old town, 10 miles to the north-east of Damoh. It possesses numerous Sati pillars, of which the oldest that I could find was dated in Samvat 1113, or A.D. 1056. There are also many carved stones and remains of temples. The jambs of a temple doorway were found built up in the entrance gateway of a Chatri, with the original sill of the door placed on the top as a lintel. The jambs have the figures of the Ganges and Jumna standing on the crocodile and tortoise, as usual.

As Hindoria is in the open country, leading from Damoh to Kundalpur and Hutta, and so on *viâ* Nagodh to Allahabad, it could not escape the destructive zeal of the Muhammadan kings of Malwa, who would appear to have been quite as tyrannical as the fanatical iconoclasts of Bengal.

16.—DAMOH.

Damoh is a large old town, situated at the foot of a high hill, 45 miles to the east of Saugor. Every old building has been destroyed, and there now remains only the shrine of the Muhammadan saint Ghāzi Miah, and the fort built of Hindu ruins.

I got a fragment of a large Sanskrit inscription of twenty-five lines, but the date is gone. I got also copies of the inscriptions from two Sati pillars, dated respectively in Samvat 1336 and 1341. The latter one gives the name of *Damoh-sthâna* at the beginning of the 2nd line, in the time of Rau Sri Jaya Sinha.

Standing at the Kacheri there is a Muhammadan inscription, which was brought from the fort, and is said to have been originally over the western gate. It is dated in the year A.H. 880, or A.D. 1475, in the reign of Ghiâs Shâh, of Mâlwa. The following is the text of this record with its translation, which has been kindly prepared for me by Maulvi Ata Rahmân.

باد محروس و مصون از فتن و ذل زوال	یارب این عرصه دمره بجهان در همه حال
که آساس همه اشرار بکرد استیصال	مقطع عرصه مذکور ملک مخلص شلک
ماحی کفرستم واهب کان زر و مال	دائی علم و علم صاحب سیف است و قلم
بادشاه همه آفاق و ملک ذرالاقبال	خاص خواس شهنشاه غیاث الدنیا

پیش دروازهٔ غبر پیش سرسس گشته   این فیصل است که مرتّب شده از مقطع حال

در سنهٔ هیصد و هشتاد و دیگر پنج برد   بست و چهارم بده تاریخ زماه شوال

ای رغامی صفت شاه و خراصش چه کنی   زانکه ناید صفت شان بیان اقوال

1. O God! May this land of Damoh remain safe in the world under all circumstances, and protected from disturbances and the disgrace of decay.

2. The donor of the aforesaid tract of land, the friend of the country, who has pulled up by the roots the sources of all evil.

3. The master of letters and banners, the wielder of the sword and the pen, the destroyer of infidelity and iniquity, the giver of mines of gold and of wealth,

4. The chosen one of the personal attendants of the king Ghiàs-ud-dunya, the ruler of the world from horizon to horizon, and the most conspicuous of monarchs.

5. Opposite the western gate of the fort this breast-work has been built by the above donor,

6. In the year 885, on the 24th of Shawâl.

7. O Raghâni (Poet) dost thou try to sing the praises and peculiar virtues of this king! His praise cannot be compassed by the descriptive power of language.

17.—BIYA–KUND.

Biya Kûnd is a hot spring in the small state of Bijâwar in Bundelkhand. It is just 40 miles due south from the cantonment of Nowgong.

The Kûnd is really a cave, and a rent has been made in the rock to let in light. The pool is 50 feet long and 32 feet broad. Rude irregular steps have been cut in the rock; and shelters have been formed in different places, by raising pillars in front of overhanging rocks.

A great mêla is held on the 15th of Mâgh badi, when several thousands of people are said to assemble.

I had repeatedly heard of this famous Kûnd, and of a Bhim-lâth, or monolith, near it; and I was much disappointed that there was nothing of any interest at so holy a place.

Near Dargoa (or Dargama), on the high road leading up to the Kûnd, there is a very long cave, but not lofty, as people are obliged to stoop constantly in going along it.

There are several pools of water. A Fakir formerly lived in this cave. It is several hundred feet long, but very narrow and very winding, and irregular in shape.

18.—SAURAI.

Saurai is a large old village, which must have derived its name from the *Sauras* or *Savaras*, as there are still sixty houses of them in this one place. It is 27 miles to the west of Shâhgarh, and 9 miles to the north of Madanpur.

It possesses three stone temples, which are said to be of the Chandel time, and are all attributed to Baniyas. The largest one is a Jain temple, dedicated to Adinâth, whose image is still inside with a bull on the pedestal.

The other two temples are Vaishnavi, with Vishnu over the middle of the door.

The best preserved of these temples is a Jaina structure, facing the north. It has a small portico in front, 10 feet 2 inches square, the whole temple being only 21 feet 6 inches long by 13 feet broad. But, in spite of its small size, it is a fine building, as it is richly ornamented outside with two rows of sculptures, of which some are the usual naked standing figures, of the Jains, while the rest are Brahmanical figures. On one face of each bracket capital of the portico there is a human figure carved, with his head downwards. These figures are sunken and appear to be of later work.

In the village there are two slab-built temples dedicated to Vishnu, whose image is over the middle of the doorway, with those of Brahma and Siva at the sides. The slabs forming the walls are 8 inches thick. Both temples have porticoes. See Plate XLII for a plan of the larger temple.

On an upright slab at a well there is an inscription of six lines as follows :—

1. Samvat 1707 varshe, Jeth sudi 7, saumavâsare ;
2. Nripa Sri Sâhi Jahân arnal, Sri Nawâb Sar—
3. -dâr Khân, Parigane Dhâmoni, moje Saurai, Chaudhari
4. Hari Chandan Lodhi Thâkur ; tasya pu. Chaudhari A-
5. * va * Dâs Kua banwayo. Likhitam Mâdho-
6. -patvâris. Bhavatu Mangalam.

"In the Samvat year 1707 on the 7th of the waxing moon of Jyeshtha, on Monday, during the reign of the king Sri Shâh Jahân, and under the government of Sri Nawâb Sardâr Khân, in the Parganah of Dhâmoni, and town of Saurai, the son of Chaudhari Hari Chandan Lodi, Chaudhari Dâs, made this well. Written by Mâdho Patwâri. May it be fortunate."

The date corresponds with Monday 27th May A.D. 1650.

Saurai must once have been a very flourishing place. It is well situated, on the high road leading from Jhânsi and Lalitpur through the Madanpur Pass to Saugar.

19.—MADANPUR.

The town of Madanpur is situated at the head of one of the principal passes leading from Saugor to Lalitpur, Jhansi, and Gwalior. It was formerly a place of much consequence, as it possessed the best stone quarries in this part of the country, and several very fine temples. To this point the army of the Chauhân Prince, Prithi Raj, advanced after his conquest of Mahoba, and carved his name on the pillars of the great temple as the conqueror of Paramârdi, King of Jejâbhukti, or Jajahuti.

There is a lake of some size, formed by throwing an embankment across the valley on the north. The embankment is from 76 to 100 feet thick, and is covered with numbers of Muhammadan tombs, generally formed of carved flat slabs.

Madanpur is said to have been founded by Madana Varmma, the Chandel Raja of Mahoba; but there is at least one inscription of Samvat 1112, or A.D. 1055, which is older than Madana Varmma, who reigned from 1129 to 1165 A.D. It seems probable, therefore, that he only renamed the place, and that the old site, now called "old Madanpur," was the original city under another name, which was changed to Madanpur by Madana Varmma. This old city was situated on the ground to the north of the village, in the neighbourhood of the Jain temples. There are traces of former habitations in numerous fragments of tiles and pottery scattered about the field. This site would naturally have been deserted for the more convenient position of the new town at the end of the lake.

There are six temples at Madanpur, all more or less ruined. The oldest of these are three Jaina temples situated to the north of the town, where the original town is said to have stood. Two others are at the north-west corner of the lake, and the sixth at some distance to the north-east of the lake.

A. The principal Jain temple is only 30 feet 8 inches long by 14 feet 2 inches broad, including the porticoes. The sanctum inside is $8\frac{1}{2}$ feet by 8 feet, and contains a naked standing figure with an inscription on the pedestal. The roof is a plastered dome of modern work. Outside there is a broken pedestal with a fish on it and an inscription dated in Samvat 1212, or A.D. 1155.

B. Close by on the west there is a second Jain temple facing the last. It also has a plastered dome. It contains five statues, of which I recognised the following :—

1. Adinâth, with a bull on the pedestal;
2. Chandraprabhâ, with a crescent; and
3. Sambhunâth, with a horse on the pedestal.

Near these temples there are two Sati pillars, dated in Samvat 1522 and 1528, or A.D. 1465 and 1471. One of them gives the name of the king Sri Sulitân Mahmud Sâhi Khalchi, with his two chief forts of Mandugarhdûrg and Chanderidûrg, and that of the governor, Phate Khân.

The long inscription in the temple consists of eight lines. It is dated in Samvat 1206, Vaisâkha Sudi 10, Bhaume, or A.D. 1149, Wednesday, 20th April, in the middle of the reign of Madana Varmma.[1] It gives the name of Swasti Sri Madanapura. But the rest of the inscription seems to be taken up with the names of Jaina pilgrims, who came to offer their adorations. There are several inscriptions dated as late as Samvat 1692.

The two Brahmanical temples at the north-west corner of the lake must have been very fine buildings. The sanctum of both temples is gone entirely, but many stones still remain to show that they were highly decorated. Both face the east. They were most probably dedicated to Vishnu

---

[1] The week day should be Tuesday, Bhaume, but the date Vaisâkh suri 10, gives Wednesday.

and Siva, as a colossal boar and a life-size bull are lying close by. The mandapa, or hall, of the larger temple was 40 feet square, and that of the smaller one 18 feet square. The floors of both were raised 13 feet above the ground, but the whole of the outer facing of these lofty plinths is now gone. The unfortunate proximity of the temples to the stone quarries, no doubt, led to the appropriation of the stones, both cut and uncut, which were lying so handy for removal.

The large temple with its spire must have been at least 100 feet high, and the smaller one about half that height. I noticed a few slightly curved and ornamented stones which must have belonged to the outer face of one of the spires; but the clearance of the fallen stones has been so complete that not even a guess can be made as to the style of the spires.

The roofs of the Mandapas are still in fair order. They are quite flat, like the roofs of temples of the Gupta period.

The colossal boar is 6 feet 2 inches long, with six rows of small figures carved on each side. The pedestal is broken, but one hind foot still remains. Below there is a very large Nâga, or snake, to represent the ocean from which the boar raised the earth, Prithvi, represented as a woman, whose two feet still remain.

The bull is recumbent, 3 feet 10 inches in length. There are also two large lions, each 4 feet long and 4 feet high.

There are several short inscriptions in these two temples, of which some are of real interest and importance, as they give the date of the victory of Prithi Râj Chauhân over the Chandel Prince Paramârdi Deva. The three records in the large temple I have already published ;* but as they are very short they may be repeated, as a mistake was made in the name of the conquered country, which, owing to the break in a single letter, was read as " Jejâkasukti," instead of " Jejâka-bhukti." These three short inscriptions are as follows :—

A. No. 9—Sri Châhumâna vansye-
        -na Prithvi Raja bhu-
        -bhujâ Paramârdi narendra-
        -sya desoya mudavasyata.

* Archæological Survey of India, Vol. X, p. 98, and Plate XXXII, Nos. 9, 10, and 11.

Here we have the names of Prithvi Raja, the Châhumâna Raja, and of his antagonist Paramârdi, the Chandel Raja, coupled together.

> B. No. 10—Aum! Aruno-râjasya pautrena Sri
>   Someswara Sununâ Jejâka-
>   -bhukti desoyam Prithvi râjenâ
>   lunitah S. 1239.

In this record we have the genealogy of the Chauhân chief given as the son of Someswara, and the grandson of Aruno Raja, with the name of the conquered country Jejâka-bhukti, and the date of Samvat 1239, or A.D. 1172.

> C. No. 11—Aum! Chandrasekhara, Bhawâniya,
>   Tryambaka Tripurântaka,
>   Chaksha Vidyâdharo Deva
>   Twam nauti pranatah sada.

Here the names of *Chandra-sekhara*, the "moon-crested," *Bhawâniya*, the "husband of Bhawâni," *Tryambaka* the "three-eyed," *Tripurântaka*, the "conqueror of (the demon) Tripura" are the titles of Siva. I conclude, therefore, that the larger temple, in which these inscriptions are recorded, must have been dedicated to Siva.

In the smaller temple there are two long inscriptions of different dates, of which the later one gives the perfect reading of the name of the country as *Jejâkabhukti mandala*, with the same date of Samvat 1239. It reads as follows:—

> 1. Aum! Jyam hisenâ Chandelam vyamâne Jejâkabhukti
>   mandalasya Sri Chahumânânwaya Kîrtti Chandra
>   Prithvi Na-
>   -rendrasya jaya prasastih ||S. 1239.
> 2.

The other inscription, which is only four years earlier, reads as follows:—

> 1. Aum! Sam. 1235 Srâvaṇa badi 1 Bikaurapathake Ma-
>   hârâjaputra Sri Alhana Deva Sri Aditya mâsaṃ
> 2. Pratidatta 2 || angrepi Sonadâsya tasya mâtâ
>   Garddabha grikshanti ||

The village of Bikaura still exists as Great and Little Bikaura, on the left bank of the Jâmini River, 5 miles to the south-west of Madanpur. It possesses some small ruined temples.* Alhana Deva must have belonged to the royal family of the Chandels of Mahoba.

The temple to the north-east of the lake is a very small one, compeletely surrounded by jungle. It is a small slab-walled building, with a spire, only 7½ feet square. Apparently it was dedicated to Siva, as there is a bull lying on the ground in front, with a group of Mahâdeva and Pârvati, and on the back wall there is a figure of Siva with ten arms, and on one of the sides a figure of the skeleton goddess Kâli, with ten arms. There is also a row of small figures with dancing girls in the angles. The temple is rather pretty, in spite of its small size. The upper part of the spire is gone.

20.—LALITPUR.

Lalitpur is a large town, about halfway between Jhânsi and Madanpur, and 20 miles to the east of Chanderi. It is pleasantly situated on the left bank of the Sajad River, a tributary of the Jâmini. Its name is said to have been given to it in honour of queen Lalitâ Devi, of whom a story is told which I have related in another place, with several variants from different localities. On this last visit the story was somewhat varied as follows :—

"Raja Sumer Singh had the disease called *Jalandhar*, or "dropsy," in his stomach, and as his case baffled the doctors, he started on a pilgrimage to Ajudhya. On the way he and his Râni stopped at a pool, on the present site of Lalitpur. Here the Râni dreamed that if her husband would eat some of the kâi (*confervæ*) of the pool, he would be cured. He ate some accordingly, and was cured. Again, the Râni had a dream that there was treasure buried under a tree on the embankment of the tank. A hole was dug under the tree and the treasure taken up. The Raja then called the tank Sumer Sâgar, or Tâl, and founded a town which was named Lalitâpura after his Râni."

In the town there is a small masjid, 19 feet 4 inches square, built entirely of Hindu materials, or, perhaps, it is part

* Markhera, on the opposite bank of the river, also has a small temple.

of a Hindu temple, only slightly altered. It is called Bâsa
and bears an inscription in Nâgari letters of the time of Firoz
Shah. The erection of the masjid must, therefore, be later
than the date of this inscription, Samvat 1415, or A.D. 1358
Feroz is called (line 6) *Râjâdhirâja pati Sri Suratân Peroja
Sâhi.* The destruction of the Hindu buildings in this part of
the country would appear to have been due to the zeal of the
Khalji rulers of Malwa, who ruled after Feroz.

The pillars of the masjid apparently must have belonged
to three or four different temples, as they are of very different
sizes, as well as of different patterns. There are six fluted
pillars of sixteen sides, which are very fine specimens of Hindu
work. Close by, in a Parwâr Baniya's house, I saw four more
of these fluted pillars. Some portions of fretted eaves now
ornament the outside of the masjid ; but the flat-roof is
hidden by a common battlement.

21.—SURAHAR.

Surahar is an old town on the high road between Lalitpur
and Chanderi. It possesses a small temple, only 12 feet 8
inches square outside, with three figures of Vishnu in niches
outside. The door faces the west. There is also an old
Sati pillar, on which occurs the name of the village.

22.—JHALONI.

At Jhaloni, 16 miles to the north of Chanderi, the road
to Gwalior passes over a low range of hills with a lake at foot.
On the top of the pass there is a tall slab, 18 feet in height,
called *chira*, or "the slab," with an inscription in seven lines
of Nâgari letters, dated in Samvat 1351 and Saki 1216, or
A.D. 1294. The letters are very badly formed, and I cannot make out the purport of the record.

23.—TERAHI.

Terahi is an old village, 5 miles to the south-east of
Ranod. It possesses two temples of considerable age and

importance, as they probably date from the beginning of the 10th century. Both temples are small, but one of them possesses a richly ornamented Toran gateway in good preservation. The larger temple, inside the village, is only 19 feet long by 14 feet broad, including its porch. The smaller temple, outside the village, is only 15 feet 6 inches long by 12 feet 3 inches broad, including its porch, but it has a fine Toran gateway in front at a distance of 18 feet, which, being 20 feet high and of the same breadth as the temple itself, adds much to its dignity.

There are inscriptions on two prostrate pillars close by, both bearing dates in the 10th century of the *Samvat*. One is *910 Bhâdrapada badi 4 Sanau*, or Saturday, 29th July, 853 A.D. On that day the *Mahâ Sâmantâdhipati* of Madhuvana, named Sri Guna Raja Unda-Bhata, a great warrior, made a gift to the temple of Sri Chândiya. Madhuban is clearly the old name of the district in which Terahi is situated, although the name is not known at the present day. The *Mohwar* River, on which Terahi and Rajapur are situated, probably preserves the old name. Ranod, which is only 5 miles distant, is in the same district, and was no doubt the residence of the chief. At Kadwâha, only 1 mile to the south of Terahi, there are four standing temples, and the ruins of nine others. This place gave its name to a parganah in Samvat 1380, or A.D. 1323. But there are short records of pilgrims on the temple pillars with the dates of Samvat 1124 and 1162, or A.D. 1067 and 1105.

The date of the second inscription is doubtful. It looks like 920 Bhâdrapada badi 14, Sanichare. But the week day does not agree with this year, nor does it agree with any other decimal year of the 10th century. It records a gift by Sri Ru * * * Bhata to the goddess Ambikâ. The name of the donor is much injured, and has no titles, as in the first record. But the latter half of the name Bhata would seem to connect him with the first record.

These temples were accidentally discovered by my draughtsman Jamna Shanker Bhatt, when searching for a village named Makhoba, which once possessed a temple with a long inscription. A small hamlet of this name was found, but it had no temple, and apparently never had one.

24.—RÂJAPUR.

Another discovery was made by the same man at Râjapur, only a few miles from Terahi. Râjapur is a large village situated on the Mohwar Nadi, 6 miles to the east of Ranod, and 4 miles to the south-west of Mayapur. About 1 mile to the north-east of the village, and on the bank of the Mohwar River, a Buddhist stûpa in nearly perfect order was discovered. The stûpa is built entirely of stone, and chiefly of small stones. It stands on a square base, or plinth, of 60 feet 9 inches side. On this rises a cylindrical drum 43 feet 8 inches in diameter and 11 feet high. Above it rises a second cylindrical drum, 35 feet 8 inches in diameter and 11 feet high, and over this rises the dome of the stûpa, 27 feet 8 inches in diameter and 22 feet high, the upper part being a simple hemisphere. The whole building is, therefore, 49 feet 6 inches in height. It is perfectly plain, without even a hand of moulding.

The people call it *Kothîla Math*, which may be translated as the "Tower Temple," but they have no tradition as to its purpose or the name of its builder. This stûpa is, I believe, the only remaining trace of Buddhism in the wide tract of the Northern Gwalior territory. There are numerous Buddhist remains at Besnagar, Bhilsa, and Udayagiri, on the southern border of the Gwalior state; but I have not seen, during the long course of my wanderings, any traces of Buddhism in the northern parts of Sindhia's dominions.

There is a strange legend attached to the Kothîla Math which would make it a monument erected over the remains of a brother and sister who had become man and wife in ignorance of their relationship. A Banjâra's wife having died, leaving two young children, a boy and a girl, the father made the boy over to one friend and the girl to another. The two Banjâras having died, the boy and girl were married to each other by the friends. After some time the girl observed a mark on her husband's head, and told him that she formerly had a brother with a similar mark. He then remembered that he had a sister very like her, and the two having become aware of their relationship prayed that their sin might be forgiven. Then the earth opened beneath them, and they were swallowed up. The Kothîla tower was then built on the spot out of the wealth which the brother and sister had left behind.

INDEX.

Govt. of India Central Printing Office.— No. 42 H. D.—9-11-85.—650.

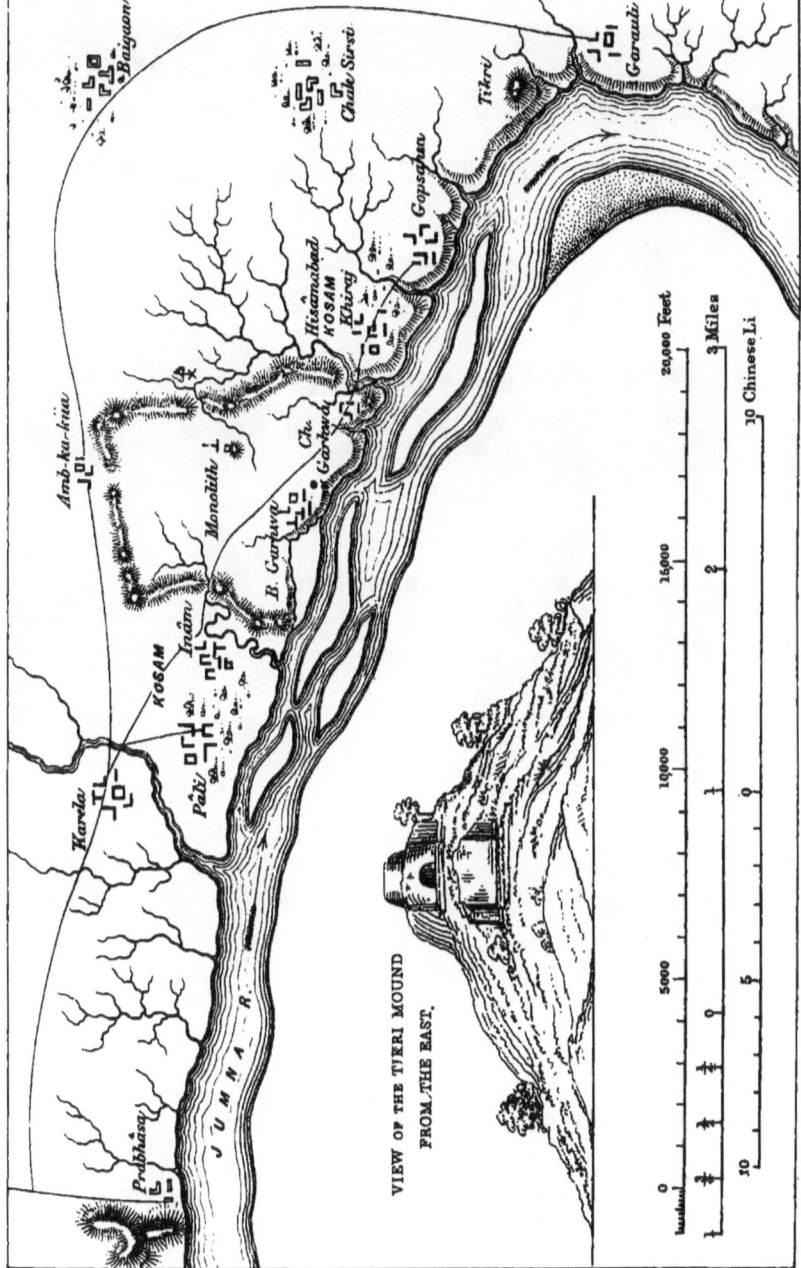

VIEW OF THE TERI MOUND
FROM THE EAST.

A. Cunningham, del.

Lithographed at the Survey of India Offices, Calcutta, September 1885.

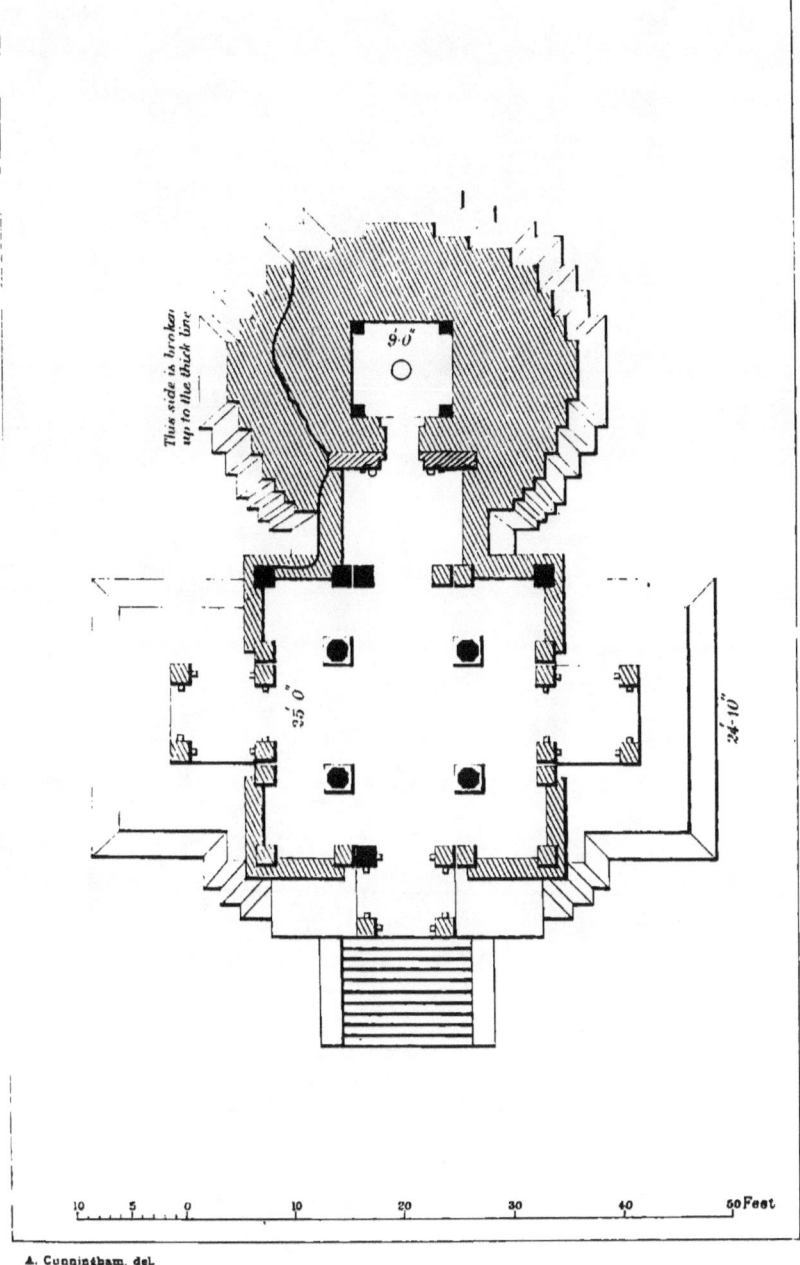

BAR-DEWAL TEMPLE on the JUMNA.

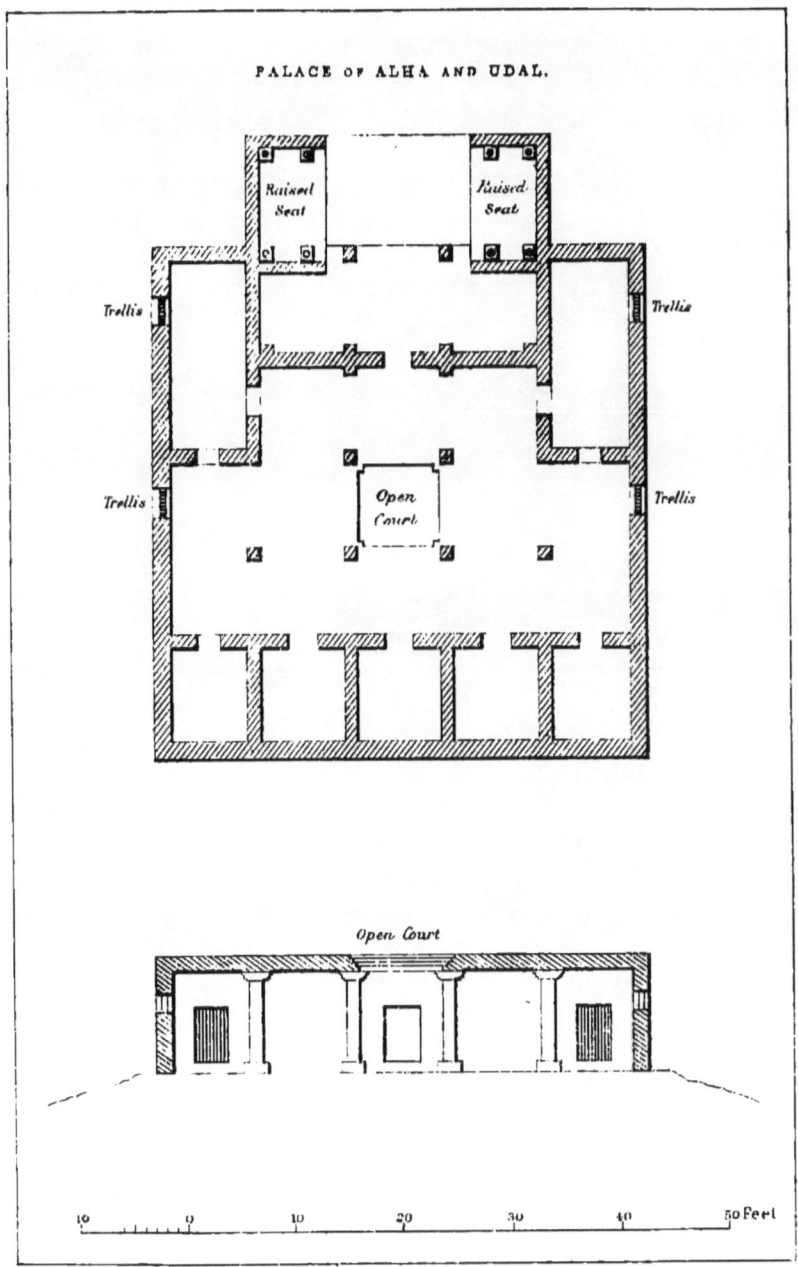

PALACE OF ALHA AND UDAL.

Raised Seat

Raised Seat

Trellis

Trellis

Trellis

Trellis

Open Court

Open Court

50 Feet

A. Cunningham, del.

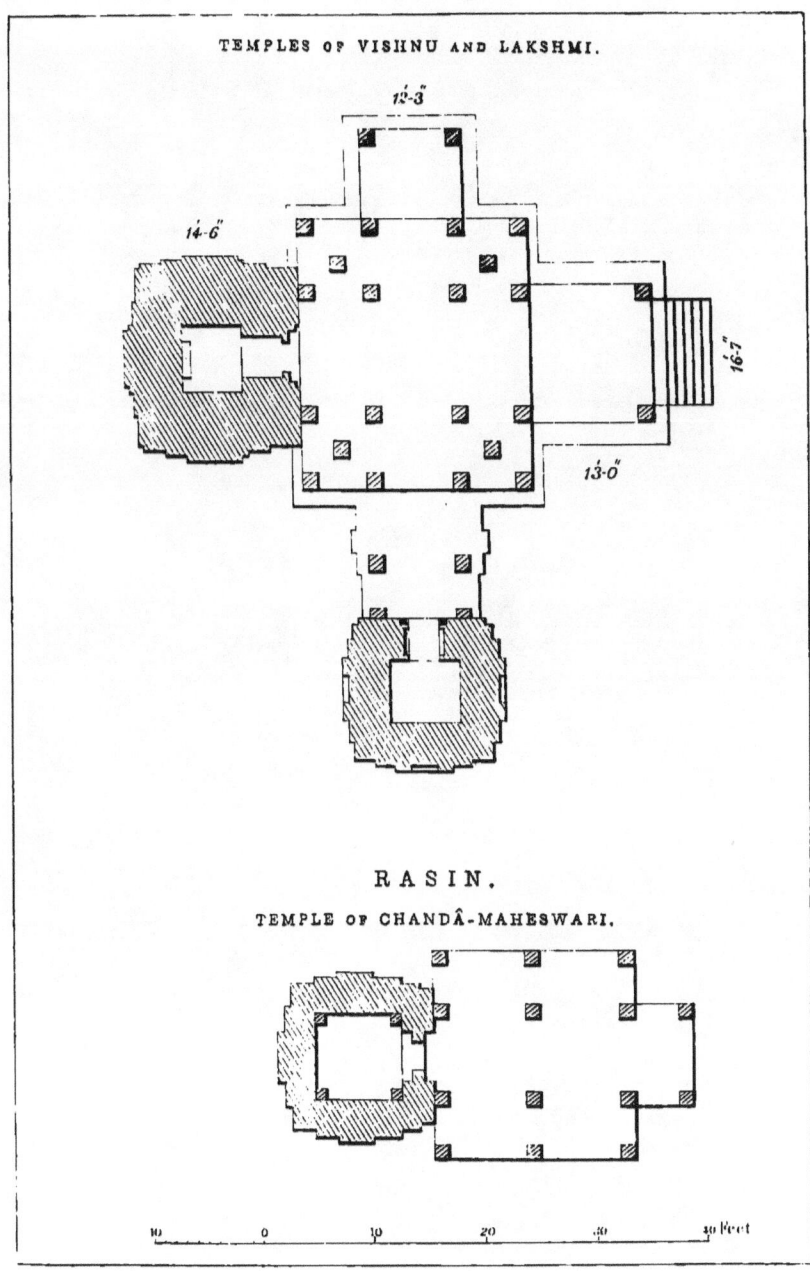

TEMPLES OF VISHNU AND LAKSHMI.

RASIN.

TEMPLE OF CHANDÂ-MAHESWARI.

A. Cunningham, del.

Lithographed at the Survey of India Offices, Calcutta, September 1885

A. Fragments and Sati Pillars.
B. Ruined Temple, Kāli-Ganes, Narsinh Hanuman.
C. Darwāza, Remains of Temple-Sculptures
D. Sivala, built of old materials.
+ Large old Wells.

Chandi Mukeswar Temple

Brick Tower

Adbhut Tāl

Chaubut Tāl

Bathihar Tāl

Ralanyian Temple

To Kurai

RASIN

Chaude Trit

KAMÂSIN M.

From Kālanjar

5000 Feet

1000   0   1   2   3   4

A. Cunningham, del

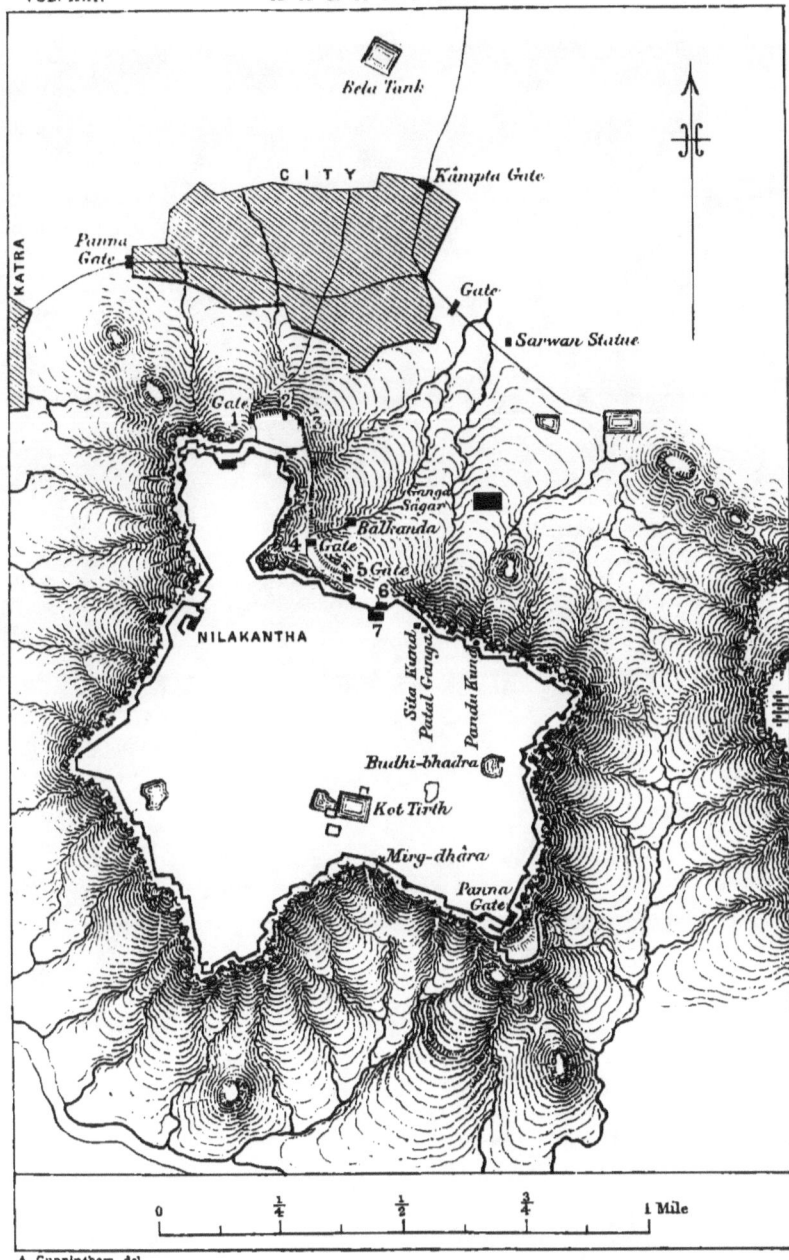

KATRA

Bela Tank

CITY   Kámpta Gate

Panna Gate

Gate

Sarwan Statue

Gate   2
1   3

Ganga Sagar
Balkanda
4   Gate
5 Gate
6
7

NILAKANTHA

Sita Kund.
Patal Ganga
Pandu Kund

Budhi-bhadra
Kot Tirth

Mirg-dhàra
Panna Gate

0   ¼   ½   ¾   1 Mile

A. Cunningham, del.

Lithographed at the Survey of India Offices, Calcutta, September 1865.

P.　Statue of Water-Carrier.

Q.　Statue of Water-Carrier.

L.　At Ganes. Gate.

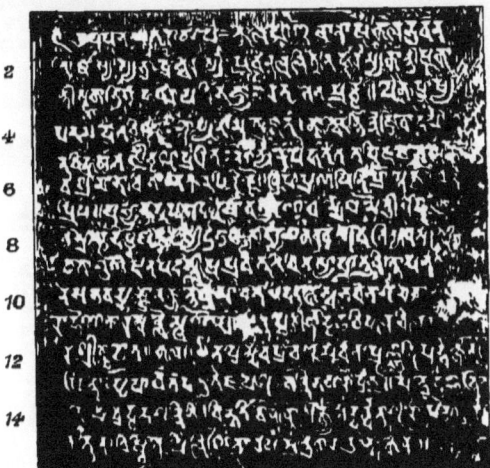

K.　In Cell near Nilakantha.

A Cunningham.　From Impressions.

A.   S. 1186.

B.   S. 1187.

C.   S. 1188.

D.   S. 1192.

E.   S. 1194.

From Impression

Lithographed at the Survey of India Offices, Calcutta, November 1885.

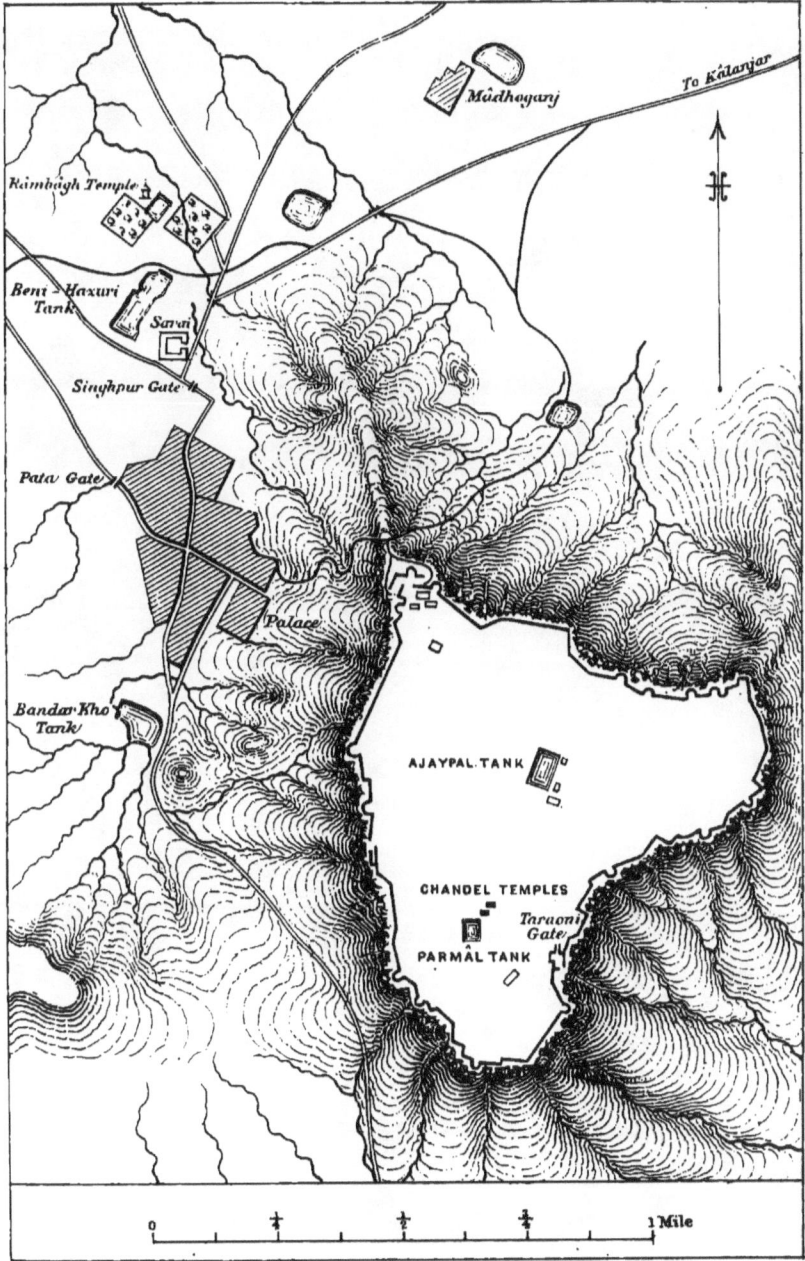

Lithographed at the Survey of India Offices, Calcutta, October 1885.

E.   Cut on the Rock.

S. 1317.

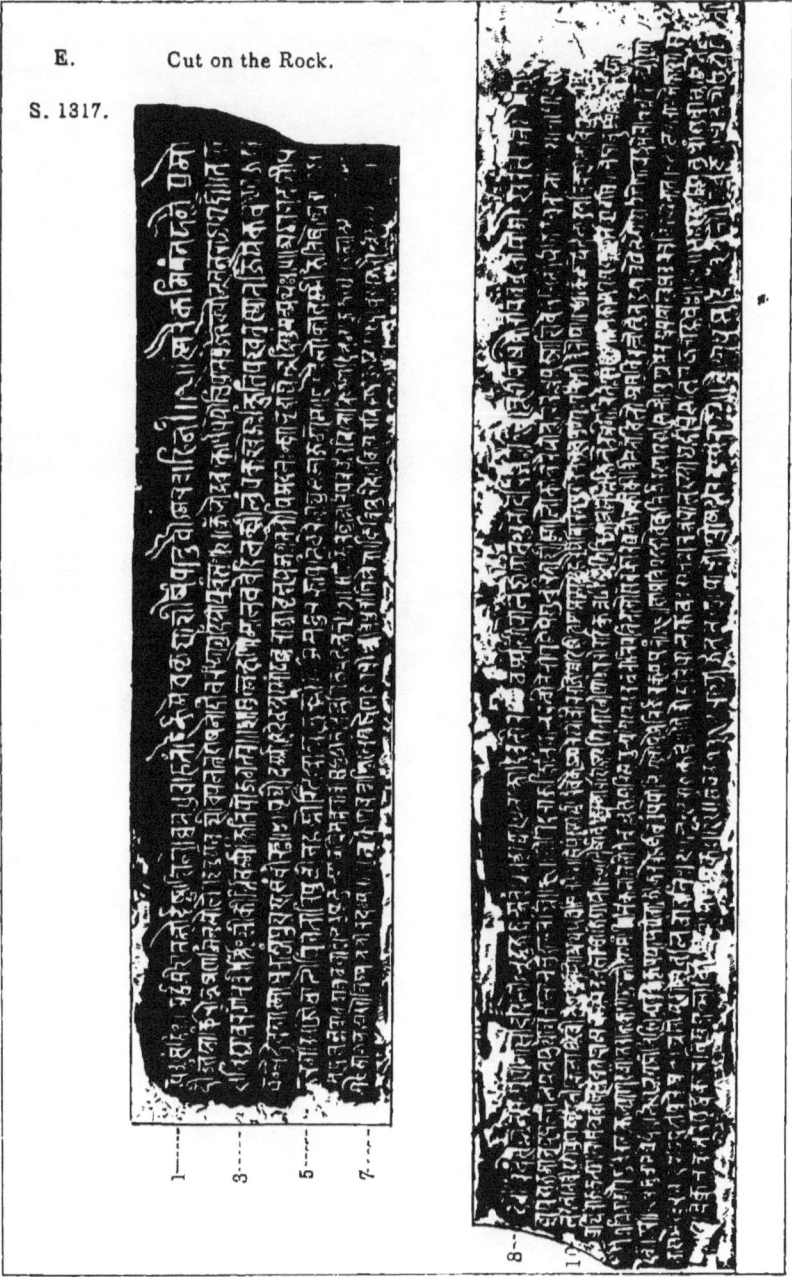

F.　　S. 1235　On Wall of Temple.

G.　　　　S. 1337.

O.　　　　S. 1372

RÂSIN.

S. 1466.

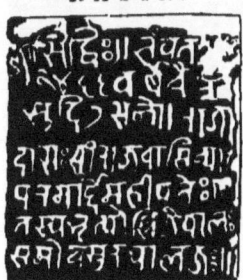

From Impressions.

Lithographed at the Survey of India Offices, Calcutta, September 1885.

Impressions.

Lithographed at the Survey of India Offices, Calcutta, October 1885.

A.   Base of Colossal Statue of Hanumân.

D.   Lakshminâth Temple.

B.   Fragment.

J.   Left door Jamb Jain Temple.

E.   Vâman Temple.

From Impression

Lithographed at the Survey of India Offices, Calcutta, November 188.

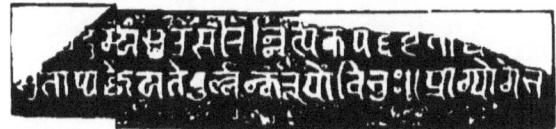

INSCRIPTION OF DHANGA DEVA.

RÁSIN.

MARPHA.

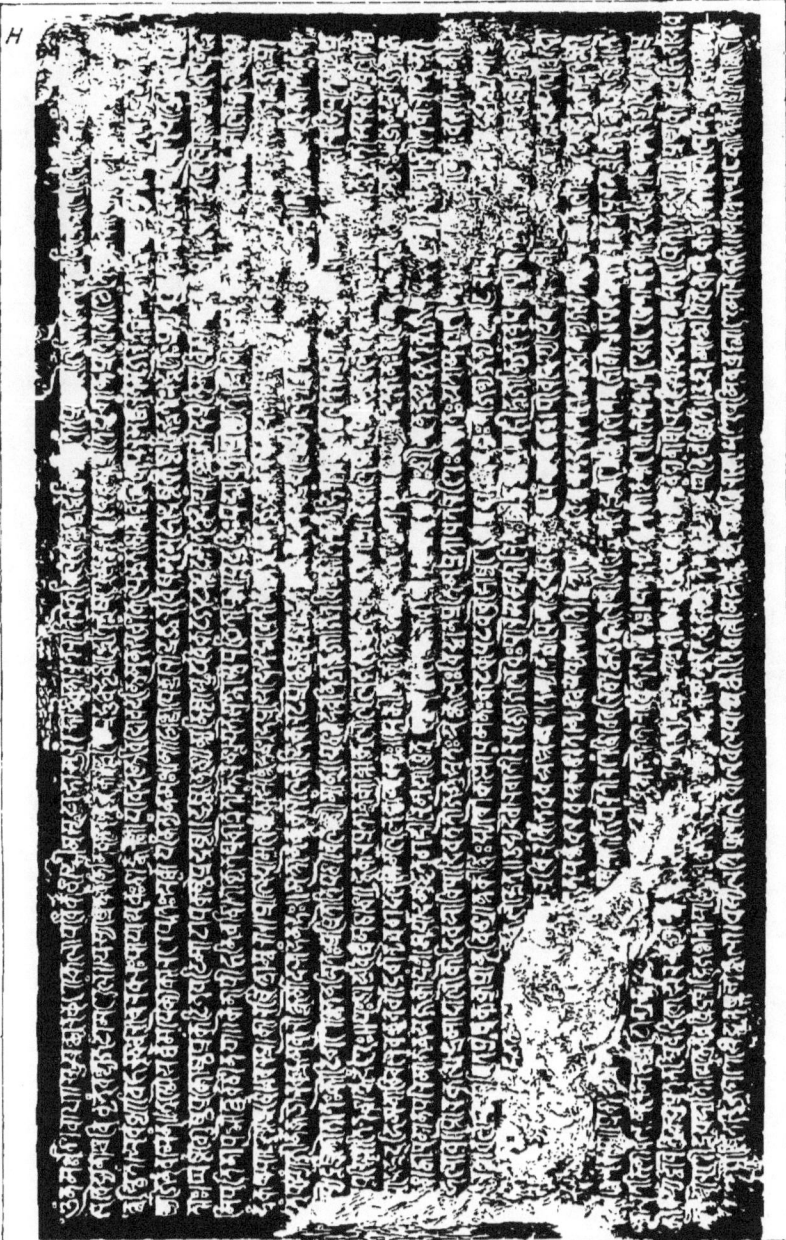

Lithographed at the Survey of India Offices, Calcutta, September 1885.

A. CHAUNSAT JOGINI.

माहेश्वरी   हेंप्लाऊ

E. GHANTAI TEMPLE.

1. ऋभिरांहुः   2. स्वस्ति श्री सा धु

C. STATUE OF SÂNTINATH.

संवत १०८ज श्रीमत – – – – – – – – – – – श्रीशांतिनाथस्य प्रतिम

D. STATUE OF SAMBHUNÂTH.

७॥ सवत् १२१५ मा पशुदि५ श्रीमन्व रन वर्क्मी देव

E. KHANDÂRIYA TEMPLE.

1. दर्शण —→ *on the under side of an Architrave*

F. CHITR-GUPT TEMPLE.

1. व्यरंदस   2. सुहृव   3. क्हील्

G. DEVI-JAGADÂMBÂ TEMPLE.

1. डिलव्व   2. इर्व्हृ ण

H. VISWANÂTH TEMPLE.

1. श्रीशक्ति   2. श्रीदिवलदस   3. श्रीमिदिराण

J. KUNWAR MATH.

वासला   *5 times*

K. STATUE OF SHANMUKHA.

देवलासलिलिवऋरूटा कंश्रीउहृ क्लिवः
अखाडे स्या॥ सह्वीपीतर्यौववःअतृरू

A. Cunningham, del.

Lithographed at the Survey of India Offices, Calcutta, September 1883.

A. IDGAH WALL.

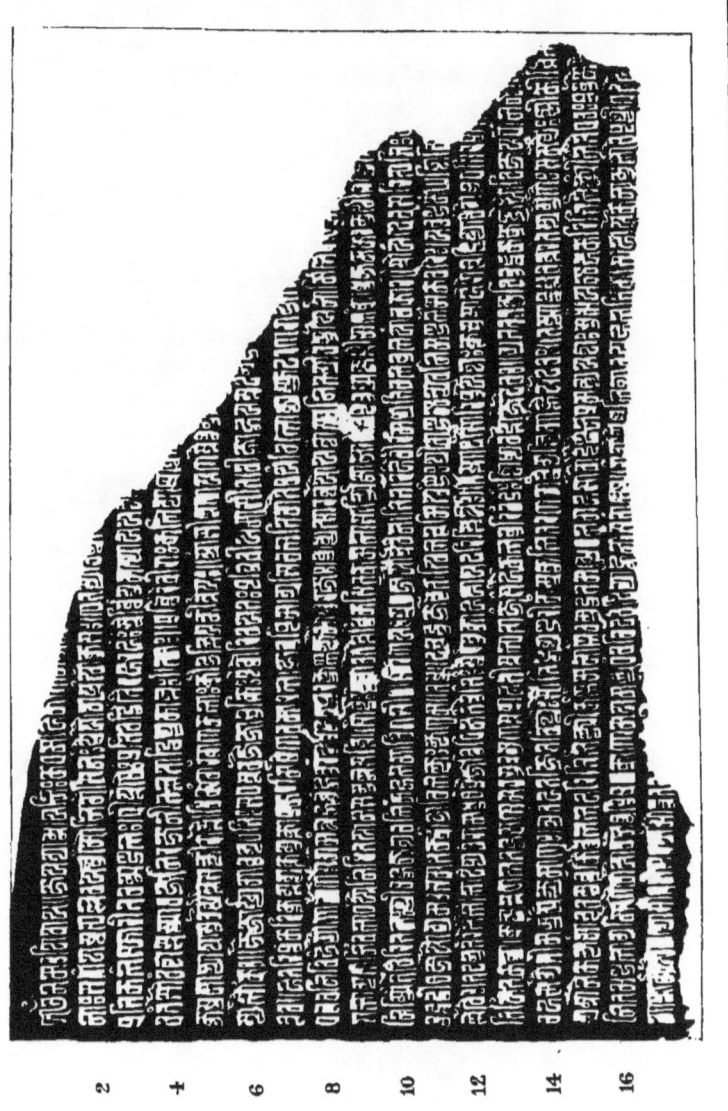

From Impressions

Wall of Fort.

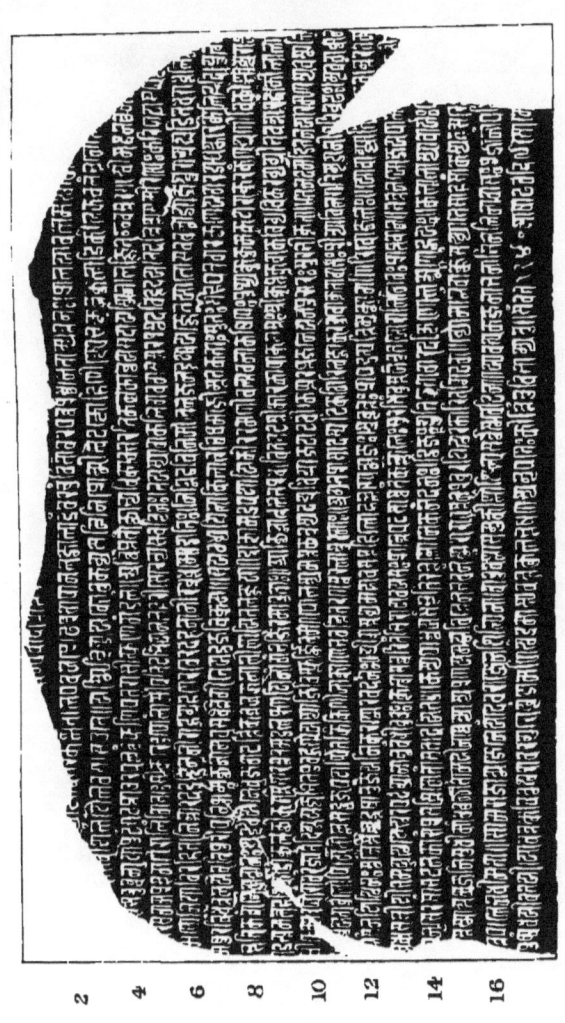

Lithographed at the Survey of India Offices, Calcutta, October 1885.

Broken Slab.

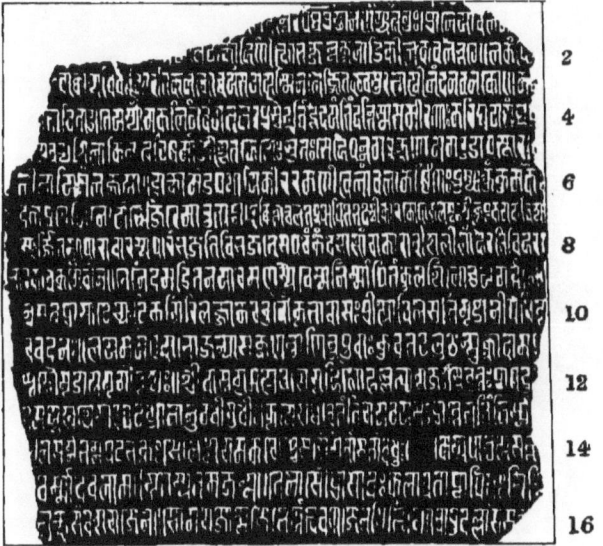

2
4
6
8
10
12
14
16

D.   Statue of Nemináth.   S. 1211.

ध गोलानर्क्रतृसेसाठुसाठेतढसाठुलारत्रूतख्रपुदेगालू

श्रीमद्मदनवर्म्मिदेवनद्रेसंग्रारर॥श्राषाढसुदिर

उदैह्क्लेझालू जीलूएण वेनित्यद्रएमत्रिाा

सनौा॥💮॥ देवश्रीनेमिना व॥रुप कार्नलाषएा॥

G.   On Pedastal with Figures.

संवत१२२४श्राषाढसु दि २न वैा॥ॐ॥ कालउराविपति

श्रीमत्यनमर्द्दिदेव पादा नामही प्रवर्द्धमान कल्याएाविज्रय राज्ये

Lithographed at the Survey of India Offices, Calcutta, September 1905

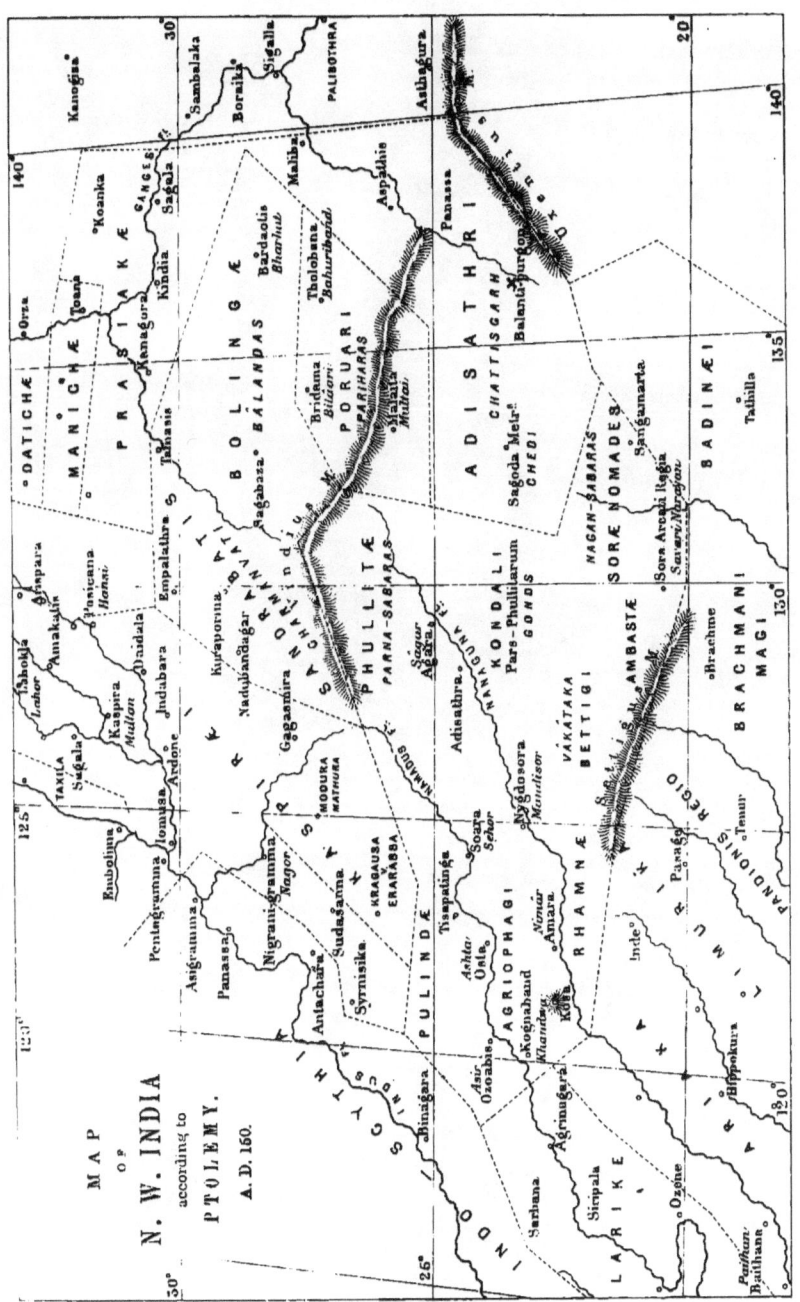

MAP
OF
N. W. INDIA
according to
PTOLEMY.
A. D. 160.

A. Cunningham, del.

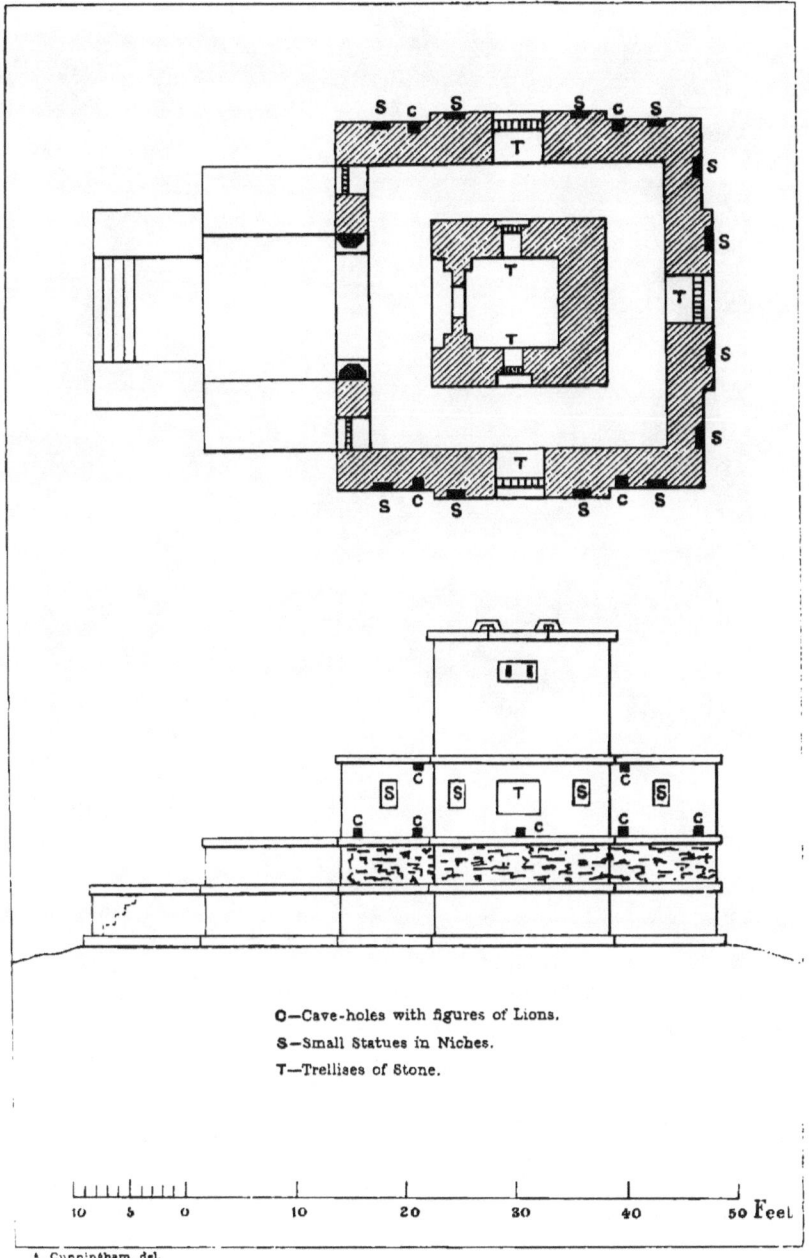

C—Cave-holes with figures of Lions.

S—Small Statues in Niches.

T—Trellises of Stone.

10   5   0   10   20   30   40   50 Feet

A. Cunningham, del.

Lithographed at the Survey of India Offices, Calcutta. November 1885.

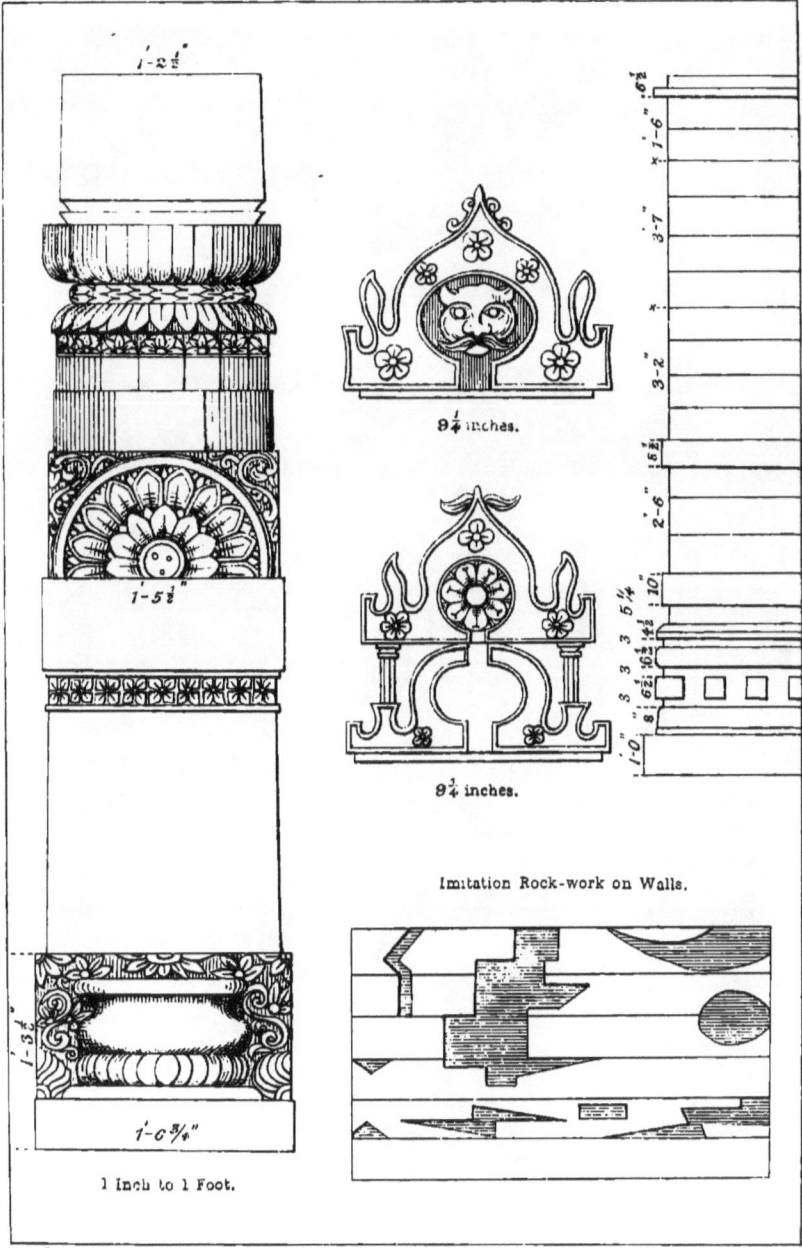

9¼ inches.

9¾ inches.

Imitation Rock-work on Walls.

1 Inch to 1 Foot.

A. Cunningham, del.

Lithographed at the Survey of India Offices, Calcutta, September 1885

NACHNA - KUTARA ·

On a loose Slab.

On the Edge of the Slab.

BESÂNI   JASSO

On a Slab.   Natural Lingam

   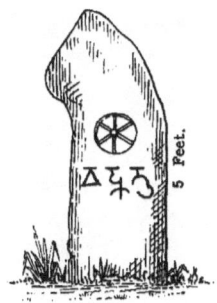

From Impressions.

Lithographed at the Survey of India Offices, Calcutta, November 1885.

CHHOTI
DEORI.

PIÂWAN
ROCK.

ALHA-GHAT.

A

B

C

D

From Impression.

Lithographed at the Survey of India Offices, Calcutta, November 1885.

View of Hill from the South.

INSCRIPTION IN RED PAINT.
Eye Copy.

Reduced Tracing.

Rude Sketches of Animals
in Red Paint.

A. Cunningham, del.

Lithographed at the Survey of India Offices, Calcutta, September 1885.

Lithographed at the Survey of India Offices, Calcutta, October 1885.

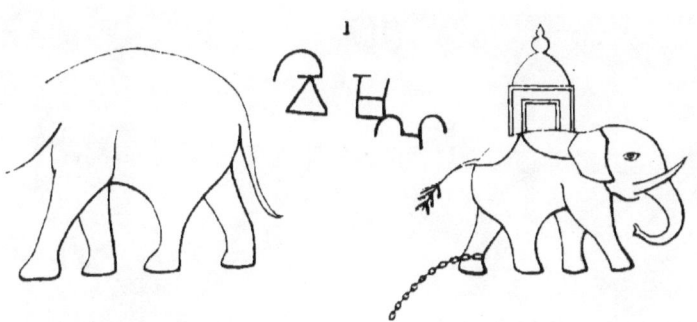

CHAURÂSI GUMBAZ.

A. Cunningham, del

Lithographed at the Survey of India Offices, Calcutta. September 1885.

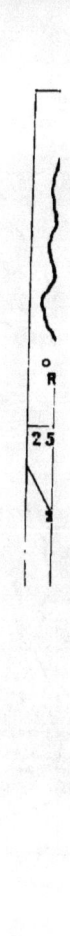

MAP OF S. W. BUNDELKHAND AND MALWA.

PLATE XXXIV.

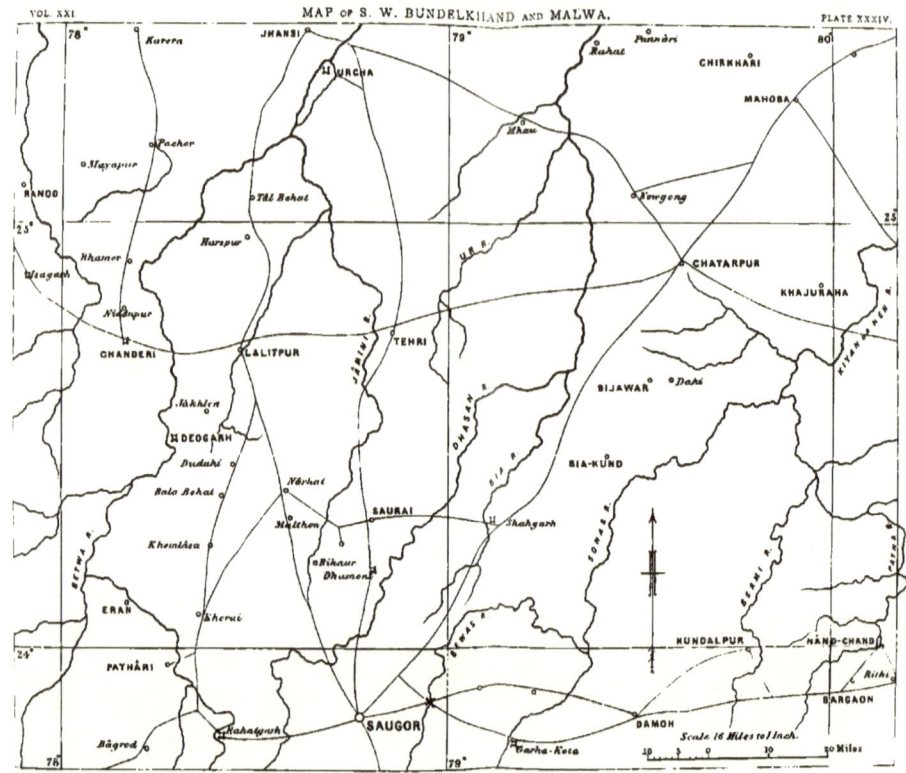

A Cunningham del

Photozincographed at the Surveyor of India Office, Calcutta, December 1892

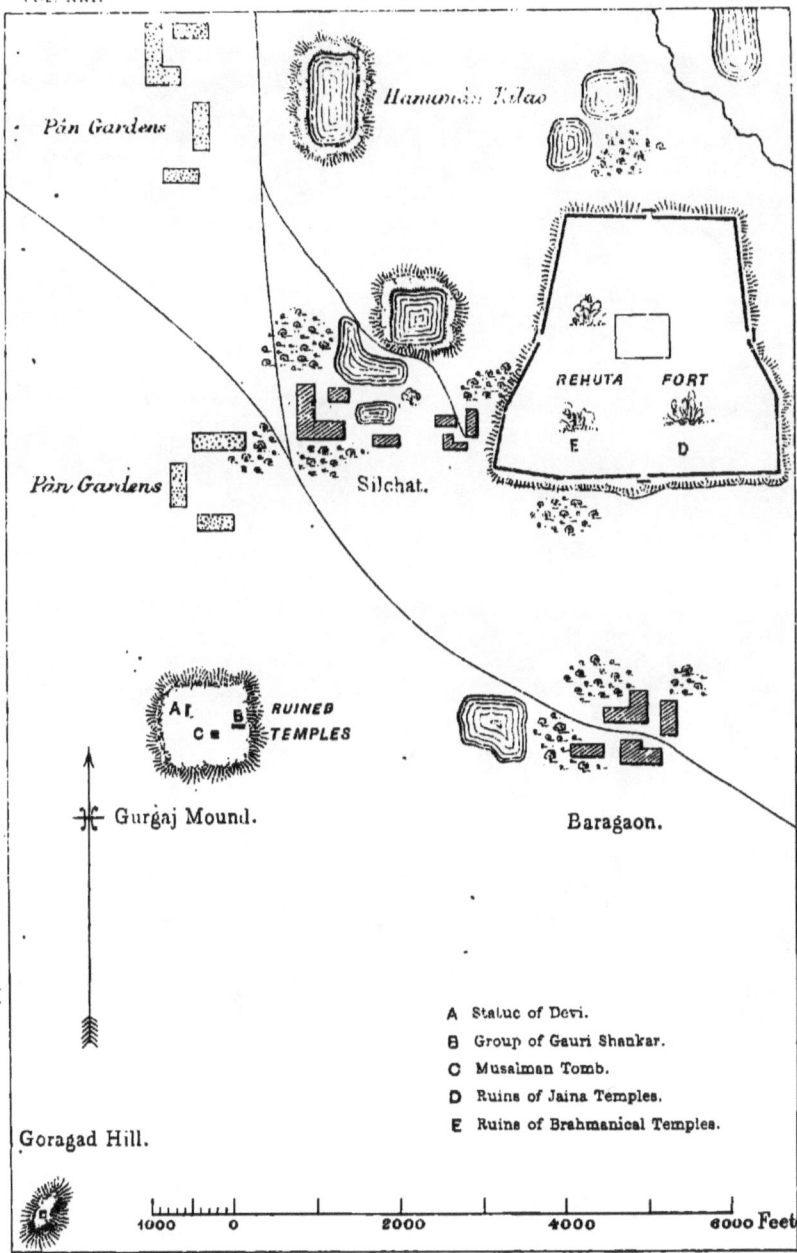

Pòn Gardens

Hanumàn Talao

Pòn Gardens

Silchat.

REHUTA   FORT

E   D

A   B   RUINED
C   TEMPLES

Gurgaj Mound.

Baragaon.

A   Statue of Devi.
B   Group of Gauri Shankar.
C   Musalman Tomb.
D   Ruins of Jaina Temples.
E   Ruins of Brahmanical Temples.

Goragad Hill.

1000   0   2000   4000   6000 Feet

A. Cunningham, del.

Lithographed at the Survey of India Offices, Calcutta, December 1885.

TEMPLE OF SOMNÂTH.

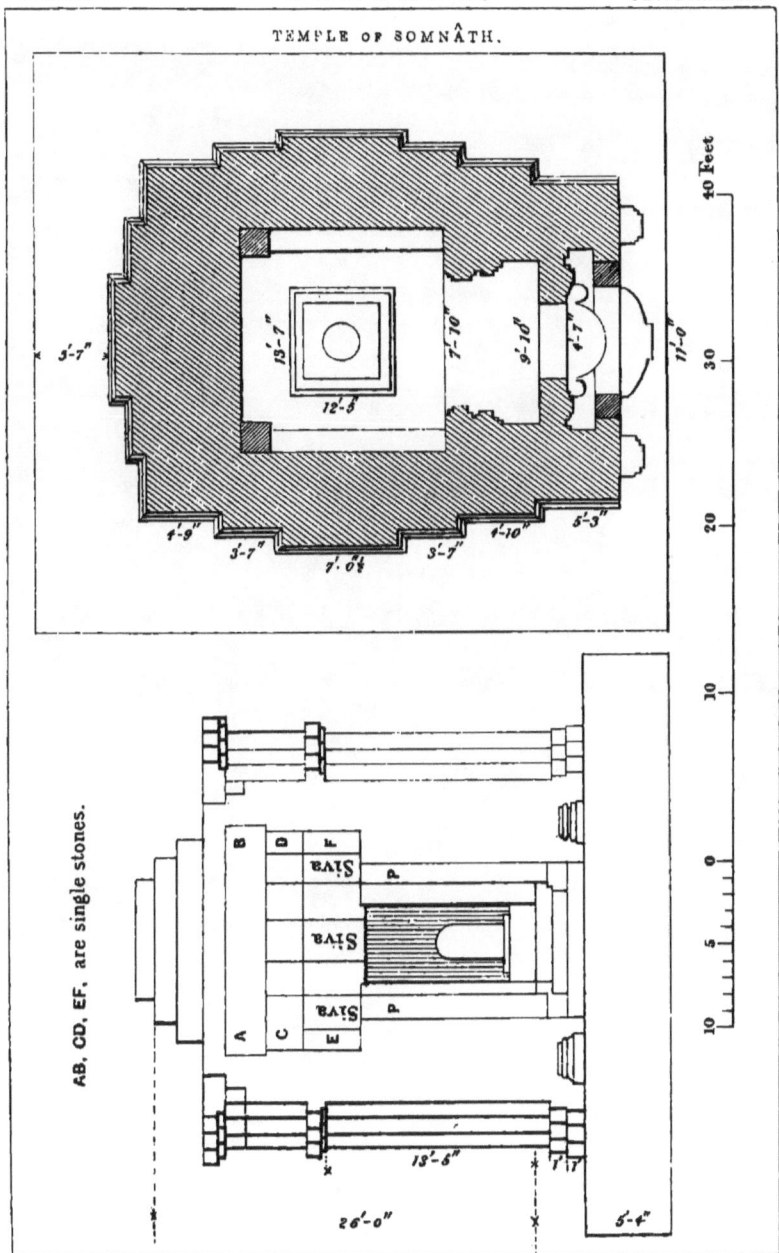

A. Cunningham, del.

Lithographed at the Survey of India Offices, Calcutta, November 1885.

SOMNATH TEMPLE.

Edge of Roofing Slabs

GARUD TEMPLE.

Face of Architrave.

A.   Long Inscription—13 lines—5 Ft. × 1' 2".

B.   Broken Inscription—11 lines—3 Ft. × 1'.

On Face of Pillar.

C.

Masons Marks on Somnâth Temple.

A. Cunningham, del.

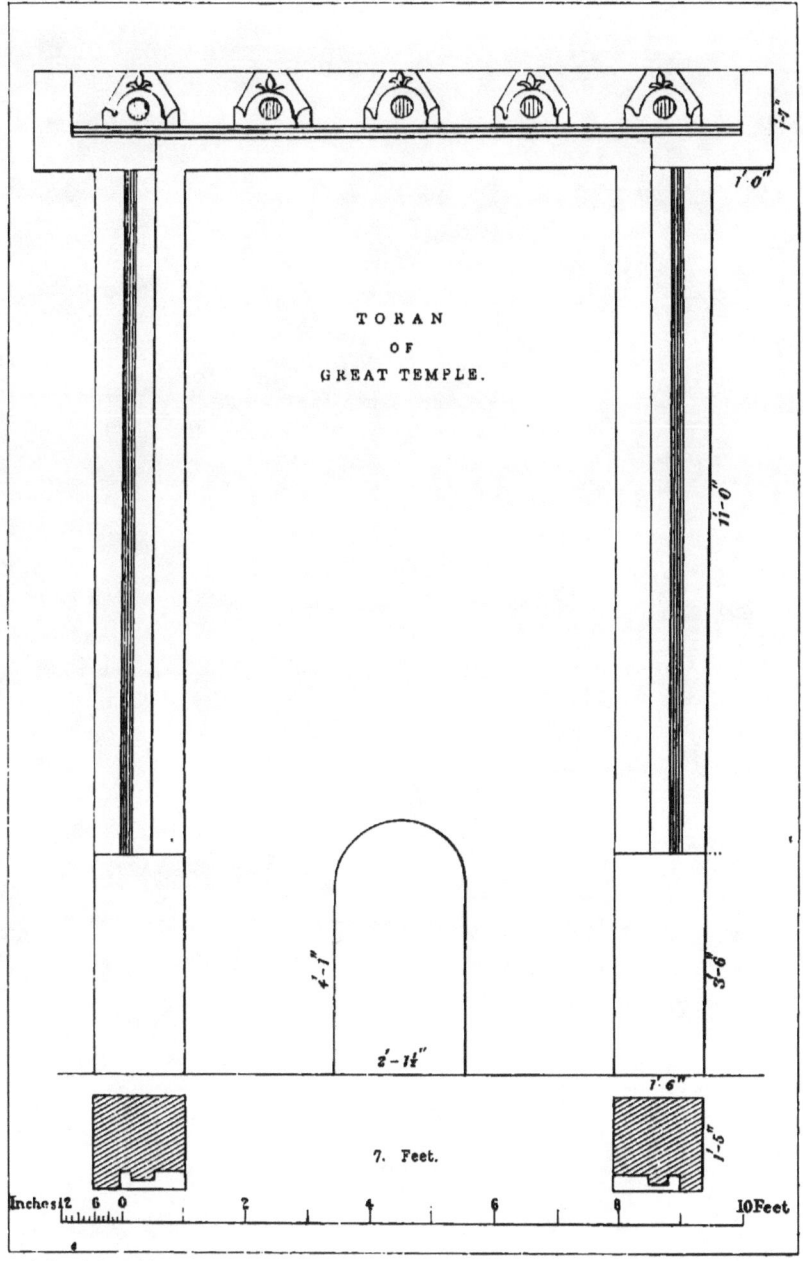

TORAN

OF

GREAT TEMPLE.

7. Feet.

Lithographed at the Survey of India Offices, Calcutta, November 1885.

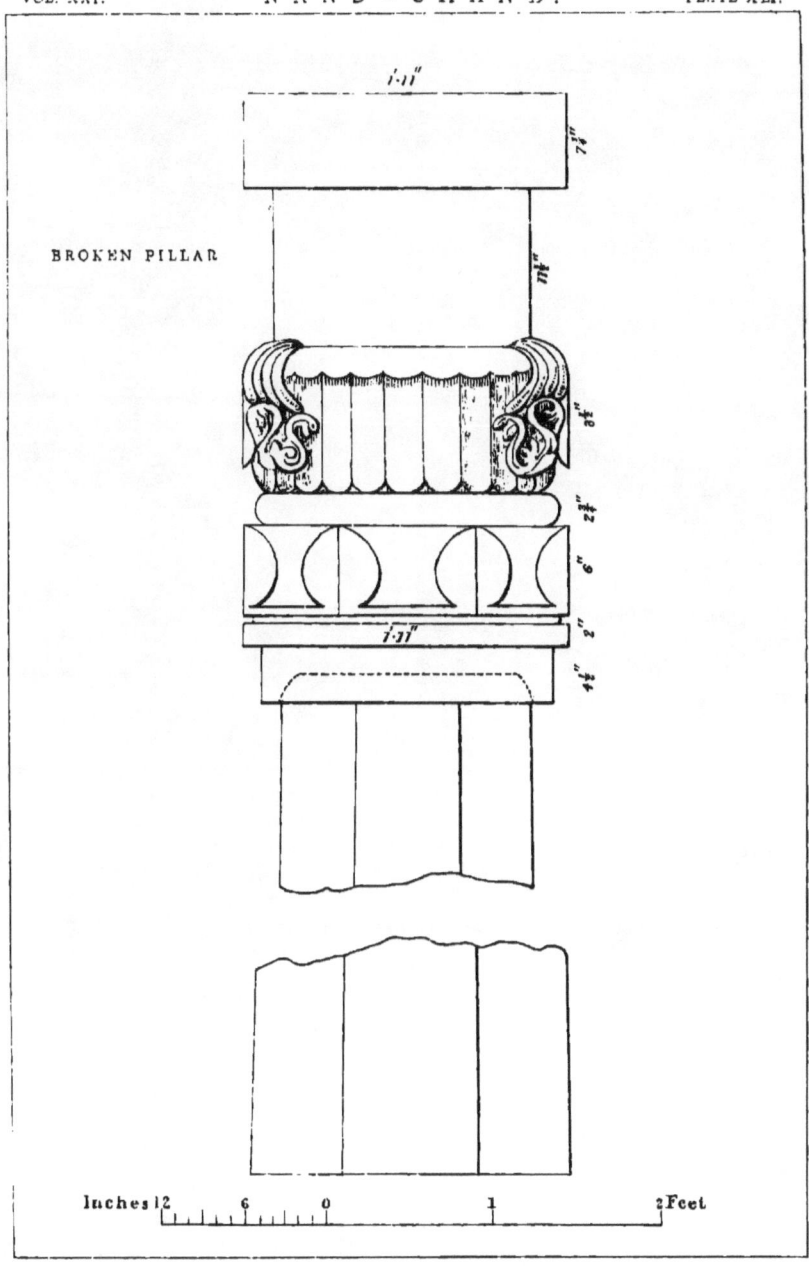

BROKEN PILLAR

Inches 12   6   0   1   2 Feet

Lithographed at the Survey of India Offices, Calcutta, December 1885.

SLAB TEMPLES.

KUNDALPUR.

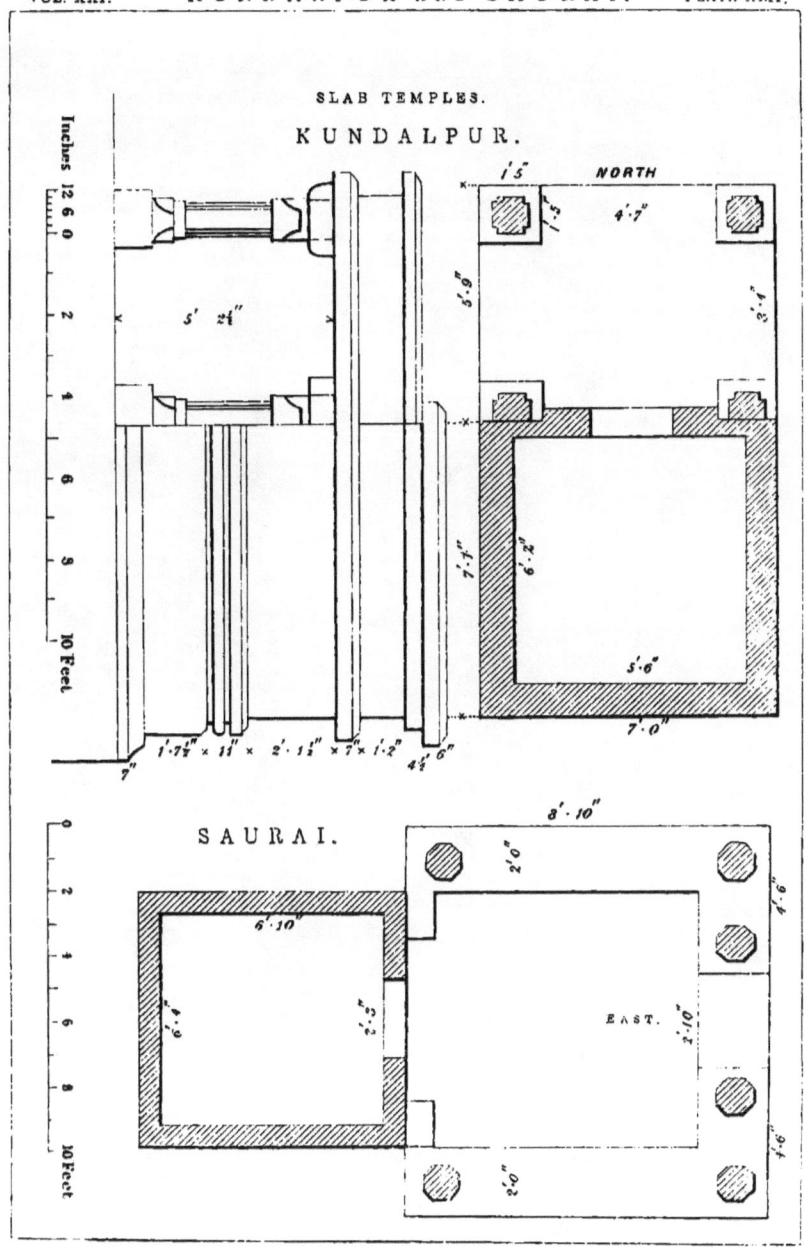

SAURAI.

A. Cunningham, del.

Lithographed at the Survey of India Offices, Calcutta. November 1885.

www.ingramcontent.com/pod-product-compliance
Lightning Source LLC
Chambersburg PA
CBHW060613030726
47498CB00005B/1663